Care Homes Are Murder

A PAUL JACOBSON GEEZER-LIT MYSTERY

Care Homes Are Murder

Mike Befeler

FIVE STAR
A part of Gale, Cengage Learning

Detroit • New York • San Francisco • New Haven, Conn • Waterville, Maine • London

GALE
CENGAGE Learning®

LIBRARY OF CONGRESS CATALOGING-IN-PUBLICATION DATA

Befeler, Mike.
   Care homes are murder : a Paul Jacobson geezer-lit mystery /
Mike Befeler. — First Edition.
      pages cm.
   ISBN 978-1-4328-2692-5 (hardcover) — ISBN 1-4328-2692-1
(hardcover)
   1. Retirees—Fiction. 2. Retirement communities—Fiction. 3.
Murder—Investigation—Fiction. I. Title.
PS3602.E37C37 2013
813'.6—dc23   2013005473

First Edition. First Printing: June 2013
Find us on Facebook– https://www.facebook.com/FiveStarCengage
Visit our website– http://www.gale.cengage.com/fivestar/
Contact Five Star™ Publishing at FiveStar@cengage.com

Printed in Mexico
1 2 3 4 5 6 7 17 16 15 14 13

For Wendy, Roger, Dennis, Laura, Paige, Asher, Kaden, and Adam

ACKNOWLEDGMENTS

Many thanks for the assistance from Wendy Befeler and my online critique groups and the editorial support from Deni Dietz, Alice Duncan, and Tracey Matthews.

Chapter 1

We made it safely to Honolulu, without the plane crashing and me drowning in the ocean or my old body being consumed by sharks. As my son Denny drove the white rental sport utility vehicle from the airport toward Waikiki, I watched the early afternoon hubbub in the streets around us. To the left a crowd of people in their brightly colored Hawaiian shirts meandered toward their next destinations. Off to the right as we passed the docks of downtown, cranes offloaded a rusty cargo ship. I spotted the local landmark tower, with its large clock near the top proclaiming four-twenty in the afternoon, right below the letters spelling out the all-encompassing greeting and farewell, "Aloha."

My wife Marion pointed toward her window. "Look, a cruise ship. Paul, we'll have to take a Hawaiian cruise some time. We enjoyed our Alaskan honeymoon cruise so much."

"I don't remember, but I'm sure I enjoyed the honeymoon part of it." I waggled my eyebrows in Marion's direction.

"Please, not in front of children." My granddaughter Jennifer, who sat in the backseat between Marion and me, put her hands over her ears.

"You're not supposed to even get what I was referring to," I said.

"Oh, Grandpa. I'm twelve you know."

My son, daughter-in-law Allison, and granddaughter had flown from Colorado to Los Angeles, where Marion and I joined them for the Pacific leg of the journey, bringing together the whole Jacobson clan. Not that I'd remember any of this if I'd fallen asleep on the plane because I suffered this little memory idiosyncrasy: I remembered the distant past and anything that happened since I last fell asleep, but anything in between, poof! It disappeared like a VW Rabbit down a Florida sinkhole.

"How old am I, anyway?" I asked Marion.

"Eighty-five and counting, dear. Your next birthday is in three months."

"What's a young chick like you doing with a geezer like me?"

She smiled. "I don't know. I guess I'm here for all the excitement."

I estimated Marion must be in her seventh decade, with sparkling silver hair, a glint in her eye and a svelte figure that inspired my old body. And amazingly, she had rescued me from widowerhood.

"Let's tell some more geezer jokes, Grandpa," Jennifer said, bouncing up and down on the backseat between Marion and me.

On the plane flight to Honolulu Jennifer and I had sat next to each other, and we passed some of the time exchanging jokes about old farts like me.

I stepped up to the challenge. "Okay, little squirt, here's one. Why didn't the geezer cross the road?"

Jennifer scrunched up her face in concentration and exhaled loudly. "I give up."

"Because he was no longer a spring chicken."

Jennifer stuck out her tongue and placed a finger into her mouth. "That's even worse than your usual bad jokes, Grandpa. I have one for you. What's the difference between geezers and tweezers?"

I stretched my remaining brain cells as far as they would go but came up with no answer. "Okay, what?"

Jennifer grinned. "Tweezers still have a grip on things."

"That's not a nice thing to say." Allison turned from the front seat to glare at Jennifer.

Jennifer held her hands open. "What?"

"That's all right," I said. "I don't mind. I'm teaching Jennifer how to tell politically incorrect jokes."

Now Allison fixed her supermom gaze on me. "Paul, we don't need that. My father would never encourage Jennifer to speak like that."

"I know. I know. I should behave myself. I'm the bad grandpa."

After Allison turned away from watching the two juvenile delinquents in the back seat, Jennifer whispered in my ear. "You're the ba-a-a-d grandpa."

Refraining from breeding further family discord, I desisted from telling any more geezer jokes for the rest of the ride. As we pulled into the circular driveway, I stared up at the shiny glass and steel structure of the thirty-story Hibiscus Hotel, my vacation home. My whole tribe clambered out as eager bellboys in their black slacks, shiny black shoes and light blue Hawaiian shirts descended on us to cart away our stack of suitcases. A trade wind blew through my remaining locks, cooling my brow from the humid air. An aroma of pikake tickled my nose.

I surveyed my new domain. My immediate attention focused on the speckled marble floor of the lobby, periodically dotted with octagon shaped carpets, displaying Hawaiian petroglyphs of stick figures, sailing canoes and spears. On top of these carpets stood glass-inlaid monkey pod tables holding ceramic pots full of bright orange bird of paradise and shiny red anthurium flowers. The whole place reeked of tropical splendor.

Jennifer skipped up to me. "This is so cool, Grandpa. Will you come watch me surf while we're here?"

"As long as I can enjoy your antics from the safety of the shore. I hate the ocean."

She stomped her foot. "We've been over this before. You need to change your attitude toward the ocean."

"It needs to change its attitude toward me. Get rid of all the water and the things that swim in it. Then we'd get along fine."

Jennifer rolled her eyes. "I don't know what I'm going to do with you, Grandpa."

"Bury me in the sand, and I'll be fine."

"Okay, we're all checked in," Denny announced, handing Marion and me card keys. "Adjoining rooms on the seventh floor."

"Cool," Jennifer said. "Do we have an ocean view?"

"Absolutely," Denny replied. "Right over the yacht harbor and Ala Moana Park."

"This will be the best Christmas vacation ever," Jennifer said, hopping on one foot. "I can't wait to get in the ocean."

"I can wait another eighty-five years," I said.

A pleasant young man wheeled our assorted luggage into the elevator with us. After a short ride upward, we strolled down a hallway to our new home-away-from-home.

Marion and I entered a room with a king-sized bed and a balcony overlooking the harbor. I scampered over to the large sliding glass door to watch as a plane took off from the Honolulu airport and made a lazy turn out to sea. I wouldn't be flying over the ocean until we returned to the mainland. In truth, I fared well being above such a huge expanse of water on our inbound flight. With Marion in the window seat and Jennifer in the middle seat, I didn't have to look out the window, and when I happened to peer that way, I mainly saw blue sky and puffy white clouds. I could do with sky, but ocean didn't appeal to me, any more than bunnies enjoyed associating with foxes.

In a moment I heard a knock on the connecting door. I opened it, and a ball of energy came bounding into our room. "How do you like it, Grandpa?"

"Not bad digs."

Jennifer put her hands on her hips. "I think it's quite nice. How can you only say it's not bad?"

Marion came over and gave Jennifer a hug. "Don't let him kid you. He loves it. He's trying to pretend to be crotchety."

"That's right," I added. "If I don't act grouchy at least twice a day, they take away my curmudgeon membership card."

Jennifer shook a finger at me. "It's not nice to fool your granddaughter."

"Yes, ma'am."

"That's more like it." She loped back into the room she shared with her parents. Marion and I followed her in so we could all give our oohs and ahs over the view. Allison removed a red Canon digital point-and-shoot camera from her purse and snapped several pictures of the yacht harbor.

"You've become quite the photographer," Denny commented.

Allison took another picture. "I never thought much of photography before but have really enjoyed it lately. Look at this panorama with the sailboats out at sea, spots of whitecaps and the various shades of blue."

Denny looked toward the ocean and sighed. "That view deserves to be immortalized in a photograph or a painting."

Marion and I returned to our room. After we unpacked and I splashed some water on my puss to refresh this old geezer, Denny knocked and informed us we needed to depart for our dinner reservation at the top of the Hibiscus.

"And we get to go up an outside glass elevator," Jennifer informed me. "Everyone's enthusiastic except Mom. She doesn't like glass elevators."

Allison stuck her head in at that mention. "I'd prefer stairs."

"It's too far to walk," Jennifer said.

"Keep your eyes closed," I added.

After heading down to the first floor, we explored around the lobby, checking out two pools and a lanai that overlooked the yacht harbor. Returning to the lobby, we approached a solo elevator, and Denny punched the button. After an interminable wait the door opened. A crowd of yakking tourists poured out, oblivious to anything around them as one man almost trod on Jennifer's foot. After the cabin cleared, we filled it up again with our trusty crew.

Allison faced the inside and immediately closed her eyes. We ascended, and the rest of us turned outward to enjoy the view.

"Cool. Mom, you should see how pretty it is."

Allison's eyes remained scrunched shut. "You can tell me after we get out."

In the way my strange brain worked, I remembered something from years before in this same elevator.

"Jennifer, this elevator is going to shoot right above the roof like in the Willie Wonka movie."

Her eyes grew wide.

As we approached the top, the elevator appeared to fly above the roof.

"Wow, you were right, Grandpa."

Allison continued to huddle against the inside of the elevator. "Are we there yet?"

The door opened and Allison shot out first, faster than Houdini escaping a pair of handcuffs.

Once I stepped out, I put my arm around my shaking daughter-in-law. "You feel the same way about glass elevators that I do about the ocean."

She gave a wan smile. "Each of us has our own unique phobias."

"Anyway, we're here. You won't have to do that again until we leave after dinner."

"Don't remind me."

While the maitre d' searched his cheat sheet to find the

perfect eating spot for us, Jennifer and I went over to the window to look out over the city.

"Your mom probably wouldn't want to look down, but it's a nice view." I watched cars snake along Ala Moana Boulevard in their parallel trails of red and white lights at dusk. Off in the distance shown the illuminated buildings of downtown. How Honolulu had grown. I remembered being here before my brain cells went kaput. Now the city had more people, more cars and more congestion.

"I like it up here. I'm not afraid of heights or the ocean."

"That's good. No sense passing on the worst traits of earlier generations. Also, try not to inherit my crappy memory."

Jennifer tapped her temple. "But I've inherited the photographic memory you have during the day, Grandpa. Both you and I could repeat the details of everything that's happened since we arrived in Hawaii. Hey, are you going to keep a journal on this trip?"

"Huh?"

Jennifer stomped her foot. "Since you forget things overnight, you've been writing in a journal. That's the best way for you to keep track of what's happened to you."

I scratched my head. "I've been doing that?"

"Yes. It helps you catch up the next day. Every night before going to sleep, you should add what occurred during the day to your diary. You can leave a note to remind yourself to read it first thing in the morning."

"Why don't I have you and your photographic memory remind me?"

Jennifer crossed her arms. "I'm not always around, and I wouldn't know all the things that you experience anyway."

"Okay. It's a good idea. I'll start tonight."

The maitre d' decided our waiting time met the regulations for the appropriate delay in a high-class restaurant and led us to a table, vacant since we had exited the elevator. He shook out napkins for Marion and Allison and left the rest of us to fend for ourselves, figuring the men and Jennifer could handle napkins unaided.

We sat near the window with an excellent view over Waikiki toward Diamond Head. Allison selected a chair with her back to the view so she could look at the solid core of the restaurant.

A large group of people sat at the next table. One curly black-haired man, who wore a yellow Hawaiian shirt, wildly gesticulated to emphasize some point he was making to his friends. Another man with a large nose hoisted a drink in a toast. They laughed loudly. Obviously, no one in that crowd felt any pain.

Our elevation allowed a view over most of the other hotels in Waikiki. The last remnant of light reflected off wisps of clouds and cast a pink glow to the sands below. I remembered walking along this beach years ago. Now my shaky memory and I had returned to Hawaii once again.

"Did you know that there's a trail to the top of Diamond Head?" Jennifer said.

"How'd you find that out?" I asked.

"I read a blurb in the Auto Club guide. There are stairs and a tunnel to go through. We'll have to hike up there."

"I'm game," I replied. "That sounds much better than going in the ocean."

"Oh, Grandpa. They're both good activities."

"I'll do the ocean part," Allison said, "but pass on the top of Diamond Head. This is enough height for me."

We feasted on seafood and various quarters of a cow. Once sated I asked, "What's the travel bureau have in store for us the next few days?"

"I'm surfing in the morning," Jennifer said, "and the next day we're going to visit Meyer Ohana and Henry Palmer at the Hale Pohai care home."

"Who the hell are they?" I asked.

"Paul, watch your language," Allison interjected.

I put my hand over my mouth. "Oops."

Jennifer scowled, and then her face relaxed. "Grandpa, you and your memory. You ate meals with them when you lived in the retirement home in Kaneohe."

"If you say so."

"I do. Meyer is a retired judge and attorney and was your best buddy there."

"Me, friendly with a dam . . . darn lawyer?"

"Yes. As strange as it seems."

"The only things I hate more than the ocean are lawyers."

Jennifer let out a loud burst of air. "I know. You hate the ocean, lawyers and taking pills."

"You have that right, kiddo."

"Meyer's a gentleman, and you like each other. You even read to him because he can't see very well anymore. Henry Palmer wasn't exactly a friend of yours, but you entertained each other." Jennifer took a sip of water.

"What do you mean by that?"

Jennifer put her glass down. "Well, Henry has Asperger's syndrome. He's very focused on baseball facts and his coin collection, but you and he enjoyed insulting each other."

I pointed to my chest. "Me, insulting someone?"

Jennifer gave a knowing smile. "Yes. Both of you were very good at it."

"I'm definitely going to have to keep a journal on this trip to remind me of prime insults."

"That's right, Paul," Marion said. "You should start tonight so you can refresh your memory tomorrow morning. Otherwise you won't remember this conversation or anything that happened today."

"This memory loss is crapola."

"Please watch what you say around Jennifer," Allison said.

"Sh . . . oops. My mouth gets engaged before my brain responds. I'll try to be more careful."

Jennifer giggled. "That's okay, Mom. I'm used to Grandpa, and he doesn't even use the 'F' word like the kids at school do."

Allison raised an eyebrow. "Things sure have changed since my school days."

"That's right, Mom. You didn't even have laptop computers and cell phones. And speaking of cell phones, when do I get one?"

"Let's not get on that kick again," Denny said. "In any case, you have your own computer."

"You can add computers to my list of dislikes," I said. "Lawyers, the ocean, pills and computers."

"Oh, Grandpa, computers are very useful. I've found all kinds of information to help you in the past."

"But you didn't uncover where my errant brain cells went."

"No. I'm afraid computers can't help you there."

I gave Jennifer a smug smile. "See, computers can't do squat."

"But they can access the Internet to find information to help solve murders."

I flinched. "Who'd want to do that?"

"Grandpa, you have this way of being around people who end up dead."

I looked around the room. "You mean like here?"

"Jennifer's right," Marion said. "It's happened before."

"I'll be hornswoggled. I don't remember anything like that."

"And I brought my laptop along so I can help with anything you need, Grandpa. I'm going to send email messages to Austin." Jennifer loudly cleared her throat. "Since my mom and dad won't let me have a cell phone to call my friends."

Allison gave her daughter a knowing smile. "You'll eventually have your own cell phone, but not yet."

"Aw, Mom. All the kids my age have cell phones."

Allison gave an eye roll. "Right. You're the only deprived seventh grader in the whole world."

"Who's this Austin you mentioned?" I asked.

Marion's face crinkled into a smile. "He's my grandson in Venice Beach. You and he became good buddies last summer, and he and Jennifer are friends. He's a year older than Jennifer."

I dabbed the corner of my eye with my napkin. "This whole world of mine that I can't remember. It's so sad."

"Now don't go feeling sorry for yourself," Marion said.

I chucked her cheek. "Only kidding. I have a good life, a beautiful bride and a great family. I need to count my blessings. As long as I don't have to use any cussed computers."

"I don't know, Grandpa. Me and my computer helped you before. You seem to have a knack for finding dead bodies and getting in trouble with the police."

I blinked. "There you go again. What do you mean?"

Marion patted my arm. "You have a checkered past."

"I remember Checker Auto Parts, a competitor to my store in Los Angeles, lo, those many years ago . . ."

Jennifer tapped the table with her fingers. "In the last several years you've also become an amateur sleuth."

I recoiled. *"Moi?"*

"But not on this trip, Paul," Allison said. "We're on vacation."

"That's right, Dad," Denny added. "This will be a calm, relaxing trip, so nothing unusual is on the agenda."

"Other than a helicopter ride," Jennifer said. "You promised that we'd go up in a helicopter."

"That's an approved event," Denny said. "I mean no one is getting involved with any criminal activity on this trip."

"And here I thought I'd steal a couple of packets of sugar

19

from the restaurant," I said.

"Tomorrow I'll look into setting up a helicopter ride," Denny said.

After dinner we discussed blindfolding Allison for the ride down in the glass elevator, but she again faced the inside with her eyes closed.

"Who wants to join me for a short stroll?" I suggested. "I need to stretch these old legs after eating such fine food."

Everyone agreed, so we sauntered over to the yacht harbor and walked along the quay.

"It would be fun to go sailing in one of those," Jennifer said, pointing to a thirty-foot sailboat named *Sallie* with a home port of Honolulu painted in large block letters on the stern.

"Not for me," I replied. "They're too damn small and close to the water."

"But, Paul. You had no problem on the cruise ship last summer," Marion said.

"Don't remember diddly about that, but I'm sure I did fine on something large with multiple decks between me and the ocean." I pointed toward the good ship *Sallie*. "But putting me on one of these flyspecks on the seven seas? No thanks."

I looked toward the street and saw a large group of revelers, obviously having partaken of too much liquid refreshment. They descended on us like a swarm of mosquitoes. Before I was able to move out of the way, a member of the rowdy crowd nudged a dark-haired, short man wearing a yellow Hawaiian shirt who in turn bumped into me. He was small enough that he bounced off, not doing me any damage. I recognized him as one of the people who'd sat at the table next to us at dinner.

He shook a fist at me. "Whatcha doing crowding the sidewalk?"

"Why are you being drunk and disorderly?" I replied.

"Drunk? No one accuses Sammy Malo of being drunk."

"Well, Paul Jacobson does, Sammy."

He swayed and aimed toward me again. "Out of my way."

"Cool your jets, Sammy. My family and I are out for an evening stroll. Don't be a jerk."

He approached me again and stuck his nose up toward my chin. "No one insults me."

"Why don't you jump in the yacht harbor and sober up," I said.

"You . . . you . . ."

"Come on, Sammy." The large-nosed man, who had been sitting with Sammy at dinner, grabbed his arm.

I turned to my family. "We should head back to the Hibiscus Hotel. Enough of the local punks."

Sammy mumbled something and gave me an impolite finger gesture before being dragged away.

Feeling heat surge up my neck, I shouted, "Drop dead!"

CHAPTER 2

I shook my head as the drunk Sammy Malo and his friends staggered off. "So much for the Aloha spirit." I hoped they would go sleep it off somewhere, but they disappeared into another bar. Some people didn't know when to stop. "There goes the reason that I don't drink in excess anymore—only a sip of wine or a beer once in a while."

"It's a shame that people like that have to foist themselves on others," Allison said. "They ruined our peaceful walk. I'm ready to go back to the hotel."

Everyone agreed with Allison, so we turned around and retraced our steps. Once in the lobby, Jennifer said, "Let's ride the glass elevator again."

Allison turned a shade of gray. "No thank you."

"I'll do it," I said. Marion also nodded her head in agreement.

"Cool."

"I'll go back to the room with Allison," Denny said.

They took off toward the regular elevators, and Marion, Jennifer and I waited by the single elevator to the top.

After watching full eaters roll out of the elevator, we ascended.

Jennifer said, "I love traveling. When I grow up, I think I'll lead tours."

"I remember you wanting to be a doctor, a lawyer, a detective, a private investigator and a tennis pro," Marion said.

"Before this trip, I last remember you being six years old," I said.

Jennifer wrinkled her nose and proceeded to ignore me. "I'm done with those professions. Old ideas from my youth."

Marion raised an eyebrow. "That was over the last year and a half."

"Eons in the past. I think I'll lead adventure travel groups all over the world. Surfing trips, jungle exploration, mountain climbing . . ."

"You can visit all the outside glass elevators in existence," I said, "but don't take your mom."

Upon reaching the top, we exited and enjoyed the view one more time. We watched lights twinkling on the hillsides.

Marion snuggled up against me. "Quite a place you've dragged me to, Mr. Jacobson."

"Only the best for my bride."

"You're not newlyweds anymore," Jennifer said. "You've been married for five months."

"A spit in the bucket," I said. "At my age that represents less than one percent of my life."

"That's the difference, Grandpa. For me five months is a major part of my life. It seems like ages since last summer."

"Ah, the wonders of youth."

After ooh-ing and ah-ing a little more, we took the elevator down so we could take the other elevator up to our rooms.

Marion and I gave Jennifer good-night hugs and adjourned to our suite.

"It's a good suggestion that I keep a journal," I said.

"Yes," Marion replied. "And I have just the thing for you." She fiddled around in her suitcase, extracted a spiral notebook and handed it to me. "Here. Write in this and leave it with a note to yourself on top of the nightstand by the bed."

I sighed. "What a way to deal with a crappy memory."

"It works. You've done it before. The only problem: you sometimes overlook reading your note to yourself first thing when you wake up."

"You'll have to remind me if that happens."

She patted my arm. "I'm your backup system."

With that decided, I documented the life and times of Paul Jacobson, Hawaiian tourist extraordinaire, while Marion performed her pre-bedtime drill in the bathroom.

As I awoke, I found myself in a room I didn't recognize. I stretched and my left arm bumped into a lump in the bed. I peered over and discerned a woman with silver hair cascading over the pillow. Something wasn't right here. I tried to collect my thoughts, but they seemed to have disappeared into an alternative universe. This wasn't my wife Rhonda. Then I remembered something from the distant past. Rhonda had died. So who was this woman next to me in bed? I noticed a wedding ring on her left hand, which rested outside the blanket.

I checked my left hand. I wore a ring as well. Did I get hitched again?

At that moment my companion shifted, opened her eyes and smiled at me. "Good morning, Paul."

"I hate to be impolite, but who are you and where am I?"

She stretched. "I'm your wife, Marion, and you're in Honolulu staying at the Hibiscus Hotel."

"I married again?"

"Yes. Last summer."

"Damn. That's a big blank."

"Why don't you read what you wrote in the notebook on your nightstand?"

I found a note stating, "Read this, you old poop. You'll wake up confused as a dog in a cat show. Don't do anything stupid. The chick in bed with you is your new bride, Marion."

It seemed to be in my handwriting. I proceeded to read the journal.

After a moment I looked up. "So my family's here as well?"

"That's right, Paul. We all arrived yesterday."

After I completed the diary, I put it down on the nightstand. "I need some time to clear my head. I think I'll take a little stroll. You care to join me?"

"No. I think I'll go back to sleep." She turned over.

I clambered out of bed and padded into the john. After taking care of various bodily processes and returning to the bedroom, I noticed a red light flashing on the phone. I punched the operator button and a kind man's voice informed me a package awaited yours truly at the front desk. I dressed, pocketed a card key and exited the room, noting the room number so I'd be able to find the right place upon my return.

Once down in the lobby, I moseyed up to the front desk and asked the clerk, who sported large bushy eyebrows, to find a package waiting for me. He reached under the counter to retrieve an envelope, which he handed over. It contained a typed note inside indicating that my family and I were the recipients of an all-expenses-paid helicopter ride, compliments of an anonymous friend. I only needed to stop by the office of Tourist Air Tours a block away and schedule a tour with Dex Tanaka this morning. I remembered reading that Jennifer wanted to go on a helicopter ride.

I chuckled as I reread the note. The anonymous friend must be Meyer, whom I had also read about in my journal. Why not take a look at this air tour outfit?

I stuffed the letter in my pocket, left the lobby, strolled past a swimming pool and out onto a deck that overlooked the yacht harbor. I felt the sprinkle of an early morning shower as orange-tinted clouds drifted down from the mountains. Out toward the ocean I spotted a double rainbow arched above the masts of boats bobbing at their moorings. Sparrows and doves pecked at crumbs left from tourists munching on bagels and sweet rolls. I listened to the cacophony of chirping, cooing and cawing as my gaze scanned upward toward the hotel with its turquoise covers on balcony railings.

As I strolled to the left end of the deck, I came to a fenced-off area below that looked like a dried-up cesspool. Obviously construction was taking place for a new hotel or set of condos or some structure to further clog the skyline. I headed down a ramp and emerged at ground level, crossed the street and peered down at the water of the yacht harbor.

A school of minnows churned the water as if expecting a handout of bread crumbs from me. "Sorry, fellows." I turned out my empty pockets. "Nothing here."

The tiny fish circled around flotsam, which consisted of paper cups, plastic bags, bottles, a blue Croc, an empty milk container and aluminum cans lazily floating along the jetty. The boats I passed possessed an eclectic collection of names: *Makani Koa, Soujourner, Seanarf, Windwalker, Crystal J, Charlene Ann, Dream Maker, Odyssey, Lisa, Pretty Woman, Waipauli, Seven Eleven, Alii Kaii II, Esoteric, Hana Hou, Hahu Kai, Valhalla* and *Jeannie*.

One boat with Christmas lights displayed a hand-painted sign identifying it as "Santa's Surf Shack." Fishing boats, yachts, and catamarans floated there in all sizes and shapes. Tethered to one sailboat, I spotted a floating rubber raft that looked like a soggy mattress.

I imagined someone getting too hot in a cramped cabin, climbing down a tiny ladder and gingerly lying on this improvised bed to sleep, rocked by the gentle swaying of the remnants of ocean swells that entered the harbor.

That wouldn't be me. I'd never be able to sleep lying there on the water. I'd be worrying about falling in or fish nibbling on my feet. Pucky. Merely watching from the shore caused goose bumps to pop out on my arms. Rays of morning sunlight peeked past the hotels towering above me and tried to warm my old body, but I shivered at the thought of the murky water in front of me. No, thank you. I was a confirmed landlubber with no hope of ever changing.

A guy almost as old as me in tattered pants and a ragged shirt shuffled up to me. He looked like he had slept in his clothes and hadn't washed for a week. He threw a dirty, gnarled hand in the direction of the harbor. "There's something out in the water."

I regarded him more carefully. He had wrinkled skin, a scraggly beard and an aroma somewhat south of dead fish. I sniffed. "What do you mean?"

"Right there." He pointed into the water.

I regarded the floating rubber raft more carefully, noticing a piece of cloth attached on one side. I moved several paces closer and peered again. Something bobbed next to the raft amid the harbor junk. It looked familiar. I scrunched up my nose and riveted my stare as a ripple surged past the raft. The minor disturbance shook the debris. My mouth went dry. The fingers of a hand broke the surface and floated there, lifeless.

CHAPTER 3

I stumbled, bracing myself against a light post, as if I were a drunken sailor. The hand in the yacht harbor bobbed in place, fingers clearly visible. The rest of the body remained hidden in the murky water. I imagined fish nibbling on whatever remained below the surface. I swallowed, doing my best to keep the stomach fluids where they belonged.

I looked around for the old bum. Nowhere to be seen. I checked to find anyone else in the vicinity. Crap. No one. Rather than trying to rouse an irate tenant living on a houseboat, I galumphed across the street and charged up the escalator to the lobby of the Hibiscus.

At the check-in desk I confronted the smiling man in a Hawaiian shirt with whom I had spoken earlier. "Call nine-one-one."

His smile disappeared. "What's the problem?"

"I just came from the yacht harbor," I gasped. "There's something human floating in the water."

He picked up a phone, punched in the three digits and spoke for a moment before handing the receiver to me. I fumbled with it as if it were on fire, almost dropping it, before I managed to thrust it against my ear.

First I heard static on the line, then a clipped female voice asked, "What's the nature of the emergency you're reporting?"

"There's no nature associated with it. It's completely un-

28

natural. I saw a hand floating in the Honolulu Ala Wai Yacht Harbor."

"And where are you calling from?"

"The lobby of the Hibiscus Hotel."

"And your name?"

"Paul Jacobson."

"Mr. Jacobson, please stay on the line, and I'll have someone meet you there."

I continued to hog the counter, but fortunately no one else demanded attention at this hour. The clerk clicked keys on a keyboard and periodically looked up at me as if willing me to disappear. The sound irritated me, but I held my duty position without complaining. How long would I have to stand here?

The woman's voice came back on the line. "I'm dispatching an emergency response team. They should be there within ten minutes."

"I'll hold tight." Good thing I availed myself of the bathroom before taking my hike.

I listened and heard a siren. Shortly, two firemen in full gear stomped toward the counter. I waved to them.

The taller of the two men approached me. "Did you place the call?"

"Yes." I handed the phone back to the clerk.

"The dispatcher said you reported finding a body."

"Not a body. But a hand floating in the water."

"Show us where."

I led them outside, across the street and pointed. "To the left side of that floating rubber raft. Where that apple core is bobbing."

We all peered.

I scratched my head. "I don't see it."

The shorter guy grabbed his radio and jabbered away.

"What's next?" I asked.

"We're calling in the divers."

As we waited, a black sedan pulled up and a man in a dark suit climbed out. He approached me and held out a badge. "I'm Detective Chun. I understand you called in a reported body floating in the harbor.

"A hand actually."

"Please describe what you saw."

I eyed Detective Chun. He stood several inches shorter than my five-foot-eleven. He had pure white hair and wore black plastic-rimmed glasses. I guessed him to be on the upper age range for an active detective. He struck me as a no-nonsense kind of guy, so I decided not to beat around the bush. "While taking my morning constitutional, I happened to spot that raft connected to the sailboat." I pointed. "While looking at it, I noticed something strange in the water. Upon closer inspection, I discovered a hand. Never saw any of the body attached to it. I hightailed it up to the lobby of the Hibiscus Hotel, and the clerk at the front desk placed the nine-one-one call."

"Was anyone with you?"

"Only a guy who looked like a bum. He directed my attention to the water, and that's when I first spotted the hand."

"And where is he now?"

"Good question." I looked around me. "He disappeared while the hand in the water distracted me. I haven't seen him since."

"May I see some identification?" Chun scratched a wart on his left hand.

"Sure, Detective." I pulled out my wallet, thumbed through the plastic insert sleeves and showed him my smiling puss on an identification card.

"No driver's license?"

"Not anymore. I have short-term memory loss, so I've given up threatening the lives of pedestrians."

He didn't smile but continued to stare at my ID. "Is this your current address in Venice Beach, California?"

I examined the card carefully, not recognizing the name of the street. "I guess so. My wife can verify it for you if need be."

"How can I reach you if I have further questions?"

"I'm in room seven twenty-five at the Hibiscus Hotel."

He jotted a note on a pad and stared at me. "How do you remember your room number? I thought you suffered from short-term memory loss."

"Very good, Detective, you were listening. My form of memory dysfunction is very specific. I remember things fine during the day, but overnight everything is as clear as the water in this harbor."

He nodded. "Okay, Mr. Jacobson. How long will you be at the Hibiscus?"

"I don't know for sure, but I imagine two weeks or so. I'm here with my family during my granddaughter's winter break from school."

He jotted some more notes on his pad and handed back my ID.

"May I be excused?" I asked.

He waved his hand. "Yeah."

Although I hadn't wandered very far, I decided, with all the time spent going back and forth between the lobby and the yacht harbor, I should see if my family wanted breakfast. I'd defer looking into the helicopter ride until later.

When I entered our room, I found Marion up and reading a newspaper. She gave me a fetching smile. "Jennifer's already been in here asking if we want to eat breakfast. Knock on the adjoining door to let them know you're back."

I rapped "shave and a haircut, two bits" and the door flew open.

"Mornin', Grandpa."

"I understand some people in here will start gnawing on the

31

wallpaper unless they have a chance to stuff their faces soon."

"You bet. Let's get going."

Our mob assembled, and we de-elevated to the lobby and moseyed into the breakfast nook filled with other rampaging tourists. We waited in line for a few minutes before a hostess led us to a table for six. I was hungry enough to eat a meal for me and for the empty seat at the table.

"Marion said you went outside, Grandpa. Did you have a good walk?"

"Short but exciting."

"What does that mean?" Denny asked.

I leaned in toward the table, cupped my hands and whispered. "I found a human hand floating in the yacht harbor."

"What?" everyone said in unison.

"Paul, you didn't mention that to me," Marion said.

"Oh, dear," Allison said.

"Dad, what have you got yourself into?"

"Only a hand?" Jennifer asked.

"No. It was probably attached to a body."

"Cool," Jennifer said. "Tell us the whole story."

So I repeated the events of the morning for the benefit of my whole family. Denny scowled while Jennifer listened with wide eyes.

"I bet they bring in divers to recover the body," Jennifer said. "Let's go watch after breakfast."

"I don't think that's a good idea," Allison said.

"Oh, Mom. I'm almost thirteen. I can handle it."

"But I can't," Allison said.

After Jennifer wolfed down her waffle, she tugged at my arm. "Come on, Grandpa. Let's go check out the divers."

Marion and Allison declined, preferring to return to the rooms, but Denny, Jennifer and I headed out to the harbor. Quite a collection of vehicles and people had assembled along the quay. A fire truck, ambulance and dive truck stood by the side of the road. Four firemen, three divers in wet suits, a two-person emergency response crew and a partridge in a pear tree (actually Detective Chun) were huddled like a football team ready to call a winning play. We ambled over to watch. The divers slipped into the water and bubbles floated to the surface as they swam underwater toward the raft.

Nothing happened for a few minutes. Then one of the divers surfaced and signaled to shore. A fireman tossed him a coil of rope. The diver submerged again, and shortly they resurfaced tugging something behind them.

We watched as one of the divers handed the end of the rope to a fireman, and together they hoisted something out of the water.

I saw a fully-clothed man in dark, dripping slacks and a torn yellow Hawaiian shirt. He had short black hair and all body parts seemed to be intact. Didn't look the least bit familiar.

Detective Chun noticed me standing there. "Curious, Mr. Jacobson?"

"My granddaughter wanted to see the divers."

He scratched the wart on his left hand. "Any other thoughts on what you discovered earlier, Mr. Jacobson?"

"Nope."

Chun handed me a genuine Honolulu Police Department business card. "Give me a call if something comes to mind."

"You'll be the first to know, Detective. And I'd lay off scratching your hand so often. You might want to have that wart surgically removed."

Chun harrumphed and turned his attention back to the proceedings.

They laid the body out on a tarp, and a woman began taking pictures. Another man slipped on latex gloves and proceeded to examine the body.

Jennifer looked at her watch. "Uh-oh. We better head back so I can get my swimsuit on. I'm going surfing this morning."

We left the crew to do their thing. I figured that would be the end of my involvement with the floating hand attached to the sunken body.

As we walked across the street, Denny said, "I just realized something. That dead man looked vaguely familiar."

Jennifer came to a screeching halt. "You're right, Dad. The man Grandpa bumped into last night wore a Hawaiian shirt with that same yellow pattern."

CHAPTER 4

"Damn," I responded to Jennifer's comment that I might have encountered the floater the night before when he was still alive. "That's all I need. Now I'm linked to the dead man."

"You didn't do anything wrong, Grandpa. The man bumped into you last night. He must have fallen in the water later. He was pretty drunk."

"We'll leave it in the hands of good Detective Chun," I said. Being on vacation with my family, I had no desire to worry about dead bodies.

Back in my hotel room I remembered the helicopter ride invitation and knocked on the adjoining door. Allison opened it. I handed the information to her. "Give this to Denny. He can set up Jennifer's helicopter ride, and it's gratis."

Allison shuddered. "As long as I don't have to go."

Denny poked his head around the corner. "And, Dad, don't forget we're going to a luau here at the hotel tonight."

"I sure don't remember that, but it's now planted in my soggy brain for the rest of the day. I'll be ready to drown my sorrows in poi."

"Are you unhappy?" Allison asked.

I patted her arm. "Not in the least. I have to complain once in a while. It keeps my blood flowing."

After my whole clan changed into various pieces of swimming attire, we slathered on sunscreen and strolled along the beach to a place where Denny arranged for a rental surfboard.

While Jennifer waited for the transaction to be completed, she bounced up and down like a pogo stick.

"Save your energy for the ocean," I said.

"Oh, Grandpa. I'm just excited."

When Denny was done, Jennifer dragged a surfboard toward the water. The two older generations plopped down on the sand with a collection of towels and beach mats to watch Jennifer paddle out and catch waves. The last time I'd caught WAVES occurred at the beginning of World War II, but that was a different story.

My eyesight being much better than my memory allowed me to keep Jennifer in view as she rode a wave almost to shore. She pumped her fist in the air in a victory salute.

"Hang ten," I shouted in my best surfer-dude fashion.

Marion looked at me askance, but, then again, I deserved it.

Jennifer paddled back out and rejoined the legion of crazies tempting their fate with Poseidon and sharks.

After watching my offspring, once-removed, accomplish something I'd never felt any desire to even attempt, Marion coaxed me into wandering down to stick my toe in the water. My toe survived, so I turned to head back to sit on the sand.

"Come on, Paul," Marion said. "Since you came this far, why don't you get wet?"

"I did. Up to my ankle."

"Don't be a sissy."

Well, with that challenge, I took a deep breath, adjusted my swim trunks to gird my loins and ventured in up to my waist. When nothing attacked me, I bent over and splashed water on my chest and shoulders.

Marion swam out into deeper water, and I returned to the safety of the sand, my bravery having expired like a parking meter with too little change. Denny and Allison entered the water while I guarded our possessions. They splashed each other like two teenagers. Kids.

Twenty yards away a beach boy loaded people onto a catamaran and launched them out to sea. They acted happy to be abandoning land, while I was content to be ensconced onshore while the insane people around me pretended they enjoyed the ocean.

Marion emerged, padded up to our towels looking none the worse for having swum in the sea, dried off and sat down beside me. "It's too bad you don't enjoy the ocean more, Paul."

"I like it fine if it stays out there and I stay here."

She leaned her soggy head on my dry shoulder. "I didn't marry you for your love of the ocean."

"Good thing. You'd be pretty disappointed. But I'm certainly honored you decided to put up with me. I'm very lucky to have such an attractive wife." I gave her my best Groucho Marx eyebrow wiggle.

Marion rewarded me with a kiss on the cheek. My heart beat faster at the thought that this wonderful woman had signed up to stick around with a geezer like me.

Not wanting to risk turning into a lobster, I put on a shirt and baseball cap and watched the young women prance by, offset by the old farts with beer bellies stumbling along. Every shape and size of human creature seemed out trying to catch skin cancer.

Eventually, Jennifer returned from her ocean expedition. Another girl, two inches shorter with long black hair, stood alongside her. "I met a new friend named Hina out there surfing."

Hina gave us a huge wide smile, revealing pearly white teeth. "Yep. It's short for Hinakuluiau, goddess of rain."

"I hope you don't bring any showers today." I looked up toward a few puffy clouds sailing past. "I'm enjoying the sunshine."

37

Jennifer rolled her eyes. "Oh, Grandpa. None of your silly jokes."

Hina giggled. "You're like my grandpa, Aliki. He loves to kid me."

"Hey, that's what we grandpas do. We're trained first as fathers to tell dumb jokes, and we have to continue the tradition with our grandkids."

"Hina's mom works at the Hibiscus Hotel," Jennifer said. "Hina will be sticking around and going to the luau tonight. Can she sit with us?"

"Sure," I replied. "The more the merrier."

Hina gave Jennifer a nudge with her elbow. "I can teach you how to string plumeria leis. We'll make them for your whole family."

"Cool. Let's go."

After they returned their surfboards, the two of them took off like crabs scuttling along the sand. The rest of us followed like tortoises crawling across the desert.

When we entered the lobby, Jennifer was waiting, bouncing from one foot to the other. "Come on. Hina and I are set up in a room behind the desk." She led us through a door to a little cubbyhole with a small wooden table on which rested a huge bowl of plumeria flowers, two long needles, scissors and thread.

Hina waved to us. "I do this all the time to help my mom. We give leis to special guests. Today the Jacobsons will be special guests, and Jennifer can make some of the leis." She threaded the long needle, snipped off the stem of a blossom and inserted the needle through the center of the flower, before pushing it to the end of the thread. Then she handed the started lei to Jennifer. "Now, your turn. Grab a flower."

Jennifer bit her lip, cut off the stem of a plumeria flower and pushed the needle through it. "Hey. That's easy."

"Now fill up the whole length of thread and I'll show you how to tie it off."

The older generations left the young girls to their work. Marion, Denny and Allison headed up to the rooms, but I went out on the hotel patio and leaned on the railing to survey the yacht harbor. Various types of watercraft headed out to sea or returned from a morning of excitement or, if it had been me, sheer terror. I turned my gaze to the road below and saw an old man in tattered clothes shuffling along the sidewalk. Wait a minute. I recognized him as the guy who had directed my attention to the floating hand this morning. A black car pulled up, and the old man climbed in the passenger's side. "Hey!" I shouted.

The driver with his arm out the open window looked up, and our eyes locked for a moment. Then the car shot away from the curb and disappeared around the corner. I hadn't gotten a good look at the driver's face or been close enough to see the license plate.

This deserved reporting to Detective Chun, so I hustled my butt up to our room and retrieved the card he had given me earlier. After placing a call and waiting for five minutes, the good detective came on the line.

"A few minutes ago I saw the old man who was with me this morning when I first spotted the hand floating in the yacht harbor." I gasped to catch my breath. "He got in a black car driven by another man."

"Did you see where they went?"

"No. I lost sight of the car."

"Describe the driver."

"I didn't see him clearly. I noticed a brown arm hanging out the window and dark piercing eyes, but that's all I can tell you."

"And the car?"

"Big and black. Maybe like a Lincoln Town Car."

"That's interesting, Mr. Jacobson. Black Lincoln Town Cars are a favorite of some of the local suspected drug dealers."

After going back to my room, showering and changing, I settled down to contemplate the latest events.

Shortly thereafter, Denny knocked on the adjoining door and stuck his head into my room, interrupting my cogitation. "Who wants to go see the imu?"

"What's an imu?" Marion asked.

"It's the fire pit roasting the pig for the luau," Denny answered.

"I'm game," I replied. "I qualify after being roasted on the beach."

The ladies declined, preferring to relax for a while, so my son and I took the elevator down to the ground level and were directed to a back lawn area. Off to one side stood a crowd of people around a sandy pit.

"We're here in the nick of time," Denny said. "They're uncovering the pig."

Smoke billowed up from the ground. Two men with shovels removed a top layer of dirt, revealing ti leaves. They raked off the leaves, and stuck long wooden spears into the cooked pig before lifting it out of the pit.

Denny and I pushed to the front of the crowd to get a better view. The aroma of succulent pork wafted through the tropical air. Red hot stones glowed underneath where the pig had been roasted. I looked up at a palm tree as the trade wind made the fronds sway like a hula girl.

I felt a shove in the back and teetered on the brink of the hot coals.

CHAPTER 5

My foot slipped, and a blast of hot air from the imu hit me in the face. My arms pin-wheeled as I tried to regain my balance. My life flashed before my eyes with visions of being burned to death.

Denny grabbed me around my waist and pulled me back to safety.

People near me gasped. As I stumbled back to solid ground, a woman put her hand to her mouth. "You almost fell into the pit."

"No. Someone pushed me." I looked wildly around, but found no one who looked guilty. "Did anyone see who did it?"

All heads shook.

"I was staring into the imu," Denny said. "I didn't notice anything until you swayed toward the pit."

My heart rate returned to its normal range, and I took a deep breath. "I think I've had enough excitement. I'm going back to the room."

"I'll join you," Denny said.

We headed into the lobby with me stopping once to look back at the crowd of people. I didn't spot anyone showing interest in my movements. Yet I knew it hadn't been an accident. Someone definitely had shoved me.

Upstairs, Jennifer had returned and showed me a display she had set up in her parents' room with five plumeria leis. It reminded me of one of the lei seller stands at the Honolulu airport that I remembered from my earlier days before my memory went on the fritz.

"You made these?" I asked.

"I made two, and Hina strung three. She's much faster than I am. I'm pretty good at getting the flowers on, but it takes me a while to tie the thread."

"They look very professional. We'll be decked out for the luau tonight. I'll have to wear my best Hawaiian shirt."

Later, we assembled and met Hina in the lobby. She stood with a young woman wearing a yellow hibiscus in her sleek black hair. Hina raced forward, gave Jennifer a hug and turned toward the woman. "Everyone, meet my mom."

The woman held out a slender hand, "I'm Grace Makoku."

Allison said, "Your daughter has been showing my daughter how to string leis. We're delighted they've become friends."

Grace graced us with a sunny smile. "Hina enjoys meeting new people. She'll probably be running this hotel when she grows up."

"No, Mom. I'm going to be a lawyer."

Jennifer giggled. "I wanted to be a lawyer at one time, too."

I groaned. "That's all the world needs. More attorneys."

"Tell them your idea," Jennifer said to Hina.

"One of the most fun things to do on this island is ti leaf sliding." Hina looked toward her mom. "Can I take the Jacobsons to do that tomorrow?"

At the same time Jennifer tilted her head to the side and opened her wide eyes to Allison. "It sounds even better than going on a roller coaster. Can we do it? Huh? Huh?"

"Slow down, you two," Allison said.

"We don't have anything planned in the morning," Denny said. "I've always wanted to try ti leaf sliding."

Allison threw her hands in the air. "I'm outnumbered." She turned to Grace. "Is this all right with you?"

Grace bit her lip. "Hina, you have some leis to make for tomorrow night."

Hina hopped on one foot. "I can do that in the afternoon."

"And I'll help her," Jennifer added.

"And if it's okay, I'll ask Keoki if he wants to come as well." Hina said. "He's my brother and knows the best places to go."

"We have plenty of room in the SUV," Denny said. "I'll put down the third seat where we stored our luggage the day we arrived."

Grace gave a sideways smile to Allison. "I know when I'm outnumbered as well. Okay, you can go, Hina."

The two girls gave each other high-fives.

"Thank you for agreeing to entrust your kids with us," Allison said.

Grace gave her a Cheshire cat grin. "You seem like nice people. Also my husband's with the Honolulu Police Department, so no one messes with my kids."

Jennifer bounced around, imitating a ping-pong ball dropped on a hard floor. "My grandpa knows detectives Chun and Saito."

I cringed. "I made the acquaintance of Detective Chun this morning, but I don't remember Detective Saito."

"You knew him when you lived in Kaneohe," Jennifer said.

Grace nodded. "I've met both of them."

"What does your husband do with the police?" I asked.

Grace frowned. "I haven't seen him much in the last month. He's with Narcotics and Vice in the Investigative Bureau and has been working undercover."

"That must be difficult," Allison said.

"That's why Keoki and Hina are spending a lot of time at the hotel." Grace peeked at her watch. "It was nice meeting you. I need to get back to work."

Hina grabbed Jennifer's hand. "Come on. Let's go find seats at the luau. We'll reserve the best place for your family." They dashed off like two firefighters going to a big blaze.

We said our good-byes to Grace and moseyed out onto the hotel grounds where a large white tent stood. Inside, we located the two girls and sat down on folding chairs in front of tables covered with white linen. Vases of purple and white orchids complimented bowls of yellow pineapple. The girls had taken the middle two of six seats. Allison and Denny sat next to Jennifer, and Marion and I plunked down beside Hina.

"This luau has the best food in Waikiki," Hina said.

"Are you the promotional manager for the hotel?" I asked.

"Nope. That's my mom's job. But we often go check out the competition. I've been to every other luau." Hina tapped the table. "We have the best lomi lomi salmon and lau lau chicken." She kissed her fingers. "And the haupia is to die for."

I regarded her carefully. "Are you sure you don't want to be an actress in Hollywood instead of a lawyer?"

Hina giggled. "No way. I may represent actors in my legal practice though."

"I can't get over kids your age considering careers already," I said. "When I was your age, future planning involved scheduling a baseball game the next day."

"My dad taught me to plan ahead."

A spotlight flashed on and highlighted three young men standing on a stage and holding sticks that burned on both ends. Drums beat from the back of the tent, and the men began a fire dance, twirling the burning batons in the air and tromping on the stage.

"That's my brother Keoki." Hina pointed. "The one on the left."

I watched as Keoki threw his fire stick ten feet into the air and deftly snatched it as it returned to shoulder level.

At the end of the dance, Hina raced up to the stage and waved to Keoki. He followed her back to our table. "Everyone, dis my big bruddah."

"Hey, howzit?" Keoki waved. "Mo betta you come Hawaii."

Hina put her hands on her hips. "Okay, big brother. We can cut out the pidgin."

Keoki bowed. "It's a pleasure to meet you." He went down the line and shook hands with each of us.

When he reached me, I said, "You've been drafted to come ti leaf sliding with us tomorrow and show us the best place on the island."

His eyes lit up. "Awesome."

"Do you work here full time?" I asked.

"Only during vacations. I'm a senior at Kamehameha School."

"And he's going to Stanford next year." Hina grinned and elbowed her brother. "He was accepted last week. Early admission."

I arched an eyebrow. "I assume you're not studying fire dancing."

Keoki laughed. "Nope. Pre-med. I have to get back to work. Thanks for coming to the luau." He headed off and passed one of his fellow fire dancers and shouted, "Hey, bruddah." They slapped hands.

I turned to Hina. "So you can turn the pidgin English on and off."

"With our local friends we speak that way, but our parents insist that we learn correct English."

"Say something in pidgin," Jennifer said.

"Hey, whatzit wid you? You no speak like da kine? You go store and buy see moi fo' me. I give you dalla fo' eighty."

"Okay, translate," I said.

"What's the matter with you? You don't speak like the rest of us. Go to the store and buy some cracked seed for me. I'll give you four dollars and eighty cents."

I shrugged. "Clear as mud."

"What's cracked seed?" Jennifer asked.

"It's dried plum and the best stuff besides luau food. I'll bring some li hing mui on our trip tomorrow."

Wait staff arrived bearing bowls and plates. I noticed Keoki wearing a Hawaiian shirt, now part of the crew. Soon, delectable treats filled the place in front of me. "Okay, Hina, tell us what everything is."

She pointed to each of the dishes. "Here's the kalua pua'a— roast pork."

"Yeah, I almost ended up too close and personal with the hot stones that cooked this."

"And that's a purple sweet potato. And the lomi lomi here consists of diced salmon, tomatoes and onions." Hina pointed to another dish. "One of my favorites—mahi mahi, the best fish in the ocean. Over there is Portuguese sweet bread. The lau lau next to it is chicken in ti leaves."

"You wrap food in the leaves and slide on them," Jennifer added.

"Yep. And the white stuff that jiggles is haupia, a coconut-flavored dessert, kind of like stiff pudding. But the most important dish." She picked up a bowl. "Poi."

I looked at the purple goo.

"It looks like library paste," I said.

"And some people think it tastes like paste as well," Hina said. "I love it. Sprinkle in a little rock salt." She picked up her own bowl of poi and added some salt. Then she dipped her fingers in the bowl. "Poi is classified by the thickness. One-finger poi is thick and three-finger poi is thin. This is two-finger poi, just right." She stuck two goopy fingers in her mouth. "Umm, good."

I thought of Goldilocks coming to the house of the three bears, finding poi instead of porridge, and Goldilocks announcing that the baby bear's poi was just right.

"My favorite part of a luau is that you can eat everything with your fingers." Hina stuck another two fingers of poi in her mouth.

Allison let out a deep sigh. "After all these years getting Jennifer to use utensils—down the drain in one day."

"Cheer up," I called across the two girls. "At least they're not eating with their feet."

"You can slug my grandpa in the shoulder for that," Jennifer said to Hina.

Hina raised a fist, and I ducked.

"Just kidding," Hina said. "I never hit grandpas."

I let out a sigh of relief. "A wise decision."

Marion and I tried the poi. "What do you think?" I asked.

She wrinkled her pert little nose. "I tried it. I think I'll stick with the mahi mahi, chicken and pork."

Now that I knew the identity of all the goodies, I dove in like a starving tourist and devoured every delicacy in sight. The poi didn't excite me. I didn't dislike it. It tasted pretty bland.

The spotlight went on and a hula troupe performed. They swayed to and fro in their grass skirts and told stories with their hands that I couldn't quite figure out since the accompanied singing was in Hawaiian. I assumed it had something to do with ocean waves, which of course weren't my favorites anyway.

At the end of the show an announcer picked up the microphone. "We're going to select several audience members to come up on stage."

Keoki appeared behind us and pulled Jennifer and me to our feet. "Come on." He propelled us up onto the stage.

I looked around. The other victims roped into this gig were either kids or young people in their fifties.

Keoki and his two fire-tossing buddies put grass skirts around us and tied them in place. I looked toward the audience but wasn't able to see anything with the spotlight shining directly in my eyes. I felt like the oldest fool in the world. Wait a minute—that was probably the case.

A hula girl showed us how to use our hands and sway our hips. I had trouble with the hip part. I wasn't that hip. She came behind me and placed her hands on my waist. With gentle assistance, I eventually made the grass skirt sway. The audience applauded.

I wiped drops of sweat off my brow. This form of exercise might not have been the best for a geezer my age. After being excused, rather than immediately returning to my family gathering, I stepped outside the tent to get some fresh air. I dabbed at my forehead with a handkerchief and took several deep breaths.

Out of the corner of my eye, I saw a shadow. It appeared to be a man holding something in his hand. At that moment two of the hula girls came out of the tent. I looked back toward the shadowy figure. It had disappeared.

CHAPTER 6

I didn't know if my mind had played tricks on me or if I had really seen a threatening figure in the shadows outside the tent. Was someone out to get me, or did I have an overactive imagination? After the experience earlier at the imu pit, my nerves remained a little frayed. I returned and sat down. The Portuguese sweet bread remained unfinished in front of Marion. "You going to eat that?"

"I'm full. Help yourself."

Having grown up during the depression, I never left food sitting. I finished off the crumbs, patted my stomach and stifled a burp. This feasting on edible island flora and fauna would hold me until breakfast.

The next morning I awoke in a muddle and raced to the bathroom so as not to cause a puddle. After reading my journal and speaking with the nice woman who had been in bed with me, everything became as clear as watching the world through multiple layers of mosquito netting—I caught the general drift but not necessarily the fine details.

We assembled for breakfast, and Denny outlined the day's agenda. "This morning we have the ti leaf sliding expedition. Later this afternoon we're going to Kaneohe so Paul and Marion can visit their friends Meyer Ohana and Henry Palmer."

"Wait a minute," Jennifer said, fixing her dad with her version of the preteen evil eye. "They're my friends too."

Denny threw his hands in the air. "As I was saying, we're going to visit Paul, Marion and Jennifer's friends."

"What should we wear for the first expedition?" I asked.

"Old jeans, tennis shoes and a shirt that you don't mind getting muddy," Denny replied.

"I can handle the old part," I replied.

After returning to the rooms to acquire the appropriate accoutrements, we reassembled in the lobby and found a girl Jennifer's age and a young man waiting there, soon identified to me as Hina and Keoki. We crammed into the SUV and took off.

"Here's some li hing mui. Jennifer, you have to try it." Hina tore open a package and handed each of us one of the wrinkled reddish-colored dried plums. "This kind is dry, sweet and sour. I like it better than the salty or wet ones. There's a seed inside. You can nibble on the meat or suck on it."

I carefully carved off a bit with my front teeth and licked my lips. Not bad. My tongue tingled and saliva flowed at the mingled tastes of sweet and sour. I ate a little more before popping the rest in my mouth and sucking on it.

After a taste, Allison wrinkled her face and placed the seed in a tissue. The rest of us kept chewing and sucking.

"What do you think?" Hina asked Jennifer.

Jennifer smacked her lips. "Different."

"It takes getting used to. Who wants another?"

"Me," Keoki shouted.

"You'd eat the whole package. I brought these for Jennifer's family."

Denny, Jennifer and I both tried another before quitting. Hina and Keoki kept going, as if they hadn't eaten anything since the luau the night before.

"Keoki knows lots of good Hawaiian stories," Hina said. "Why don't you tell us one, big bruddah?"

"That would be cool," Jennifer said.

Keoki nodded. "Okay, since I do a fire dance, I'll tell you a story of Madame Pele, the goddess of fire and volcanoes."

"From what I read in my journal, I almost met her accidently yesterday," I said. "I almost fell in the luau fire pit."

"You have to be very careful around Madame Pele," Keoki continued. "She mainly lives on the Big Island of Hawaii, since that's where the active eruptions take place. She expects tribute from people who go into her territory. One of her special places is the Saddle Road that goes from Waimea to Hilo."

"I've driven there," Denny said. "A rough road."

"Exactly," Keohi replied. "So here's a true story. One night a malihini, which means newcomer, was driving over the Saddle Road. He had bought a pork sandwich for a snack and set it on the passenger's seat of his car. It was a dark night with no moon. He came around a bend, and his headlights shone on a woman with long flowing black hair standing in the middle of the road. Before he could even put on the brakes, the car engine conked out and he came to a stop. The woman, who had glowing red eyes, approached the driver and said, 'No one comes through here with pork. You must leave it for me.' The man at first refused to give up his sandwich. He tried to start his car, but it wouldn't turn over. The woman remained at the side of the car, smoke coming out of her mouth. The malihini became so scared that he tossed the sandwich out the car window. The sandwich and the woman disappeared in a ball of fire. The man sat there speechless. Then the car started by itself. The malihini took off and never drove that road again."

"I don't blame him," I said. "Who wants to be held up for a sandwich? I bet the poor guy was hungry the rest of his trip."

Jennifer, who sat behind me on the third seat with her friends, leaned forward and said, "I have a new geezer joke for you, Grandpa."

I turned my head. "Any geezer joke you've told me in the last six years will be new to me anyway."

"Oh, Grandpa. I want to tell one that's new to me."

"Well, don't keep me in suspense. Let's hear it."

"Okey-dokey. A doctor, a lawyer and a geezer take a walk together. They start talking about the most important things they could do."

"Wait a minute," I interjected. "A lawyer wouldn't have any clue."

"Grandpa, please contain your prejudice against lawyers and don't interrupt."

"Yes, ma'am."

"As I was saying, these three were talking together about doing something important. The doctor said, 'I'd like to cure cancer.' The lawyer nodded and added, 'That's important. I'd like to prove the innocence of all people wrongly jailed.' The geezer looked at the other two and said, "I'd like to find a restroom.' "

In spite of myself I laughed. "Good one."

"No more geezer jokes," Allison shouted from the front seat.

"Besides, don't tell that one around Meyer," Marion said. "With his incontinence problem, he might not appreciate it. And don't let your grandfather be a bad influence."

"I'm the ba-a-a-d grandpa," I said.

Keoki directed Denny into Nuuanu Valley and up the Old Pali Road. "Pull over right here," Keoki said. "I know a shortcut through the trees."

We climbed out, and I looked up at the clouds sailing by. Leaves glistened from a recent shower, but the rain held off for the moment.

"Shouldn't we have umbrellas or ponchos?" Allison asked.

"Nah." Keoki said. "We're going to get wet anyway, and it's warm." He began pushing his way through the undergrowth, and we followed single file. Marion and I brought up the rear.

"Where are we going?" Marion asked.

I shrugged. "I'm following the crowd."

"What if we get lost in this jungle?"

"Let's keep up with the youngsters so that doesn't happen."

We emerged from the undergrowth at a stream.

"We're at the bottom of the run," Keoki said. "There's a trail up to the right."

I peered at a hillside, slashed with a streak of mud running down it. "Where do we find the ti leaves?"

"We'll pick them along the trail."

"I'm not hiking up there," Allison said.

"I'm with you," Marion added. "We can wait by the stream."

"Suit yourselves," Denny said. "You going to try it, Dad?"

"I'll come along for the hike."

We trudged up the hillside. Periodically, I latched onto a vine to help pull my old body over a muddy spot on the trail. We stopped at one point.

Keoki picked a two-foot long, emerald-green leaf, shaped like a giant feather with a rib down the middle. "Here are some good-sized ti leaves. Everyone grab one."

We did as commanded and continued on until we reached a plateau. From here I saw the muddy slope for sliding.

"I'll go first," Keoki said, "to make sure there are no rocks in the way." He set the ti leaf on the ground, dropped onto it and shot down the slope with a loud whoop and disappeared out of sight. In moments I heard a splash and a shout, "It's safe and clear."

"You want to go next?" Hina asked Jennifer.

"You go. I'll watch one more time."

Hina sat down and adjusted the ti leaf. Using her hands, she pushed off and zoomed down the slope. "Yeah hoo!"

After we heard her splash into the stream, Jennifer made her run. Denny turned to me. "You going to try it, Dad?"

"I don't know. Let me take a closer look." I shuffled to the lip of the hill and peered down. It didn't look too bad. Back when my memory still worked, I'd gone down one of those water slides steeper than this.

I took a step closer for one more peek down the slope. My feet shot out from under me, and I thudded down on my butt, careening down the hill without a ti leaf. "Yikes!" My arms flailed as I tried to align my body. The only saving grace—I plunged down the mud feet first. Trees and vines shot by me. I didn't know if my old body would survive this. My tailbone took a bump. I pictured every bone in my body broken. The next thing I knew, I landed in the stream. Water splashed into my face. "Help, I'm drowning!"

"Grandpa, it's only a foot deep."

"Oh." I checked to make sure I had no broken bones. Everything seemed to be in the right place and still connected.

"Cool ride, Grandpa."

Keoki held out a hand and helped me to my feet. "Next time I'd suggest using a ti leaf rather than just your jeans."

"Good advice." I wiped the mud off my backside.

Denny came down and splashed into the steam. He shook off the water and joined the rest of the group.

"Ready to go again, Grandpa?"

"I'll join the ladies and watch from down here."

"Before you go back up the hill, I want to get a picture," Allison said. "Everyone gather by the stream."

We huddled together like a collection of muddy clams, and Keoki gave the Hawaiian shaka sign indicating "hang loose" by holding up his right hand with the pinky finger and thumb extended and the other three fingers curled.

"Squeeze a little closer for one more. Smile on three. One, two, three." Allison pointed the camera and clicked.

Jennifer, Hina, Keoki and Denny charged up the trail again. I watched as they each shot down and plunged into the stream. Denny gave up after a few more rides, but the kids kept going.

"Don't you ever get tired?" I asked Jennifer.

"Nope. This is as cool as surfing." She raced up the trail again.

Allison wandered along the stream, taking some pictures of plants and flowers. I followed and stood watching as she leaned over to get a close-up. "Good subject?"

She gave a start. "Paul, I didn't hear you coming."

"You were pretty intent on that fern."

"What incredible scenery. I want to take pictures of everything. Digital cameras are wonderful. I can take as many pictures as I want and not worry about wasting film."

"You seem to be enjoying photography."

"I love it."

She continued shooting photographs, so I decided to meander back to the group. Allison soon returned, and we oldsters and middlesters watched the kids slide for another hour.

Eventually, Denny looked at his watch. "We better head back to town."

As we hiked back to the car, Denny and I brought up the rear. He grabbed my arm. "Dad, I've been wanting to speak with you."

"I do something to embarrass you?"

He gave a forced laugh. "No, you haven't done anything. It's that . . . uh . . . I've been thinking about my job."

"Ah, a career discussion."

Denny wiped mud off his face. "Yeah. I'm making good money, but not enjoying what I'm doing that much anymore."

"I hate to say it, but I don't remember what you've been doing these last few years."

"Aw, Dad, you and your memory. I have clients I help with

their investments. I even have a few on Maui that I visit once in a while. But I don't know if I want to keep doing this forever."

"I remember that feeling back before my memory stalled. I can't say I loved the auto parts business, but it paid the bills."

Denny came to an abrupt stop and faced me. "That's it exactly. It's become only a job. I want to do something I really love."

"Midlife crisis time." I patted him on the back. "I don't claim to be an expert, but it seems to me you have two choices. First, you can continue what you're doing, support your family and enjoy your outside-of-work activities. Second, you can decide on your passion and go for it. What do you really want to do?"

"This may sound silly, but I want to paint."

I swatted a mosquito using my arm for a buffet. "As in houses or art?"

"Oil painting. I painted some pictures before Jennifer was born and really enjoyed it, but haven't had time to pursue it since."

"You were quite the artist in high school. At one time I thought you might pursue a career along those lines."

"I put it aside. In college, business seemed like a reasonable major, and I decided to make some money rather than be a starving artist. I'm wondering if I should take up painting again."

Raindrops fell from one of the low-hanging clouds. I wiped my face with the back of my hand. "To become an artist will take time. I can't see you supporting your family by the efforts of your artistic talent for a number of years. One idea—you could take classes and set aside some time to paint. When Jennifer goes off to college, you'll be able to do more. I know I had more time on my hands after you moved out on your own. You can see if painting will be a hobby or something you want to pursue seriously. It can be something you retire into."

"I like that. Retire into." Denny shook water off his soggy

head. "That would give me something to aspire to."

"Yeah, in hindsight my early retirement years were kind of a mess. I sat around trying to figure out what use I was. After your mom died, I really was at a loss."

Denny groaned. "And now you spend your time with detectives and murder victims."

I swatted another mosquito. "That's not an avocation. I happened to be at the wrong spot at the wrong time. Have you discussed your interest in painting with Allison?"

"No. She might get uptight if she interprets it that I'm considering quitting my job. She's very concerned about financial security."

"I don't know. You might be surprised. You two make a good team. Her photography and your painting."

Denny opened his mouth to say something and then snapped it shut as we reached the rest of the group, huddled in the rain by the car.

Allison shivered. "Wouldn't you know it? The person with the key arrives last, and we're soaked to the skin."

Denny took the key from his pocket and beeped the doors open. "Thanks for listening, Dad."

"Any time you want to chat, you know where to find me."

We climbed in the SUV and Denny tried to start the engine. It made a clicking sound but didn't turn over.

CHAPTER 7

"Uh-oh," I said when the car wouldn't start. "Does someone have a pork sandwich in here that Madam Pele wants?"

Denny only glared at me before popping the hood. He, Keoki and I went to brave the continued downpour and have a look.

I scratched my head. "I sold auto parts for years, but never learned to be a mechanic myself. Also, I don't know anything about these new-fangled engines." Denny had never been a car person, so I didn't hold much hope that he'd be able to figure out the problem.

Keoki reached in and fiddled with a wire. "I've worked on an SUV similar to this. Someone has tampered with your wiring. "There, that should fix it temporarily." He dusted his hands. "You should take it back to the rental agency to get another SUV while they fully repair this one."

Denny tried the ignition and it started.

Along the way we stopped at a neighborhood store to buy some sandwiches. The proprietor didn't express any surprise at seven soggy people invading his establishment. In fact, no one in the store paid any attention to our group of muddy people.

"No pork," I reminded everyone.

Hina pointed to some pastry. "Malasadas. You have to try these."

We bought a dozen and sank our teeth into the sweet fried dough covered with granulated sugar. It tasted like a donut but without a hole. I decided I could survive indefinitely on island fare. I imagined being shipwrecked and having hula girls bringing me pineapple and malasadas.

"Dad, why are you standing there with a goofy expression on your face?" Denny asked.

"Oops. I guess I was daydreaming."

As we drove toward Waikiki, Hina said, "Keoki, tell us another story."

"Okay. Here's one about Menehunes, which are small and, like leprechauns, play tricks on people. One day a haole surfer dude, while resting on the sand at Makaha, saw something sparkling up on the hillside and went to investigate, leaving his board on the beach. After scrambling up the slope, he discovered what he thought were three kids shaking dice and betting with what looked like diamonds. He grabbed a handful of the sparkling rocks and ran back toward the beach. He didn't get very far before he tripped over a vine and dropped the diamonds. He discovered that two of the 'kids' held the vine across the trail. They scooped up the jewels and shook their fists at him. When the surfer dude got back to the beach, his surfboard was gone. He looked out in the water and saw three 'kids' surfing on tiny boards. They came to shore and ran into the jungle. The surfer dude picked up the three small boards and saw they were pieces of his original board. The lesson is, never mess with Menehunes."

"I understand," I said. "Say away from Madame Pele, pork sandwiches and Menehunes."

Back at the Hibiscus Hotel, Hina and Keoki went to find their mom, and we took the elevator up to our rooms to shower and change. While Denny took the SUV back to be replaced, Jennifer and I sat in the lobby, watching people.

"With my mom not here, let's tell geezer jokes."

"Okay with me, but your mom doesn't appreciate my ba-a-a-d influence on you."

Jennifer giggled. "She's not here."

"What the heck? Since I'm the bad grandpa, why not? Here's one inspired by Keoki's reference to Menehunes and leprechauns. What's the difference between a leprechaun and a geezer?"

Jennifer closed her eyes in concentration and then opened them. "I give up."

"One has a pot of gold and the other is a pot of old."

She turned her thumb down. "A one on a scale of one to ten. Here's one for you. What's the difference between a geezer and the Easter bunny?"

"You got me."

"A geezer has fuzzier ears."

"I resemble that remark." I tweaked my ears.

Someone cleared his throat, and I looked up to see a man standing there who said, "May I speak with you, Mr. Jacobson?"

"I suppose. Who the hell are you?"

He smacked his lips as if tasting something sour and held out a badge.

I peered at it. "Oh, Detective Chun. I remember your name from my journal. What can I do for you on this fine Hawaiian day?"

"If we can step to the side, I'd like to show you a picture." He motioned toward a deserted part of the lobby.

I accompanied him and he pulled a photograph out of a manila envelope. "Can you identify this man?"

I stared at a picture of an old codger with a dirty salt and pepper beard. He didn't look very healthy.

"Can't say as I recognize him. Kind of pasty."

"That's because this was taken at a homicide scene. He was

knifed and his body found early this morning. He's a transient and may be the man you mentioned being at the scene when you found the body floating in the yacht harbor."

"I remember reading a reference to that event in my journal, but I have no way of identifying the man who told me to look in the water."

Chun scowled. "I was afraid of that." He returned the photograph to the envelope. "The body you spotted in the yacht harbor. It's been identified as a man named Sammy Malo. Does that ring a bell with you, Mr. Jacobson?"

I gulped. "I read that name in my journal."

"And you were reported to have had an argument with him the night before you found him in the yacht harbor. Interesting coincidence."

I shrugged. "Yeah, I wouldn't have noticed the hand in the water if the transient hadn't pointed it out to me."

"What did you do after the argument with Sammy Malo?"

"From what I read in my journal, I went back to the hotel and slept all night. You can verify that with my wife."

"I'll do that. What else do you know about Sammy Malo?"

"As I said, only the reference to what I'd written in my diary."

Chun gave me an intense stare. "He was reputed to be a kingpin in the illegal drug business on Oahu. And by the way, he was murdered."

Yikes. "Uh . . . I'm not involved with drugs. I even hate taking pills."

At that moment Allison and Marion showed up. "Detective Chun, meet my wife and daughter-in-law. You said you wanted to speak to my wife."

Chun nodded. "If I could have a word with you, Mrs. Jacobson."

They stepped aside.

"What's that all about, Paul?" Allison asked.

"Some questions regarding a murder investigation."

"Murder?"

"Yeah. The body I saw in the yacht harbor."

Chun and Marion rejoined us. "Anything else you'd like to share with me, Mr. Jacobson?" the detective asked.

I swallowed hard. "No. Nothing else."

"Until we next speak." Then he strode away.

Jennifer came hopping over. "What's going on, Grandpa?"

"Detective Chun talked to me regarding two murders. A transient and the body dredged out of the yacht harbor. That guy turned out to be a suspected drug honcho."

"Wow." Jennifer's eyes grew wide. "Grandpa, you almost got in a fight with him."

Marion turned to me. "And the detective asked where you were the night before last after you got in that argument. I told him you went back to the hotel with us and slept all night."

I didn't want to think of the consequences of these latest revelations. Fortunately, we had things to do and places to visit. Allison informed us that Denny would be here momentarily to pick us up.

As advertised, Denny drove up with a shiny new white SUV, and we piled in. Within twenty minutes, we ground to a halt in traffic on H-1 on our way to visit Meyer and Henry.

"What's with so many cars in this Pacific paradise?" I asked.

"Honolulu's a big city now, Dad."

"I remember this being a tiny burg."

Denny clicked his tongue. "Even when you first lived here twenty years ago, the city wasn't that small."

"Yeah, but I like to exaggerate."

We made it safely through the puka in the Pali, known to people on the mainland as a tunnel, and headed down the green north-facing slope. I spotted a section of the old Pali road that had been a winding, narrow route along the cliff before the tunnel existed. Allison would have gone nuts riding on that.

Heading into Kaneohe, Denny navigated us into a residential neighborhood off Kamehemeha Highway, down a long driveway and into a parking area by a large two-story house.

"Meyer and Henry live here, Grandpa. Aren't you excited to be seeing them again?"

"I don't know. You and Marion mentioned them, but I wouldn't recognize them if they had their names tattooed on their foreheads."

Jennifer wagged a finger at me. "Remember, Meyer used to be your best friend. And with Henry, you enjoyed insulting each other."

"I'm ready for that. I feel an upwelling of snide comments."

"Good, Grandpa. You're prepared."

Denny and Allison decided they needed to make a run to the store to buy some more sunscreen, so they dropped off Marion, Jennifer and me and said they'd return shortly.

A plumeria tree in full bloom stood along a cement path that led to a covered patio and entryway. A monarch butterfly lighted on my shoulder. "Hey, look what found me."

"You were once given a collection of mounted butterflies," Jennifer said.

"It's on Paul's dresser at home," Marion said.

I shrugged. "Doesn't ring a bell with me."

"Detective Saito gave it to you, Grandpa."

"If you say so."

Our delegation entered the house to be greeted by a tall, smiling woman with an orange hibiscus in her gleaming black hair.

"Good afternoon," I said. "We're the health inspectors from the mainland."

Her smile disappeared.

Marion poked me in the ribs. "We are not. Please ignore my husband. We're friends of Meyer Ohana and Henry Palmer here to see them."

The woman's smile returned. "Oh, yes. Mr. Ohana said he'd have some visitors today. Please come in. They're in the living room."

Two large couches faced a blaring television with a western shoot-'em-up playing. Two men and four women sat there quietly. One of the women knitted and two other women appeared asleep or dead, their heads lolling to the side with their mouths wide open.

Jennifer raced over and grabbed the arm of one of the men. "Guess who's here to see you?"

He smiled. "I can't see you that well but it must be Jennifer Jacobson. Did you bring that old coot of a grandfather with you?"

"Sure enough. He's right here."

The man stood up and shuffled toward me. "As I live and breathe, is that you, Paul?"

"I am living and breathing as well. It's me."

He didn't look familiar, but I assumed he had to be my old buddy Meyer. I gave him the onceover. White hair and beard, my height, good posture, seemed healthy.

We clasped hands.

"Welcome back to the islands, Paul."

"It's good to be here, Meyer. You keeping this place jumping?"

"It's pretty calm without you to add excitement."

"And this must be Henry," I said to the squat, bald-headed man.

"Hello, jerk," Henry said, adjusting his metal-rimmed glasses. "Are you as stupid as you used to be?"

"Such a warm greeting," I replied. "Henry, you have a split

personality—a mix of obnoxious and repulsive."

"Nice try, jerk, but you're as useless as an elevator in a one-story house."

Meyer chuckled. "I'm glad to see you two hitting it off like you used to."

"I don't even remember the SOB and he's insulting me." I faced Henry and eyed him. He reminded me of a bowling ball with arms and legs. "Henry, why don't you take your ugly pill and climb into a hole somewhere."

Henry smiled. "Not bad, but it's a shame you missed a button on your shirt."

I looked down. "Damn. You're right." I fastened the bottom button on my Hawaiian shirt. "How'd you notice that so quickly?"

"Henry's very observant," Meyer said. "Also, do you have any baseball facts you want to test him on? He may have slowed down after his heart attack, but he still knows his baseball."

"Yeah, Henry," I said, "who's on first?"

He proceeded to spiel off the whole Abbott and Costello gag routine about the St. Louis team with Who's on first, What's on second and I Don't Know on third.

Jennifer listened with rapt attention. When Henry finished we applauded.

"I have some friends at school who used that routine in a comedy show last summer," Jennifer said. "That was cool, Henry."

He actually blushed.

"Nothing wrong with your memory, Henry," I said. "It's unfortunate that your couth quotient remains so low, though."

Henry gave a dismissive wave of his right hand and returned his attention to the western on TV as if we had been mere buzzing flies.

"Let me introduce you to the people here," Meyer said. "Mrs.

Wilson, meet my old friend Paul Jacobson, his wife Marion and his granddaughter Jennifer."

Mrs. Wilson looked up from her knitting and gave us a pleasant smile. "I'm a widow and my husband died in 1998. I have two sons who live on the mainland, one in Los Angeles and one in Salt Lake City. They're both lawyers, and each has a son and daughter, so I'm blessed with four grandchildren."

"This is my full contingent of grandchildren." I pointed to Jennifer.

Mrs. Wilson's eyes dropped to her knitting.

Meyer skipped over the two other old biddies, who were sleeping with their mouths hanging open, and put his hand out toward another woman sitting on the couch. "Mrs. Hirano, meet my friends Paul and Marion Jacobson and Jennifer."

Mrs. Hirano nodded a gray head. "Did you know that melted ice water is best for you?"

"Huh?" I replied.

"Yes. I only drink water that's first frozen, and then the ice cubes are melted in the microwave."

Meyer jumped in. "Mrs. Hirano has some very advanced views on health."

"That's right," she said. "The combination of freezing and thawing ensures the water molecules will bind to your cells and prevent cancer. See, I'm ninety-one and cancer free."

I nodded my head, and Mrs. Hirano's attention returned to John Wayne plugging an outlaw.

"And our nurse on duty is Pamela Newsome." Meyer waved in the direction of the woman at the desk. "She's here in the afternoon and early evening."

"Yes, Paul made a good first impression with her." Marion gave me a wifely elbow to the ribs.

"Let me show you around the grounds," Meyer said. "Henry, you want to join us?"

Henry flicked his hand as if dispatching an unwanted mosquito.

Meyer headed toward the door and felt along the wall to retrieve a white cane. "I'm using this so I won't fall down. My macular degeneration has reached the point where I can't see where I'm walking very well."

"Your eye cells and my brain cells obviously disappeared into the same black hole."

"Paul, you and I made quite a pair back in the old days at the Kina Nani retirement home before you ran off with Marion."

"Meyer, you should hook up with one of the ladies here. There's Mrs. Wilson. She seemed nice and with it."

"Oh, she's nice all right, but you talk to her again and decide what you think of her mental state."

I punched my right fist into my left hand. "I'll do that. The Jacobson matchmaking agency is now open for business."

Ignoring me, Marion said, "This place is nicely landscaped, Meyer. Quite a collection of flowers. Who maintains it?"

"There's a regular gardener, but also Mrs. Hirano and Mrs. Kwan enjoy working outside. They're responsible for the orchids."

And sure enough. One section of garden below a hedge displayed quite an array of purple and white petals.

"Cool," Jennifer said. "You have a Jacuzzi."

"Yes, like at Kina Nani. It's kept covered so no one falls in inadvertently, but between two and three in the afternoon one of the staff members mans the tub so we can use it. I didn't use it today."

"Perfect for soaking your old bones," I said. "And the authorities here dish out the hot tub like a controlled substance."

"Exactly, Paul. You have to be careful with old people."

"Who's old? We're merely experienced."

Jennifer pointed to two cardinals hopping through the pili

grass, their red heads bobbing. "Look at the birds."

"And you have wildlife on your estate, Meyer."

"Until the neighbor's cat chases them away."

We completed the tour of the yard and headed back inside. I decided to check out Mrs. Wilson for Meyer.

"Hi, Mrs. Wilson."

She looked up from her knitting. "I'm a widow and my husband died in 1998. I have two sons who live on the mainland, one in Los Angeles and one in Salt Lake City. They're both lawyers, and each has a son and daughter, so I'm blessed with four grandchildren."

Uh-oh. "Nice speaking with you Mrs. Wilson."

I moseyed into Meyer's room, where he was showing Marion and Jennifer a scrapbook. The sparsely furnished space contained only a bed, dresser, nightstand, lamp and bookshelf. Three seascapes hung on the otherwise white walls.

"Meyer has a collection of letters to the editor," Jennifer said.

"I used to vent to the press when something irritated me."

"Sounds like a strange hobby, but to each his own. I found out the problem with Mrs. Wilson. Her record player is stuck in the same groove."

Meyer chuckled. "That's right. Same story every time you speak with her."

"I guess I prefer my form of mental dysfunction. I don't repeat myself because I can't dredge up what I said the day before." I paused. "At least I don't remember repeating myself."

"Same old Paul." Meyer closed his scrapbook.

We ambled into the living room and, shortly, Denny and Allison returned from their store excursion.

"Let's take this old fart out for an early dinner," I said. "Show him some Jacobson hospitality."

Meyer's damaged eyes lit up. "I'd enjoy a meal out." He

leaned toward me and whispered. "The food here is okay but not much variety."

"What would you like, Meyer?"

"Somewhere that offers good seafood. Shall we invite Henry?"

"Sure. The more the merrier. Denny rented an SUV so we can all fit."

We found Henry still vegging out in front of the television.

"Get your butt off the couch, you little hunk of crud," I informed him in my most polite manner. "We're taking you and Meyer out to dinner."

Henry looked up. "Where?"

"We haven't decided yet but somewhere with good seafood."

He stood up and stretched his stubby arms. "Haleiwa Joe's serves excellent food."

"Sounds better than Waianae Willie's."

We assembled our whole crew in preparation for departure when Pamela Newsome informed us we needed to sign her log to let Meyer and Henry out.

"Why the hell do we need to do that?" I asked. "You afraid we'll lose them?"

Pamela gave me an indignant glare. "It's the procedure here."

"Don't get riled up, Dad. I'll sign." Denny affixed his scrawl to a sheet on a clipboard resting on Pamela's desk.

"Do we need to keep them on a leash or can they be trusted unfettered?" I asked.

Nurse Pamela ignored me, and Marion gave me another well-deserved poke in the ribs.

After we were safely seat-belted in, Denny asked, "Where to?"

"Turn right on Kamehameha Highway, make a left on Haiku Road, and it's one point two miles on the left side," Henry said.

I regarded Henry in amazement. "Damn. How'd you know that?"

"I went there once before."

"And you remember all that?"

Henry smiled. "Of course. I'm not a mental degenerate like you."

"Grandpa has a photographic memory during the day, but it doesn't work overnight."

I gave my granddaughter a thumbs-up for supporting me.

Denny followed Henry's directions and we arrived at a parking lot with a Haleiwa Joe's sign. A plain-looking building stood at the side of the parking area.

"Doesn't look like much," I said.

"Just wait, jerk," Henry replied.

"Okay. I'll hold my water."

And Henry was right. Inside, we sat at a table overlooking a green, lush garden thirty feet below the restaurant with a view of the equally verdant mountains behind. Birds chirped and the aroma of sizzling steaks and fresh bread permeated the air.

We hunkered down to peruse the menu selections, a good cross-section of edible options from the sea and pasture.

After we placed our orders, Jennifer said, "Grandpa found a dead body in the Honolulu yacht harbor yesterday morning."

Meyer put his water glass down. "Up to your old tricks again, Paul?"

"What's that supposed to mean?"

Meyer looked toward me, his eyes not quite making correct contact. "You have a propensity for being involved in police investigations."

"I don't remember anything like that. I'm merely a retired old poop who used to run an auto parts store in Los Angeles."

"Meyer's right, Grandpa. You've found dead bodies before and been accused of murder."

"Well, that won't happen this time. I only saw a floating hand. Didn't even recognize the fingers."

"Remember to avail yourself of legal assistance if somehow you become further involved," Meyer said.

"I don't need any damn lawyers."

"Grandpa, Meyer used to be a lawyer."

"Well, I'm sure he was a good one. He's fine, but I don't want any attorney with his meter running breathing down my neck."

"They should lock you up and throw away the key," Henry said, then went back to munching on bread.

"Thanks, Henry. Maybe they can put you in the slammer as my accomplice."

Henry let out a burst of air as if trying to eliminate a foul smell from his lungs. "I'm not as dumb as you are."

"I want to go see the garden close up," Jennifer said. "Anyone want to come with me?"

"I'll go stretch my legs," I volunteered. "Henry, don't stuff your repugnant yap with all the food while I'm gone."

"Don't get eaten by mongooses, jerk."

"Come on, Grandpa. You and Henry can insult each other later. I want to explore."

We took the stairs down to the lower level and wandered around a grassy area with vivid green plants surrounding us. Jennifer twirled around like a ballerina. "What a beautiful place, Grandpa. And since it's only you and me, we can tell geezer jokes. I found a good one on the Internet."

I came to an abrupt stop. "I don't care if you found it on the inner net, the outer net or the in-between net."

"Oh, Grandpa. When are you going to become computer literate?"

"In my next life. Let's hear your joke."

"Okay. Why didn't the geezer vampire bite the young woman's throat?"

"I give up."

"Because he forgot his false fangs."

I laughed. "Good one. I have one for you that I remember from my old days when the brain cells still connected. "What's happy hour for a geezer?"

Jennifer looked upward thoughtfully. "I don't know."

"Happy hour for a geezer is taking a nap."

On that note we returned to rejoin the rest of our group. Henry greeted me. "Hey, jerk, you look like a slob. You have grass all over your shoes."

I looked down, and sure enough, green blades, from traipsing with Jennifer, covered my shoes.

"You look as well dressed as a homeless bum," Henry added.

Our food arrived before I wrung Henry's neck, but my hands itched to do so. We settled in to munching and slurping.

When Meyer finished his salad, he pointed a fork at Henry. "Did you know that Henry has a girlfriend?"

"No kidding," I said "She as obnoxious as you, Henry?"

"I wouldn't know," Henry said.

"Huh?" I replied in my most inquisitive fashion.

"They've never met," Meyer said. "They're carrying on a romance over the Internet. She lives in Florida."

"You going to marry the broad and make her an honest woman?" I asked.

"Yup." Henry gave us a wide grin. "We're engaged."

"What?" I almost spat out my dentures, except I didn't have any. "How can you do that if you've never met?"

"I like her picture, and she's smart, not like you, jerk."

Jennifer whacked her fist on the table. "My grandpa is smart."

"Ah, my granddaughter to the rescue. See, Henry, not everyone shares your opinion."

"Jennifer's smarter than you are, jerk," Henry replied.

Meyer chuckled. "Jennifer is the only person who ever stumped Henry with a baseball question. He respects that."

Henry began buttering another piece of bread. "She was lucky."

"No way." Jennifer gave her head a thorough shake. "I got you good, and I can do it again if I want to."

Henry glared at her for a moment and then went back to chewing.

I couldn't contain myself and had to poke more into the strange engagement. "I bet this woman is after your money, Henry. She obviously doesn't want to marry you for your sweet personality."

"We'll see." Henry picked up a bread crumb from the table and popped it in his mouth. "She's paying her way to Hawaii so we can get married here. She's arriving tomorrow."

"We'll have to come back to meet her," Jennifer said.

"Her flight gets in at one, and she's renting a car," Henry said. "She'll be here around three. Then we can finalize our marriage plans."

"So you found a woman who still drives," I added.

"Yup. She's a pip."

"I wonder how long she'll put up with you, Henry. After five minutes, she'll probably call off the engagement."

Henry snorted. "We're made for each other."

"She must be a piece of work. We'll see if she recants."

"Where are you going to live?" Meyer asked.

"I've pretty much recovered from my heart attack. We'll get an apartment at the Kina Nani retirement home."

Meyer frowned. "Back where all of us first met."

"That's going to leave Meyer all on his lonesome," I said. "Meyer, you'll have to hook up with Mrs. Wilson."

Meyer rolled his failing eyes.

Jennifer wiped her mouth with a corner of her napkin. "I think Grandpa and Henry should have an insult contest."

Henry looked up from his food and waved his hand toward

me. "Sounds fun. Jerk, you can even take the first shot."

Having to rise to the occasion, I thought for a moment and then focused on Henry's bald head. "Henry, you have the social graces of an evil spawn born of a wolverine mated to a rattlesnake without the benefit of being fuzzy or the ability to have your skin made into boots."

Henry turned up his nose in my direction. "Not bad, jerk, but not good enough. Jacobson, your memory is so bad that when people meet you, they only have a second, third or fourth chance to make a good first impression."

Jennifer put her hand over her mouth to stifle a giggle.

"Whose side are you on, anyway?" I shot my most disgusted dagger-stare at my granddaughter.

"Sorry, Grandpa, but that was funny."

"Henry doesn't usually do funny," Meyer said.

"He must have been inspired by being engaged," Denny said.

After we practically licked every last morsel off our plates, we indulged in a round of dessert before I slapped down a piece of plastic as ransom for the food. Afterward, we waddled out, content as some of the cattle before being turned into filet mignon.

Back at the care home Meyer raced in to use the bathroom, and Henry followed without paying any attention to the rest of us.

"We'll come back here tomorrow afternoon to meet Henry's fiancée," Marion said.

I groaned. "I can't believe that doofus is marrying someone he's never even seen in person. I'm sure they deserve each other."

Marion patted my arm. "It's not much different than you being married to someone who you don't recognize most mornings."

"Most?"

"That's right."

I crinkled an eyebrow. "I sense there's a story there."

Once inside, while overseen by the warden nurse, I signed the sheet to indicate the inmates had returned. Allison, Denny and Jennifer went over to watch one of the residents painting a watercolor on a short easel mounted in front of her wheelchair.

Meyer and I passed Mrs. Wilson, seated near the nurse's desk with her knitting in her lap. She looked up at me, smiled and said, "I'm a widow and my husband died in 1998. I have two sons who live on the mainland, one in Los Angeles and one in Salt Lake City. They're both lawyers, and each has a son and daughter, so I'm blessed with four grandchildren."

"That's nice," I said and hotfooted away from her.

Meyer pulled me aside. "I think Mrs. Wilson has her eye on you, Paul. If Marion ever tires of you, you have a new fan."

"Wouldn't work. I need a young chick like Marion who has all her marbles. I'll leave Mrs. Wilson for you, since you don't have me around that much for entertainment. Do I need to tuck you in bed before we leave?"

"No. I'll listen to the television for a while before retiring."

"As long as it won't be too exciting for you."

"No, Paul. You're in charge of excitement for this crowd."

I watched the watercolor lady pack up her paints and easel and return to her room. The entertainment possibilities were diminishing here by the minute.

At that moment Henry piped up. "Hey, I'd like a snack."

"You just ate dinner," I replied.

"That was an hour ago, jerk."

"There are usually some cookies left in the kitchen," Meyer said. "Paul, you want to go take a look?"

"Sure. Since Henry's too lazy to get off his butt, I might as well."

I sauntered into the kitchen and turned on the light. A woman with her throat cut lay on the floor in a pool of blood with a knife resting on her chest.

CHAPTER 8

My old ticker ramped up lickety-split at seeing a dead woman and blood on the kitchen floor of the care home. I heard a door slam and rushed toward the outside exit of the kitchen. I pushed open a screen door and looked out to see a man running into the bushes. "I saw you!" I shouted. "The police will nail your sorry butt."

I turned back inside, and the sight of the body made me lose my appetite, but somehow I kept from spewing my dinner. "Help," I gurgled.

I heard footsteps behind me. I turned around to see Denny there. I heard him gasp loudly as he covered his mouth with his hand.

Then the attending nurse, Pamela Newsome, stuck her head in the kitchen and shrieked, "Oh, no. It's Louise Kincaid."

I didn't know Louise Kincaid from a kumquat, but she had met her maker. I cringed at the bloody sight. What a way to go.

I shouted, "Call nine-one-one."

Shaking, Denny pulled out his cell phone. I looked down at the floor and noticed a piece of paper off to the side of Louise's body. Bending over, I knew better than to touch it, but I plainly saw writing on the face-up side. I read, "It's working, Louise. Time to expand our operation," and was signed "Sammy Malo."

Uh-oh. A reference to the guy found in the yacht harbor. How did I keep getting involved in these absurd coincidences?

Denny and I stumbled out of the kitchen, and I dropped

down onto a couch. Our pleasant evening had turned into a disaster. I hoped this didn't ruin our vacation.

"What's happening?" Allison asked, shooting to her feet.

Denny put an arm around her shoulder and whispered in her ear. She turned as white as the nurse's uniform. Allison grabbed Jennifer and pulled her to her breast.

Jennifer gasped. "Mom, I can't breathe. What's going on?"

"No one go into the kitchen," Denny said in a quavering voice.

Jennifer's eyes grew as large as the coaster holding a glass of water on the table. "Oh, no. Did Grandpa find something bad?"

Allison clutched Jennifer tightly again.

Marion came over and put her arm around me. "Paul, you're shivering."

Denny paced around the room like a little boy lost in a storm. I'm sure he felt he should do something but didn't know what.

Henry sat in a chair with a blank expression on his face while Meyer nervously ran his hand through his white beard.

Oblivious to all the strange behavior, Mrs. Wilson kept knitting.

In minutes a siren wailed, and moments later two EMTs and three firemen charged into the home to be directed by Pamela into the kitchen. I heard some banging and stomping. Nothing anyone could do for the poor woman. Two cops and a woman carrying a black bag and a camera arrived.

One of the police officers asked if we had seen anyone leaving the scene.

I waved my hand and explained that a man had fled out the back door. The policeman took off lickety-split.

We all sat in the living area in our various states of stupor.

Later, a man in a crumpled suit appeared. He went into the kitchen and in a few minutes returned to the living room. While vigorously chewing gum, he spoke to Pamela Newsome.

After a moment, Pamela pointed to me.

The man's eyes narrowed as he stared at me, and then a faint smile crossed his face. In two quick strides he stepped over to where I stood. "Mr. Jacobson. I never expected to see you again."

"I guess I didn't expect to see you again either since I don't know who the hell you are." I regarded the man, shorter than me with an intense expression on his face.

He gave a snort that reminded me of a horse with allergies. "Same old bad memory. I'm Detective Saito."

Denny came to life. "I remember you. You investigated the murder in the retirement home over a year ago."

"That's the one," Saito said.

I shrugged. "Doesn't mean anything to me."

"You and I got to know each other very well at that time, Mr. Jacobson. I heard that you'd left the Islands. Back again for a visit or to stay?"

I peered into his dark eyes. "My family and I are here on vacation."

"I understand you found the dead body." Saito pointed toward the kitchen. "Up to your old tricks?"

"What's that supposed to mean?" I said in my most surly manner.

"Oh, you seem to have a way of getting yourself involved in crimes," Saito said. "I see some other familiar faces. Mr. Ohana and Mr. Palmer. You both used to live in the Kina Nani retirement home with Mr. Jacobson."

Meyer jumped in. "That's right. We graduated to this care home. Paul's visiting us and had nothing to do with the death you're investigating."

"I'm sure he didn't," Saito replied. "But I'll need to get statements from everyone here. First, I want to start with you, Mr. Jacobson, since you found the body. Let's sit down at the dining room table by ourselves."

Once seated, Saito asked me to recount what I'd seen. I explained that I found Louise with her throat cut and saw someone run out of the care home.

"One of our officers checked the neighborhood but couldn't find any sign of an intruder. Our crime scene investigator will check for footprints outside the back door. What else did you notice?"

"There was a note." I bit my lip before launching into a point of clarification. "You should know, Detective, that I also discovered the body of the man whose signature is on that note—Sammy Malo."

Saito's eyebrows rose so high, I feared they'd shoot above his forehead. "Do tell."

"You can check with Detective Chun in Honolulu. He has the details. I can assure you I'm not responsible for either murder."

Saito held a hand up as if trying to stop a runaway bus. "I know, Mr. Jacobson. A coincidence."

I let out a deep sigh. "Yeah, and you and I don't believe in coincidences. I can't figure out what's going on and why these two events occurred and how I happened to be at the scene both times."

"Detective Chun and I will get to the bottom of it."

"I sure hope so. I want to enjoy my vacation without dead bodies."

"Now I need to complete my interviews." He stood and signaled Pamela Newsome. "I'd like to speak to the members of the staff on duty."

"I'm the only one here," Pamela said. "That is, besides Louise, who's dead. I've called to have someone else come assist, given the . . . uh . . . unfortunate circumstances."

Saito pulled Pamela aside to speak in private while the rest of us remained on the couches and chairs that faced the television with some sitcom in a bar. Pamela had turned down the volume so I could only hear muted tones.

Jennifer sidled up to me and whispered in my ear. "This is creepy."

"Yeah. I'm sorry you had to be here when this happened."

I could see tears form in Jennifer's eyes. "I hope the police catch who did this."

I put my arm around Jennifer's shoulder. "I'm sure Detective Saito will track down the culprit."

When Saito asked to speak with me again, I reiterated that I had done nothing more than go into the kitchen and inadvertently discover a dead body.

"Yes, and I've verified that you spent the evening at a restaurant with your family and friends so you couldn't have committed the murder."

"You have that right."

"Did you notice the type of knife found on the victim?" Saito asked.

"One of those fancy Swiss Army knives."

He shook a finger at me. "That's right. In spite of your short-term memory disappearing when you go to sleep, you have a photographic memory during the day."

I pointed back at him. "You have a good memory."

"Oh, you're someone I'd never forget, Mr. Jacobson."

"I don't know if that's good or bad. By the way, you should give up chewing gum. It's a bad habit."

Saito regarded his right hand. "I used to smoke, which resulted in nicotine-stained fingers for years. You convinced me to change that bad habit. Unfortunately, now I chew gum instead."

"I guess gum's better for your health than tobacco. But a young pup like you can give up that bad habit as well."

"Thanks for the vote of confidence, but chewing gum is better than chewing too many malasadas and ending up too fat to fit through a doorway."

At that moment Henry came dashing out of his room. "I can't find my Swiss Army knife. Someone stole it."

Chapter 9

With Henry's missing knife as the suspected murder weapon, Detective Saito asked us to tell him our recollections of Henry's whereabouts. The problem—none of us had paid attention to Henry after we returned to the care home.

Denny, Allison and Jennifer had watched the watercolor artist, a woman named Ritaestelle Christiano, for a few minutes before she had disappeared into her room. I had been distracted at Pamela Newsome's desk while signing in the two inmates we had helped temporarily escape for dinner, and then Meyer and I had spent time speaking with Mrs. Wilson.

I couldn't believe this was like the Clue board game—Henry in the kitchen with the knife. My photographic memory wasn't able to dredge up any image of Henry being in the room or being elsewhere after we returned until the time he said he wanted a snack. I reviewed the sequence of events again. Nope. If called to testify at a trial, I couldn't swear to Henry's presence in the living room the whole time. It was frustrating. I smacked the side of my head, but it did no good in shaking up anything useful.

"Henry wouldn't have asked someone to go in the kitchen if he'd committed the murder," I explained to Detective Saito. "In addition, he wouldn't have called attention to his missing knife if he had done it. Besides, I heard a door slam and spotted someone running away. That's the person who must have committed the crime."

"That's one explanation, Mr. Jacobson. Or you might have seen a neighbor or someone not related to the homicide."

I rolled my eyes. "Give me a break. Henry might be a pain in the butt, but he's not a murderer. No, if I were a betting man, I'd put my money on the running man and not Henry."

"You told me you didn't get a good look at the man outside."

"That's right. I tried to give him the impression I had seen him, but I really only caught a glimpse long enough to tell it was a man."

"Now, regarding Mr. Palmer," Saito said. "I'm still trying to find someone who saw him after you returned from dinner. There's a gap of ten minutes when no one can give Mr. Palmer an alibi. That's plenty of time to slit a throat and return to the living area. Any further thoughts on Mr. Palmer's whereabouts?"

"What's Henry say?" I asked.

"I don't have to share any statements with you, Mr. Jacobson."

"I know. I know. I don't want to pry into your investigation. I'm only trying to help clarify the situation."

Saito sighed. "You'll be able to verify this with him anyway. Mr. Palmer claims he went into his room to use the bathroom and then came back out into the living room. He says all of you were looking the other way and probably didn't see him leave or return."

"That seems pretty reasonable to me. Speaking of which, I better use the facility so I don't have an accident." I charged off to visit the guest restroom.

When I came out of the bathroom, my clan and Meyer were gathered around Henry. Saito was nowhere to be seen. "What's up?" I asked Denny.

"We're concerned that Detective Saito suspects Henry."

"I didn't do anything," Henry mumbled.

"The only people in the room here were Pamela Newsome,

Mrs. Wilson, Ritaestelle Christiano, Marion, Allison, Jennifer, you and me," Denny said. "None of us can say for sure we saw Henry between the time we arrived here and when Henry said he was hungry."

At that moment someone tapped me on the shoulder. I turned around to see Mrs. Wilson standing there.

"Did you notice where Henry Palmer was this evening?" I asked.

She shook her head. "I was busy with my knitting."

"It's really important, Mrs. Wilson. We're trying to find out if anyone saw Henry."

"Didn't notice him. Has anyone seen Louise?"

"Uh . . . sh . . . she's not around," I stammered.

Mrs. Wilson put her knitting down on a chair. "I need to find her. She's supposed to bring me my brownies."

All eyes turned to stare at her.

"Brownies?" Meyer blurted out.

Mrs. Wilson put a finger to her lips. "Oh, it's a secret. She gives me special brownies to help with my arthritis pain. They make me feel good again." Her pleasant self turned surly. "Now where are my brownies?"

"She's giving you medical marijuana?" Meyer asked.

"Oh, no. I don't use drugs, and I never take pills."

"I'm with you on that," I said. "I hate pills."

Mrs. Wilson looked around our conclave and let out a deep sigh. "Louise has these special brownies that make the pain go away. I pay her fifty dollars every day." She pulled a bill with the picture of Ulysses S. Grant out of her pocket. "Go find her. Tell her I'm ready."

"I'm afraid she's had an accident, Mrs. Wilson," Meyer said. "She won't be giving you brownies anymore."

She frowned and rubbed her wrist. "That's too bad. It was the only thing that really helped my arthritis."

Detective Saito reappeared. I waved him over. "You better hear what Mrs. Wilson has to say. It may shed some light on the murder victim."

CHAPTER 10

Detective Saito began to grill Mrs. Wilson. Although he didn't want us to be part of the conversation, my snoopy personality required that I keep an ear open to the interrogation as we sat in the living area of the care home. Mrs. Wilson proceeded to play her tape about her children and grandchildren for Saito. I didn't watch him, but I could almost hear his eyes roll like a pair of dice.

Mrs. Wilson asked again to have her brownies, and Saito inquired if she knew the ingredients. Mrs. Wilson replied that brownies contained her happy juice. Maybe she had withdrawal symptoms and attacked Louise because her happy juice was too late in being delivered. That made as much sense as Henry slitting Louise's throat.

After Saito heard Mrs. Wilson mention her children and grandchildren for the third time, he gave up and went over to speak with Pamela Newsome at the nurse's station. She continued to oversee the living area like a mother hen protecting her chicks. Another nurse had arrived a few minutes earlier and was checking with each of the residents not in the living area to make sure everything was copacetic.

I considered what we had seen and heard. Denny, Allison, Jennifer, Meyer and I provided alibis for each other. Henry had the missing period of being unnoticed by all of us. Mrs. Wilson had been off on the side knitting, but I hadn't paid any attention to her after Meyer and I had spoken with her briefly. Could she have gone into the kitchen and dispatched Louise? And what about Pamela Newsome? I hadn't noticed if she had stayed at her desk the whole time between our arrival from dinner and my discovery of the body. Or maybe the murder had occurred right before we showed up. Still, the best bet remained the running man I'd seen outside the kitchen.

Detective Saito would be checking on Louise's background to see if any alienated boyfriends or enemies wanted her out of the way. Or did her sideline of marijuana brownies lead to her demise? She obviously possessed a source for the ingredients. That meant she bought it from someone who didn't have it legally. Did she get crosswise with a drug dealer? And the note from Sammy Malo? What business dealings did Sammy and Louise have? How did her death tie to Sammy's death? I couldn't sort out this big muddle.

An idea occurred to me. I leaned over to Meyer who sat next to me on the couch. "Is medical marijuana legal in Hawaii?"

He whispered back in my ear. "Hawaii was the first state to pass a medical marijuana law. There are dispensaries throughout the islands."

"But Mrs. Wilson wasn't an authorized patient."

"Apparently not."

Something didn't make sense to me. "I wonder why she used the backdoor route to get her pain relief."

"People have many reasons for not pursuing medical marijuana. Possibly her doctor wouldn't prescribe it. Also, Medicare and medical insurance won't cover it."

"I don't think we'd get a straight answer if we asked Mrs. Wilson."

Meyer bit his lip. "No. I've never been able to get her to say anything other than reciting her children and grandchildren routine."

"Still, Mrs. Wilson chose to pony up good money for her

drug of choice. Meyer, what do you know about the victim, Louise Kincaid?"

"She came every evening to dispense pills. Apparently, she had a contract to go to a number of care homes to provide medication."

"Plus the sideline of brownies for Mrs. W. I wonder if she did that with any of her other patients. The police will have lots of interesting things to look into."

Detective Saito returned to our little enclave. He stared at Henry. "Mr. Palmer, I need to ask you to accompany me to police headquarters."

Henry glared at him. "I don't want to."

"This isn't a request."

"Henry, you need to get a lawyer," Meyer said.

Henry crinkled up his nose. "As Paul used to say, I don't need any stinkin' attorney."

Meyer shook his head. "That's not a wise decision. Tell you what. I may be a little rusty, but I can come along with you to provide legal counsel. Would that help?"

Henry nodded.

"Do you want the rest of us to join you?" Denny asked.

Saito held up a hand. "Mr. Palmer and his . . . uh . . . legal representative will suffice. The rest of you can remain here or are free to leave."

"Meyer, give us a call when you and Henry finish," Allison said. She reached in her purse and pulled out a notepad and jotted on it. "Here's my cell phone number." She handed it to Meyer.

"How will Henry and Meyer get back here?" Denny asked.

"We'll provide transportation for them," Saito replied.

We watched them head out and followed to get in Denny's rental car. On the way back to Honolulu through the Pali tunnel, Jennifer leaned toward my ear and whispered. "When you found bodies before, I always thought it was kind of a game to try to solve the crimes, but this time being so close made my stomach queasy."

"You and me both."

Jennifer grabbed my arm probably to assure herself more than me. "You're around another murder investigation."

"Another murder investigation? Besides that floater I found in the yacht harbor, I don't do murder investigations."

Jennifer bit her lip. "Oh, Grandpa. You've forgotten all the crime cases you've been involved in." She began counting off on her fingers. "In Hawaii, in Colorado, in California, on an Alaskan cruise and now back in Hawaii. Detective Saito will welcome your assistance again. Back over a year ago he suspected you of a murder, but you actually helped him solve it."

"If you say so. I can't remember any of it. I'm a retired old poop with a head full of sushi instead of working brain cells."

"You're lucky you wake each day and don't remember the day before. I'm not going to forget this tomorrow and will probably have nightmares tonight. At least this time you're not a suspect, Grandpa."

"You act like I have a criminal past."

"Well, yeah. You've been implicated in all sorts of crimes." She gave a determined toss of her head. "You've been a person of interest a number of times."

"And here I never considered myself that interesting."

Jennifer groaned. "Stick with geezer jokes, Grandpa. But you eventually helped track down the bad guys and were cleared of suspicion."

"That's a good thing. Someone my age shouldn't have to be subjected to a police investigation. It could have a bad effect on the old ticker."

"But now Henry has to deal with being a suspect. Grandpa,

we're going to have to help clear him."

"I don't know what we can do. Meyer can put his legal background to work, and we'll see what happens next."

We sank into silence. I thought over what Jennifer had said. If something bad occurred, I could avoid any future pain by not writing about the event in my journal. Then I thought back to scanning through my journal this morning before all the shenanigans of the day. Reviewing a journal provided distance as well. If I described something disastrous, upon reading, it had the feel of having happened to someone else and not me. Whereas, at the moment, as I relived the events in the kitchen of the care home earlier, my stomach was tied in a bowline, two half-hitches and a sheep shank.

As we entered the lobby of the Hibiscus Hotel, Allison's cell phone jangled. She grabbed it out of her purse and began a conversation punctuated with lots of "Uh-huhs." After a while, she snapped it shut.

"Well?" Jennifer tugged at her mother's sleeve.

Allison sighed. "Meyer called. Henry was fingerprinted, interrogated and released. He's a person of interest but wasn't arrested."

"The police probably didn't want anyone with such a sweet disposition as Henry's clogging up their jail cells," I said.

Jennifer stomped her foot. "Henry's innocent. They have no evidence to hold him. Even if his knife was used to commit the crime, it doesn't mean that he had anything to do with it."

"Thank you, Judge Jennifer," I said. "But Henry's fingerprints are on the knife from when he last used it. If the murderer used gloves, Henry could still be in deep yogurt."

"We'll have to wait to see what Detective Saito comes up with," Denny said.

I yawned. "I think it's time my bride and I got some shuteye.

What's on the agenda for tomorrow?"

A little more life returned to Jennifer's eyes. "Surfing in the morning. I'm going to ride for hours. That will help me forget what happened tonight."

"As long as I don't have to go in the ocean."

"Grandpa, you can watch from the safety of the sand while I catch waves."

We took the elevator to our floor and said our good-nights. Inside our room I sat down at the desk and documented the life and times of Paul Jacobson and his clan.

After changing into my pajamas, I climbed into bed with Marion. "With all the commotion tonight, I forgot to tell you about a talk I had with Denny on our way back from ti leaf sliding."

"Oh?"

"My son is going through a minor midlife crisis. He's questioning his job and wants to become an artist." I recounted my conversation with Denny.

"You gave him sound advice, Paul. Denny will listen to what you said and make the right decision, I know."

"Speaking of which, what do you want to be when you grow up?"

Marion's eyes glittered. "I want to help people with short-term memory loss."

"What?" I almost spat out my teeth, but, fortunately, they were still attached. "How long have you wanted to do that?"

"The last seven months. But I think I'll concentrate on only one person."

I laughed. "I'm glad I can provide a fulfilling experience for you."

"Oh, you do."

After we turned off the lights, Marion snuggled up against me. I rubbed her back as I tried to push aside the trauma of the evening. She pressed against me, and I held her tight. She returned the hug. Something in my pajama bottoms came alive, and before I knew what was happening, my bride and I were engaged in comfort sex and making the mattress bounce to a happy tune. I upheld my part of the marital agreement and lay there, spent and amazed, at what a geezer my age could accomplish. Wonder of wonders.

The next morning upon awakening, I remembered everything from the day before—going ti leaf sliding, dealing with a car that wouldn't start, visiting Meyer and Henry and finding the dead body in the care home kitchen. My gut clenched at that memory. I recalled my conversation with Jennifer. For once a bad image from the day before had not disappeared.

Marion sat up in bed, rubbing her eyes.

"Something unusual happened." I leaned over and gave her a kiss on the cheek. "My memory has somehow started working again."

Marion nodded. "It happens under a special circumstance."

"And that is?"

"Think back to last night."

I scratched my head. "We ate dinner and then took Meyer and Henry back to the care home." My chest double-clutched like an old unsynchronized manual transmission. "Uh-oh. Does it have something to do with the murder?"

Marion scowled. "No, silly. It's the result of something pleasant."

"Let's see. We came back to the hotel, went to bed and then . . ."

"Now you're on the right track."

I gasped. "You mean our encounter under the sheets?"

"That's right." Marion gave me a hug. "It caused a special effect in you and jogged your memory."

"I'll be damned."

"But it only lasts for a day. After you next go to sleep, you'll reset and lose your short-term memory for anything that recently happened before you fell asleep."

"So unless I turn into a sex machine, my memory will be crapola again?"

"That's right."

"What a predicament. My mind's willing to give it a go again tonight, but I can't say the same for my body."

"We'll see when all of you is ready again."

"I can hardly wait."

After feasting on papaya, banana pancakes with coconut syrup and Kona coffee, we headed out to watch my offspring tempt the waves of Waikiki Beach.

Jennifer charged ahead with Denny and Allison trying to keep up with her. Marion and I trailed behind, holding hands like newlyweds—wait. We were still newlyweds after only five months of marriage.

"Jennifer seems to have bounced back after the awful event of last night," I said.

"She's resilient. It's good she has surfing to look forward to today."

We slathered on gallons of sunscreen to ward off any evil effects of the sun, and the two older generations sat down on the sand to watch Jennifer paddle her rented surfboard out into the shark-infested ocean. No, that was only in my overactive imagination. With so many people in the water, any self-respecting shark would have hightailed it six miles out to sea.

I watched as Jennifer in her bright red swimsuit reached an area of breaking waves, turned her board around and began paddling. She caught the first wave and rode into shore. I applauded the amazing feat of my granddaughter. She waved and paddled back for more.

Hina came down the sand, carrying her surfboard, and stopped to greet us. "Is Jennifer already out there?"

"Yep. Right over there." I pointed.

"I'll see you later." Hina took off, threw her board in the water and paddled away.

"Let's go in the water," Marion said.

"You have to be kidding. That ocean is teeming with man-eating surfboards, skin-tearing coral and slithering things ready to pounce on me."

"Don't be such a sissy. Come stick your toe in."

Marion stood and reached out a hand to me. With my manhood thus challenged, I clambered up, dusted off the sand from my legs and eyed the ocean. Yikes. It was huge and uninviting. "Don't you want me to make a drink run?"

Marion furrowed an eyebrow. "No. I want you to come in the water with me."

I gave in to the inevitable as she led me to my doom. I put one foot in. It felt warm. "Not too bad. Okay, now I've been swimming."

"Paul!"

"Yes, ma'am?"

"You can come in farther."

I looked out to sea before returning my gaze toward the safety of the beach. I gritted my teeth and went in up to my knees. A wave rolled in and splashed my stomach. Okay, now I was wet.

Marion grabbed my hand and pulled me in up to my chest. My heart began to race. I gasped for breath. "I think I'm having a heart attack."

"Don't give me any more guff. You can handle this." She splashed water in my face. I returned the favor and suddenly we were engaged in a water fight like two little kids. Once we quit, I sank down in the water.

Marion again grabbed my arm and tugged me out until I stood up to my neck. And I was still alive.

"Why don't you try floating on your back?" Marion said.

"I don't float so hot."

"Give it a try. I'll hold you up."

So I flopped out, and Marion put her hand under my butt. I looked up at a fluffy cloud sailing from the land out to sea. I actually floated.

When Marion took away her hand, I plummeted like an anchor. My head went under, and I kicked my legs trying to find the ocean floor. I finally stood and spat out a mouthful of water.

"You really do sink like a rock," Marion said.

"I warned you. I don't have any baby fat. Only lead."

I used this opportunity to scurry to shore, toweled off and sat on the blanket to enjoy the ocean being where it belonged and me being on the sand. I put on my straw hat to protect my face and watched Jennifer catch more waves. The ocean and I had reached a truce with neither of us having any more to do with the other.

When Jennifer and Hina gave up, hunger overcoming their love of surfing, we headed back to the hotel to change. The message light was flashing on our telephone, so while Marion showered, I checked and found a message from Detective Chun asking to give him a call ASAP.

I punched in his number, and after the third ring, he answered.

"What can I do to help the Honolulu Police Department?" I asked.

"I want to check with you to see if you recall anything new regarding Sammy Malo and the events leading to his death."

"With my short-term memory loss, there's nothing new that will pop up."

"I received a call this morning from Detective Saito in Kaneohe. Your name came up in connection with a case he's investigating as well, the murder of Louise Kincaid. Through an informant, I've verified that Sammy Malo provided illegal drugs to Ms. Kincaid. Very interesting that you discovered both bodies, Mr. Jacobson."

CHAPTER 11

Here I was somehow tied to two murder victims who were involved in some form of drug dealing. "The only drugs I'm involved with are the pills my wife crams down my throat twice a day, and I'd happily give those up."

"Detective Saito indicated he met you a year and a half ago regarding another case of his," Chun said.

"I don't remember the details because of my short-term memory loss, but everyone keeps telling me I've been around crime investigations before. I have no background or inclination to deal with this sort of crap."

"I want to hear your thoughts on how you came across two murder victims who work together, Mr. Jacobson."

"Just a coincidence."

"Yeah, right. Coincidence. I've never met a coincidence I didn't distrust. If you think of anything more you'd like to share, give me a call."

"You'll be the first to know, Detective."

I sat there in stunned silence. What was going on? I witnessed the aftermath of two murders, and the two victims worked together in the illegal drug trade. Who killed them? Why had I found both bodies? I could still make no sense of any of this.

I failed to notice my bride beside me, clean and dressed. "You seem lost in thought, Paul."

"Yeah. I'm trying to sort out what's happened with the two

murder victims I've happened upon."

She patted my shoulder. "I'm sure Detectives Chun and Saito will find out."

I let out a heartfelt sigh. "I hope you're right."

With no additional useful insights, I showered, and then we reconvened to grab some chow.

After sating our appetites, Jennifer regarded me thoughtfully. "We need to go find out how Henry's doing."

"Are you sure you want to go back to the scene of the crime?" I asked.

Jennifer shivered. "Not particularly, but I wonder if Henry's been cleared of suspicion. We also need to meet his fiancée."

"This should be quite an event," I replied. "Henry and his computer romance. Care to take a bet on what this woman is like?"

"Oh, Grandpa, don't be such a curmudgeon."

"Hey, that's what I do best. If she's interested in Henry, she has to be some kind of wacko. No one else would put up with him."

With that endorsement, we assembled the troops in the SUV, and Denny drove off for the wilds of Kaneohe. We barely missed an accident when the driver of a pickup waved to a friend and veered into our lane. "Sorry, bruddah," the man shouted and continued on his merry way.

With no dents or scratches, we arrived at the care home. Inside, everything looked normal—no crime scene tape, no police patrol, no Henry in handcuffs. Henry, Meyer and a platinum blonde sat in the living room. Henry and the woman both stood when we entered. I guessed her age to be early seventies, and she towered over Henry by a good six inches. She wore enough gold bracelets to finance the national debt, and her bright blue muumuu covered a solid, but not hefty, frame. She had bright red lipstick and a healthy pink to her cheeks. In a booming voice she announced, "I'm Madeline Hightower." She stepped over and grabbed my hand. "You must be the jerk. Henry mentioned you." My knuckles crunched, and I grimaced under the vise-like grip. She released my hand and put her arms around Jennifer, pulling my granddaughter to her ample bosom. "And Jennifer. We'll have to exchange baseball facts."

"Ain't she a beaut?" Henry said with stars in his eyes, completely bedazzled. Was this love at first sight?

After the completion of the introductions, I asked, "Are the police going to incarcerate you, Henry?"

He gave a dismissive wave of his hand. "Nope. I'm free to be with my honey bun." He made goo-goo eyes at Madeline.

I'm sure my mouth dropped open at seeing the goofy expression on Henry's face. "Are you two really getting hitched?"

"Right after Christmas." Madeline held her hand out to display a diamond the size of a marble. She turned to Henry, lifted him off the ground and gave him a kiss on the forehead. "My honey bunch and I are going to have a civil ceremony. Meyer will preside."

"Is that legal?" I asked.

"I was a judge," Meyer replied.

"Any of your relatives coming for the ceremony?" Allison asked Madeline.

"Nope. My brothers and sisters have kicked the bucket. I was married once before, but we never had any kids, so I'm solo. I'm appointing Jennifer my maid of honor. And you." She jabbed me in the chest. "You get to be best man."

I rubbed the spot where I'd been poked and checked to make sure I wasn't bleeding. "With an invitation like that, how can I refuse?"

"Don't mess up our ceremony, jerk," Henry said.

"I wouldn't think of it. But Madeline, you should be aware that your fiancé is under suspicion with the police."

She waved her arm, and I ducked to avoid being knocked flat. "I've heard the story. Henry didn't kill that woman. The police will find the real culprit. Now we need to go get some food. I haven't eaten in an hour. I'm treating." She grabbed Henry under her arm and headed for the doorway as if carrying a stuffed animal.

Pamela Newsome at the front desk held up a hand. "You need to sign out first."

Madeline slapped the nurse's hand aside with her free arm and barged out the door with Henry's legs kicking in the air.

"Ain't she a beaut?" came the faint refrain as the door slammed shut.

"I'll sign," Denny said and went over to the nurse's desk.

Marion grabbed my arm and whispered in my ear. "I'm ready to get out of here. I still find it creepy being in this home after what happened last night."

We headed outside. By this time, Madeline and Henry were tucked in a red Corvette with the engine gunning.

"Where to?" Madeline shouted.

"Let's try Buzz's Steakhouse in Kailua," Denny replied.

"I'll punch it in my GPS," Madeline said. "Okay, got it. See you there." The Corvette shot off in a cloud of gravel.

"Ain't she a beau-u-u-t?" drifted back from the distance.

"I think Hurricane Madeline struck us," I said.

Meyer shook his head. "That woman will give Henry another heart attack if she doesn't squeeze him to death first."

"Nah," I replied. "Henry's tough. But I do believe he's met his match. Those two will cut a swath like a tornado rampaging through a Kansas cornfield."

We seat-belted in, and Denny drove at a leisurely pace to the restaurant. When we arrived, Madeline was striding around the parking lot like a wild lioness. "The cussed place doesn't open for half an hour," she informed us.

"We can go to Kailua Beach across the road for a while," Jennifer said. "Let's take a walk."

So our entourage strolled across the street, with Madeline planted on the centerline with her hands out stopping traffic in both directions. This was not a woman to mess with.

Jennifer removed her shoes and raced down to stick her feet in the water. "Look. People are windsurfing. Dad, we have to do that."

"It's not that easy," Denny replied. "I tried it once and couldn't stay up for more than thirty seconds."

"It'd be no problem for me." Jennifer gave a determined nod. "It's like surfing with a sail. All it takes is good balance."

"You'd never get me out there," I said. "Besides, I'm not that balanced."

"What's the matter, jerk?" Madeline elbowed me, leaving a dent in my ribs. "You don't like the ocean?"

"Can't stand it."

"I was in the Navy with the WAVES. I love the ocean." She spread out her arms as if to summon Neptune. Fortunately, he didn't respond.

The steady breeze provided enough fresh air to raise my spirits. I pushed aside the thoughts of dead bodies as puffy clouds nestled above the horizon.

We continued our promenade and watched two young men throw a Frisbee back and forth. One of them came running toward us to make a catch and ran smack into Madeline. He bounced off her as if striking a rock cliff and lay flat in the sand. She didn't even flinch. "Watch it, slimeball." She picked the man up as if lifting a toothpick and shoved him stumbling back toward his companion. The man gaped at Madeline once and staggered onward.

"Ain't she a firecracker?" Henry said.

Jennifer collected several hunks of driftwood, and I found a piece of drift glass before we headed back to the restaurant, now open. We sat at a table for eight and settled in to survey the menu.

When the waiter came for our orders, Madeline bellowed out, "I want your largest steak, rare, and throw in a side of a lobster tail and crab legs. Get the orders from the rest of these yahoos and bring me the bill at the end."

No one dared argue with Madeline.

As salads arrived Madeline took a huge bite of lettuce and punched Henry in the shoulder. "Ready to trade baseball facts?"

He rubbed his arm and gave a crooked grin as if he'd been kissed rather than slugged. "You can ask first, honey bun."

Madeline hit her fist on the table, causing the glasses to shake. "Okay. From 1901 through 1909 what three National League teams won pennants?"

"Easy." Henry rubbed his hands together. "Pittsburgh, New York and Chicago. Here's one for you. Who was the league home-run leader with the lowest total for a year in the twentieth century?"

"Hmmm." Madeline waved her napkin around as if trying to cool off. "Several only hit seven in the American League. But the lowest was Thomas Leach of Pittsburgh in 1902. Six home runs."

"Dang. I thought I might catch you on that."

"No way, sweet cheeks." Madeline practically pinched a piece of flesh off the side of Henry's face.

They continued the battle until Henry waved his hand in the air in submission. He had become too bruised from Madeline's affection, practically turning into a purple bowling ball.

Madeline ate every scrap on her plate plus half of Henry's. To complete the meal, we devoured Buzz's Ice Cream Pies for dessert. Madeline asked if anyone wanted seconds.

Jennifer raised her hand, so she and Madeline scarfed another dessert.

Madeline let out a satisfied belch and planted a kiss on Henry's cheek.

Henry wiped his mouth with a napkin. "Ain't she a beaut?"

CHAPTER 12

Back in our room that night, I knew there would be no repeat performance for Paul Jacobson in the erotic zone. I was too tired. I managed to update my diary before crashing into bed.

I awoke not recognizing my surroundings. A woman with silver hair lay next to me in bed. Who the heck was she, and how did I end up in bed with her? She didn't seem to be here under duress, for she slept with a smile on her face as she periodically licked her lips. Must have been having a good dream. I got out of bed and looked out the curtains. I spied a yacht harbor. It looked like Hawaii. I thumped the side of my head. Think. What was I doing here? I remembered living in Hawaii. Then something came back to me. I had become a widower after my wife Rhonda died. But this woman now sharing a bed with me? I spotted a note on top of a spiral notebook on the nightstand by my side of the bed. I read, "You'll wake up not remembering your fanny from a fandango so read this diary of what you've been up to, you old coot."

Since it was my handwriting, I followed the directions and caught up on the life and times of Paul Jacobson, soon to be best man for some fruitcake named Henry. I had also accumulated a new wife named Marion, the woman next to me. I peeked under the covers. Not bad. I guessed I could go with this new situation. Roused by the fresh air being let in under the sheets, she awoke and smiled at me. That was a good sign.

She seemed to accept having an old poop with a memory like seaweed sleeping with her.

We met my son, daughter-in-law and granddaughter for breakfast. I ordered scrambled eggs and papaya. I suddenly shivered, as if feeling the eyes of someone watching me. I surveyed my domain and saw a man in a blue Hawaiian shirt standing in the lobby with his back to me. No one seemed to be paying any attention to yours truly. I returned my attention to my family to catch up on the latest report from the world of a twelve-year-old, which included lobbying for a cell phone and reporting on the latest email from her friend Austin in Venice Beach.

When the food arrived, I looked at the papaya and wrinkled my nose. "I don't think I'll eat it after all."

"I'll take it, Paul." Marion reached in front of me and removed the plate with the papaya. She took a few bites but pushed it aside as well.

After breakfast Jennifer took off to meet her friend Hina for a morning of surfing. Denny and Allison decided they'd go to the beach as well.

"You want to stroll on the sand?" I asked Marion.

"No. I'm not feeling that well. I think I'll rest in the room this morning."

"I'll keep you company."

My bride and I adjourned to our room. "What seems to be the problem?" I asked.

"I'm having a little trouble breathing."

"What? I better call a doctor."

Marion fluffed up her pillow. "That isn't necessary."

"Don't be a jerk! If you're not feeling well, we need to do something right now."

"Paul, don't shout at me."

"Of course I'll shout at you. You need medical attention."

Marion pounded her fist on the bed. "Go away. You're bothering me."

I stepped closer ready to speak my mind, before thinking better of it. "I'll go sit out on the balcony." I stomped to the sliding door, opened it, stepped outside and plunked down on one of the two chairs. I adjusted it to give me a view over the yacht harbor and watched a large catamaran motor out into the channel. It unfurled its sails and proceeded into the briny deep.

What was the matter with me? Why'd I let my hair-trigger temper get the best of me and yell at Marion? She didn't feel well and how did I act? Like a jerk.

I took a deep breath and smelled an aroma that mixed seaweed, salt spray and jasmine. *Calm yourself.* Okay, I needed to go make amends.

Returning to the room, I saw Marion huddled in bed and heard her gasping for breath.

"Paul, I'm having more trouble breathing."

"That does it. I'm calling for help." I dialed the operator and told her my wife was having trouble breathing. I was informed that a call would be placed to 9-1-1 and a staff physician would be up immediately.

After hanging up, I scrambled over to Marion. "Can I get you a glass of water, a wet washcloth or anything?"

"No," she croaked.

I paced around the room, waiting, my heart beating lickety-split. I felt helpless. What could I do for her?

Hearing a knock, I raced over and thrust the door open.

A woman holding a black bag stepped in. She stood approximately five-foot-two but walked with the authority of a giant. She went to Marion, checked her mouth, put a stethoscope to her chest and took her pulse.

"How is she, Doc?"

"I think it's best that we have her taken to the hospital. An ambulance will be here momentarily."

While waiting she checked Marion's blood pressure.

I stood there wringing my hands, feeling as useless as a flashlight without batteries. Finally two EMTs arrived, wheeling in a gurney. They helped Marion aboard and strapped on a face mask connected to an oxygen tank.

We headed down the elevator and out the front door to the waiting ambulance. The doctor informed us that she would call ahead to Queen's Medical Center with her information, and I climbed in the back of the ambulance with Marion. As we took off and the siren wailed, I held Marion's hand. "It's going to be fine," I said, more to reassure me than Marion. "I got a little carried away earlier. I'm sorry I yelled at you."

Marion squeezed my hand, the best feeling imaginable.

We arrived at the emergency room entrance, and two attendants whisked Marion into the hospital. I followed to take care of paperwork and was directed to a waiting room to do of all things, wait. A dozen people sat there, some speaking in low tones and others rigidly silent. I found a two-year-old medical magazine and read an article on dementia. It described people with short-term memory loss who consistently misplaced their car keys or glasses. I certainly didn't know anyone like that. The only thing that exempted me—I didn't need glasses and had already given up my car keys.

I threw the magazine down and placed my palms against my forehead. *Pull through, Marion.* Although I remembered knowing her for only a day, somewhere inside I realized she had become the most important person in my life. We belonged together, and she couldn't die here in a hospital in the wilderness of Honolulu.

"Hey, man," a voice said. "You got someone in there?"

I looked up to see a guy, probably in his thirties, wearing torn jeans and a T-shirt that read, "Wow." His hair looked like he combed it with a cake mixer.

"Yeah. My wife is having trouble breathing."

He gave a sympathetic nod. "I know. It's a pisser when someone you know has problems. The doc is patching up my girlfriend."

"What happened?" I asked.

He let out a deep sigh. "My ex-wife tried to do a number with a knife, but she never was very good with kitchen utensils."

After what seemed like two days but was two hours, a doctor in scrubs appeared and led me down a hallway.

"How's she doing, Doc?"

"She's fine. Heart is strong, breathing has improved. She suffered an allergic reaction and is on medication to open her airway."

He parted a curtain, and I beheld a beautiful sight—Marion resting in bed with a smile on her puss. I went over and gave her a kiss.

"Thank you for making the call, Paul. I shouldn't have argued when you first suggested getting help."

"And I apologize again for flying off the handle. Me and my temper. I was so damn worried."

The doctor tapped a clipboard he held. "Mrs. Jacobson, I need to ask again if you have any food or medication allergies."

"None that I know of."

He stared at me. "Mr. Jacobson, have you noticed any previous allergic reactions from your wife?"

"I wouldn't know, Doctor. I have short-term memory loss. But nothing that I've noted in my journal."

The doctor tilted his head in my direction.

"Paul keeps a diary so he can reacquaint himself with his recent activities," Marion explained. "He remembers things fine during the day but overnight forgets the recent past."

Arching an eyebrow, the doctor stared at me more intently. "Interesting. I have a colleague who would love to discuss your symptoms."

I made a crossing motion with my hands. "No way. I'm on vacation. As soon as we can get Marion released, we have some serious relaxing to do. Speaking of which, when can I spring her?"

"I'd like to check her once more in an hour. We can discharge her at that time if the symptoms don't return."

I sat down in a chair next to Marion and held her hand. "You scared the living bejesus out of me."

"I feel fine. Look." She took a deep breath and exhaled loudly. "For a while I could only take little gaspy breaths."

"I wonder what caused it."

She shrugged. "Maybe some pollen I'm not used to. Or something I ate."

Then it struck me. Marion had eaten some of my papaya and soon afterward started having trouble breathing. Did someone poison it, and was it meant for me?

CHAPTER 13

I kept my concern to myself that someone might have spiked my papaya at breakfast. There would be no way of determining anything now. The papaya would be long gone in some trash bin with no way to figure out who had poisoned it. It was a good thing Marion only took a few bites. If she had eaten the whole thing, she might not have made it.

Marion got out of bed and walked around briefly before returning to lie down. "No trouble breathing at all."

When the doctor returned, he checked her lungs with his stethoscope and ruled her fit to leave the hospital. He handed her a slip of paper. "Here's a prescription you can have filled at the hospital pharmacy. Take it if your symptoms flare up again."

After Marion changed into her street clothes, we purchased the medicine, and I requested the front desk call a cab for us.

A black car with an orange sign on top saying "Moki's" pulled up in front. A man hopped out and came up to me. "Hey, bruddah. You call a cab?"

"That we did. To the Hibiscus Hotel."

"You got it, bruddah."

We climbed in and in a blink of an eye shot out of the parking lot and headed back to Waikiki to be reunited with the rest of our family.

"You interested in a tour of the island sometime?" the cabbie asked.

"Not today," I replied.

He reached back and handed me a card. "You eva need any-ting, call Moki." He thumped his chest. "I give da best taxi service on da whole island."

"I'll remember that, Moki."

Marion elbowed me. "You'll forget by tomorrow."

I gave Marion my best geezer smirk. "Not if I write it in my journal." For insurance, I handed the card to Marion for safe-keeping.

Moki brought us right under the portico at the Hibiscus Hotel and hopped out to open the door for Marion.

Once I completed the payoff with ample tip so as not to be blackballed by the Taxi Association of Honolulu, we strolled into the hotel and headed up to our room.

Denny stood in the doorway between our adjoining rooms. "Where have you two been? We were worried sick. We couldn't find you, you left no note, and we didn't know if something happened to you."

"A little medical emergency, but everything's fine," I explained. "In the heat of the moment I never considered a note or anything else."

"It would be a lot easier if you used a cell phone," Denny said.

Jennifer bounded into the room like a jackrabbit on steroids. "See, Dad, that's why I should have a cell. I could report in so you'd always know where I was."

"This is different," Denny said.

"I don't want one of those itty bitty phones to stick to my ear like all the crazies I see on the sidewalks," I answered. "You can give my hypothetical cell phone to Jennifer instead."

"Great idea." Jennifer tugged on her dad's arm. "Grandpa has a good suggestion. What do you think?"

He sloughed off her hand. "No, this concerns your grand-father, not you getting a phone."

"Hey, I get by fine without that kind of gadget. Sorry that you worried. We came back as soon as the hospital released Marion."

"Hospital?" Allison said, sticking her head into our room.

"Okay, the whole clan's assembled," I said. "Let me give you the News at Nine report." I recounted Marion's allergic reaction, trip to the hospital and recovery, leaving out my speculation of tainted papaya.

"And you're fine, Marion?" Allison asked.

"Yes. And I have some pills to take if I suffer any further breathing problems."

"Hah," I said. "Justice is served. You may have to take pills rather than trying to stuff them down my throat."

Marion shrugged. "I don't mind taking pills if I have to. It's no big deal. I can dry-swallow pills with ease."

"Maybe you can. I can't even down the dang things with water."

"I know, Grandpa. You hate the ocean, lawyers and pills."

"Exactly. But I like my granddaughter."

Jennifer came over and gave me a hug. "That's good because I like you too."

With us all lovey-dovey, we made plans to have dinner at a nearby restaurant and spend a quiet evening.

The next day at the crack of dawn after digesting the account in my journal, I listened as Denny informed me that an early morning helicopter ride awaited us.

"Only the representatives of the three Jacobson generations," Marion said. "Allison and I will forego that pleasure."

"That's right," Allison added, "since I like heights as much as Paul likes the ocean, there's no way I'm going up in something that flimsy."

"I'm fine with flying as long as we don't crash into any bodies of water," I said. "Fortunately, Jennifer didn't inherit fear of oceans or heights."

"Darn right. I love both." She waved her arms. "I can spend hours in the ocean and will go up in the air whenever I have the chance."

Denny had ordered sweet rolls, coffee and juice from room service. After a quick repast, Denny, Jennifer and I departed for the helicopter ride and boarded our craft at the Honolulu airport. Our pilot introduced himself. "I'm Dex Tanaka. Dex stands for dexterous." He wiggled his fingers. "I've flown helicopters for thirty years without one mishap."

I eyed him warily. "Let's keep it that way. Don't have your first accident and crash into the ocean."

Dex laughed. "No way, bruddah. I always land on the helicopter pad."

We climbed aboard, with Denny sitting up front with the pilot and Jennifer next to me in the seats behind. We buckled up and put on headsets to hear Dex's spiel and to be able to speak to each other above the sound of the blades.

After taking off, we circled over Keehi Lagoon, and my heart jumped into my throat at the sight of the water below us. We passed over a sandbar, and a person there waved to us. What was someone doing out in the middle of the ocean on that small spit of sand? You'd never get me out in a place like that.

As Dex flew us along Waikiki Beach, Jennifer pointed. "I went surfing there yesterday, right where the waves are breaking."

"And next to shore is where I risked life and limb going in the water up to my neck," I shouted above the whooping sound of the blades.

We passed Diamond Head. "We have to climb to the top while we're here," Jennifer announced into her headset.

"That's fine with me. Your mother wouldn't like the height, but it's better than being in the ocean."

"You folks are lucky today," Dex said. "You've signed up for the deluxe tour. We're going all the way around the island."

Not that the island was that big. We passed Koko Head, Hanauma Bay, the Blow Hole and continued on past Kaneohe. I mentally waved to Meyer, Henry and the Amazon Madeline Hightower. Jeez. What a pair she and Henry made. They'd be able to out-insult and out-muscle the whole island if ever challenged.

We flew into a valley and Dex pointed out Sacred Falls. Next, we passed the northern tip of the island at Kahuku Point. At Haleiwa we jogged inland and Dex gave us a running commentary on the land once growing sugar cane and pineapples. I felt relief at not flying over water for the moment.

But this was short-lived as we doubled back and proceeded around the western tip of the island at Kaena Point.

"I've never been here," Denny said into his headphone.

"Few people have," Dex replied. "No road so you have to hike around the point. I'm going to show you another area that doesn't have many visitors." The helicopter veered inland over a forested area and, once again, I gave a sigh of relief to be no longer over water.

"We're flying over Waianae Valley." Dex chuckled. "Home of some of the most popular unauthorized pot growing on the island."

I thought of Mrs. Wilson and her brownies. Maybe some of the ingredients originated in this valley.

What sounded like a gunshot interrupted my cogitation. Dex grabbed the controls and the helicopter dipped. "Uh-oh," he said.

I didn't like the sound of that.

"Hold on tight, folks," Dex called out.

The engine coughed as the helicopter vibrated and descended.

I heard what sounded like automatic weapon fire. "Holy crapola. Someone's shooting at us."

"We're going to land in that small clearing," Dex shouted.

I looked out and saw the postage stamp–sized opening in the jungle. My stomach lurched as we dropped and made contact with a resounding thud that caused my whole body to shudder. I counted limbs and determined that all pieces survived and remained in the right places.

"Everyone okay?" Dex asked.

We mumbled, "Yes," into our headsets.

"Now what?" Denny asked.

"We get out," Dex said.

We unbuckled and clambered outside. Dex had managed a miracle. The helicopter rested on a grassy patch with not more than five feet clearance from trees on all sides.

"How the hell do we get out of here?" I asked in my most irate tourist manner.

"That's the least of our worries right now." Dex pointed to five men emerging from the forest. They wore camouflage shirts, ragged jeans and boots and carried rifles. Definitely not military. One who was obviously the leader put a hand up to hold the others back and stepped up to our motley group. He was tall and muscular with a shaved head and wore a drab brown and olive bandana around his forehead. "What you doing here?"

"Uh . . . someone seems to have damaged our helicopter," Dex replied.

"This area is off-limits. No one flies over us."

Dex gulped. "Yeah. I see that. I was showing these tourists around the island."

"We no need no haoles snooping around here. You come with me." He pushed us toward a faint trail into the trees. I decided not to ask for the nearest restroom.

We marched along for twenty minutes with the rifle-toting

men behind us. Denny and I exchanged eye signals. He stepped in front of Jennifer, and I got behind her to hide her as much as possible from the armed men. Jennifer bit her lip when she turned around to see me, but I was amazed at how brave she was in this unwelcomed situation.

We reached an encampment, replete with half a dozen dirty pup tents, an extinguished campfire, and a pile of pointy-leaved plants. These weren't your garden-variety horticulturists, so to speak.

"You sit there." The leader pointed to a patch of dirt near the fire ring. We plopped down while two of the men stood guard with their rifles at the ready. Several other men milled around on the other side of the clearing. This certainly wasn't a good place to be for an old poop like me, a middle-aged financial advisor like my son and a young squirt like Jennifer. Speaking of whom, she leaned over and whispered in my ear. "I recognize one of the men with rifles. The one with the big nose way over by the trees. He was with Sammy Malo the night you and Sammy argued by the yacht harbor."

CHAPTER 14

I squinted at the man identified by Jennifer. He possessed a distinctive large nose, but that didn't jog my useless memory, since I couldn't remember several nights ago from string cheese.

I thought back to my journal entry about encountering Sammy Malo and discovering Sammy's body in the yacht harbor the next morning. Damn. What a mess. I hoped the armed big-nosed guy didn't recognize me. I tried to make myself inconspicuous by huddling behind Denny.

I turned my head and glanced at him out of the corner of my eye. Big Nose stood there with no evidence of recognition. He seemed preoccupied with guarding the pile of leaves. Hopefully, he thought all old haoles looked alike.

I shifted my gaze to Dex. He didn't look that worried. Maybe he was used to landing in the jungle with gun-toting drug growers.

Off to the side I heard the leader speaking to another man sporting a patch over one eye. Fortunately, my hearing was much better than my memory, so I tuned in to their conversation. They were debating what to do with us. Eye-patch guy thought we should be shot and buried in the jungle. My mouth went dry, and my heart beat a ragged tattoo. The leader thought we might be candidates for ransom. I swallowed hard at this idea. Neither of these men suggested my vote of letting us go on our merry way. The leader's argument seemed to hold sway. Certainly better than being shot.

The leader stepped over and pointed a rifle at us. "Okay, you rich haoles. How much money are you worth?"

How to deal with this? In spite of our desperate situation, one idea seized my weirdly wired brain. I reached in my pocket and pulled out my change, which consisted of two quarters, a dime and a nickel. "Looks like sixty-five cents."

He knocked the coins out of my hand, sending them scattering toward the fire pit. "Don't give me no crap, old man."

"You have the old part right. I'm a retired geezer on Social Security. I get a check from the government every month."

He turned to Denny. "I bet you one rich businessman."

Denny shrugged. "Nope. Only a regular guy with a job, paying my mortgage and food bills. I'm trying to save a little money to put my daughter through college."

"I have a piggy bank with nine dollars and forty-six cents in it at home," Jennifer said, getting in the swing of things. "You can have that."

Eye Patch tapped the leader on the shoulder. "Maybe my way be betta."

Uh-oh. I didn't want him going back to the worse alternative. I waved my hand like a kid in school with the right answer.

The leader pointed at me. "Yeah?"

"I'm sure some reasonable reimbursement can be arranged."

"What you mean?" the leader asked.

"We could set up monthly payments like my Medicare Part B deductions from Social Security. You know, take out a hundred dollars a month from my bank account."

He raised his arm like he wanted to whack me, but at that moment the sound of automatic fire rattled though the jungle.

A man ran up and ground to a halt in front of the leader. "Kenny, cops are coming. We gotta get outta here."

The leader nodded his head in acknowledgment and motioned to his men, who grabbed most of the pile of leaves and raced into the jungle before you could say, "Maui wowie."

The guy with the big nose remained as the last one after the others skedaddled. He aimed a rifle toward me and fired a shot. It hit a rock next to my foot with a ping. I dropped to the ground and covered my head as my heart played a staccato beat.

I heard clomping sounds in the jungle, and three men appeared wearing body armor and holding some mean-looking automatic weapons. Not a smile on their faces. "On the ground," one of them commanded. "Police."

The others dropped like swatted flies. I was already on the ground.

I felt someone frisk me. It tickled, but I refrained from giggling. Then a gruff voice told me to stand up. As I wiped some dirt off my pants, one of the officers pointed to the remnants of the leaves. "This belong to you?"

Dex stepped forward. "Officer, I'm Dex Tanaka of Tourist Air Tours. These are my passengers. We flew over this area and were shot down by some men who took us hostage. We ended up in their camp, and they ran off when you arrived on the scene."

"Let's see some identification from everyone."

Denny, Dex and I handed over our IDs, and Denny explained that Jennifer was his daughter. The officers perused our laminated cards and handed them back.

"The men hurt you in any way?" one of the officers asked.

"They threatened us, but no physical harm," Denny explained.

"Please describe what they looked like."

Jennifer stepped forward. "Someone called the leader of the group Kenny. He was tall, muscular and bald. He had a tattoo of a surfboard on his right arm and a scar on his left index finger. And black boots."

"Wow," I said. "You noticed all that? You're pretty observant."

"Yep. And he wore ragged jeans and a brown and green short-sleeved shirt with a bandana wrapped around his forehead."

"One guy wore a patch over his eye," Denny added. "He acted like he was second in command and wanted to kill us."

"Another had a big nose," I said.

"He stayed in the background, but we saw him with Sammy Malo in Waikiki five nights ago," Jennifer said.

"What? You know Sammy Malo?"

"Um . . . I happened to be there when Sammy's body was pulled out of the Honolulu Ala Wai Yacht Harbor," I pitched in.

"And we saw Sammy the night before he died," Jennifer said.

One of the officers motioned us toward a faint trail into the jungle. "Now I need you to accompany me to the Waianae Police Station for further questions."

"What about my helicopter?" Dex looked around nervously.

"You better call your headquarters to get a mechanic out here to fix it."

With that we marched down the hillside until we came to three police SUVs. Jennifer and Denny went in one, and Dex and I were locked in the back of another one.

"Your spotless record has been tarnished with this little episode," I said to Dex. "First crash landing."

He frowned. "And that's not all. I haven't been shot at since my tour of duty at the end of the Vietnam War."

"Cheer up. No one was injured. You made a good landing."

"But I don't know what it will take to fix the helicopter. It could be out of commission for a long time. None of our mechanics will want to traipse into a known marijuana growing area. It's too dangerous. I'll have to see if I can fix it myself."

"Maybe the police will provide an escort. They won't want the drug dealers to get their hands on your helicopter."

We remained in silence while we bounced along a rutted dirt road. I thought serious damage would be done to my coccyx. Eventually, we emerged from the undergrowth and came to a paved road. It felt as smooth as a silk kimono.

Minutes later, we entered the Waianae Police Station, Jennifer elbowed me. "Here we are again, Grandpa. You spent time here once."

"What? Police stations? I don't do police stations."

"When you lived in the Kina Nani retirement home and we visited you a year-and-a-half ago, you were suspected of stealing an automobile. You were detained for a few hours here, but it was a misunderstanding and got cleared up."

Maybe it was a good thing I didn't remember squat. I looked around. Not the least bit familiar, but I wouldn't have remembered it from yesterday much less a year-and-a-half ago.

We were separated and individually questioned. During my interrogation, the detective in charge, a large man with a pointed chin named Silva, honed in on Sammy Malo. "Tell me again how you met Sammy."

"See, Detective, I have short-term memory loss, so I don't remember the events. But I keep a journal, which I read this morning. I literally bumped into Sammy after dinner, and we shouted at each other. In the jungle, my granddaughter recognized a guy with a big nose who was with Sammy that evening."

Silva furrowed an eyebrow. "I thought you couldn't remember things."

"I remember fine during the day, but overnight everything goes blotto. I can recount everything that's happened to me today."

"Keep going with how you know Sammy."

So I covered discovering the hand in the water and watching the body being recovered. "You can check with Detective Chun. He has the scoop."

Silva jotted a note. "Anything else I should know?"

I considered mentioning how I found the body of Louise

Kincaid but figured that would further muddy the already murky waters.

He left me alone for a while and then returned. "I spoke with Detective Chun. He also directed me to Detective Saito in Kaneohe. It seems you've been linked to another murder as well. How come you didn't mention that?"

Uh-oh. Sweat began to form on my aged brow. "I figured it didn't relate to what just happened."

"Pretty suspicious set of circumstances. An altercation with Sammy Malo, a leading suspected drug dealer. You find his body. Then you report finding Louise Kincaid, also suspected of drug dealing with Sammy. Finally, you're discovered in a drug camp in the Waianae Mountains, with some of the same gang. Quite a set of coincidences."

"And like the other detectives I've dealt with, I bet you don't believe in coincidences."

"You have that right."

CHAPTER 15

An hour later I sat in a room with the triumvirate of my favorite detectives—Chun, Saito and Silva. They acted like they wanted to draw straws to see which one would have the honor of tearing off my first limb. Chun began the latest round of interrogation. "Mr. Jacobson, let me review some of the relevant facts. You had an altercation with Sammy Malo and the next morning reported finding his body in the Honolulu Ala Wai Yacht Harbor. Correct?"

"I can't remember the details, but that's what I read in the journal I keep."

"You also discovered the body of Louise Kincaid at the care home where your friends live," Saito added.

"Guilty as charged."

Silva tapped a large, wrinkled finger on the wooden table between us. "And now you're found in a camp with marijuana all over the ground and identify one of the men there as an associate of Sammy Malo. Care to speculate on how these circumstances tie together?"

I shrugged. "I guess I have a knack for being in the wrong place at the wrong time."

Saito turned to the other two detectives. "As strange as these events seem, they don't surprise me. I considered Mr. Jacobson a one-man crime wave a year ago last summer. He professed his innocence the whole time and turned out to be correct. He even helped me solve the case. But this current situation is very disconcerting."

"Hey, nothing unusual here. I'm up to my old tricks, I guess. I'm not linked to any of these scumballs, but I've been in their presence through no fault of my own."

Detective Silva leaned forward. "We'd like to show you some pictures to see if you can identify some of the men suspected of growing marijuana in the mountains. They're part of a large drug gang we're trying to bring down."

"Fine by me."

"I thought Mr. Jacobson suffered from short-term memory problems," Chun said.

"I do but only overnight. I can remember things fine from today so will have no trouble picking out anyone I saw in the jungle camp."

Silva pulled out a picture from a manila folder and slid it across the table.

I squinted at it. "Yep, this guy was the leader of the group that captured us. Strong, muscular guy who wanted to ransom us."

Silva nodded. "His name is Kenny Keonu. Quite a past. A star football player in high school and a state champion wrestler before going the gang route."

"I wouldn't want to mess with him," I said.

Silva passed another picture to me.

"Oh, yeah. The pirate guy with the black patch. He's a nasty one. He wanted to kill us, but Kenny talked him out of it."

"That's Snake Laka. A mean son-of-a-bitch."

"How'd he lose his eye?" I asked.

"Knife fight. The other guy didn't fare as well. Here's one last picture."

I stared at it. "Ah, Mr. Big Nose. He was there as well. My granddaughter recognized him as someone she saw with Sammy Malo the night of our confrontation."

Silva tapped the table. "That's Manuel Hiaka. He's been an enforcer for Sammy Malo. There's some indication that he may be involved in some action to split off part of the gang."

"He stayed in the background but took a potshot at me as they scurried away when your officers arrived. Why are these maniacs still on the loose?"

Silva leveled his gaze at me. "Good question. The three of them have been arrested at one time or another, but no convictions. No witnesses stepped forward."

I gulped. "They probably wouldn't be very keen that I could identify them."

Silva nodded. "Be sure to stay with your family and not wander off on your own, Mr. Jacobson. A few more photographs."

I looked at several other pictures but didn't recognize anyone. Finally, I yawned and stretched my arms. "It's been a long day."

Saito chewed his gum for a moment and turned to his companions. "Do either of you have anything other than circumstantial evidence to hold Mr. Jacobson any longer?"

Both heads shook.

"In that case you're free to leave." Chun worried the wart on his hand. "But we'll be talking to you again."

"Thank you, gentlemen. And, Detective Saito, my friend Henry Palmer didn't have anything to do with Louise Kincaid's death either."

"We'll see, Mr. Jacobson. We'll see."

I rejoined Denny and Jennifer. Jennifer hopped over and gave me a hug. "That was so cool. The police interrogated me, and I told them we were innocent bystanders."

"What kept you such a long time, Dad?" Denny asked.

"Hey, the police like to spend time with old geezers, I guess. Where's Dex?"

"He's waiting," Denny answered. "Someone from his

company brought a van to take us back to the Honolulu airport."

Outside, Dex said he would stick around for another person to arrive with a four-wheel drive so he could go check on his helicopter. The rest of us climbed into the van.

On the ride, Jennifer leaned over and whispered in my ear. "That was so scary but exciting. We were right in the middle of an attempted drug bust."

"I don't know. We were the ones almost busted. You sure are one plucky young lady."

A faint smile crossed Jennifer's face. "I take after my grand-father."

"I don't know about that. We're fortunate the police showed up when they did. We might still be captives, or if that Snake guy had his way, dead. The police are suspicious of yours truly for being involved with these drug types."

"But we know you're innocent, Grandpa."

"The one piece of positive news—Detective Saito showed up and actually put in a good word for me."

"He should. You helped him out before."

"Everyone keeps referring to my past crime investigation career. Unfortunately, I remember diddly on that subject."

"You were awesome, Grandpa. You brought the perps to justice."

"If you say so."

After a transfer to Denny's vehicle, we returned to the Hibiscus Hotel to reunite with Marion and Allison up in the room.

"What did you two do while we gallivanted around?" I asked.

"We spent the time at the pool," Marion replied. "I read a magazine, dipped in the water and sipped a Mai Tai."

"How boring." I covered my mouth to stifle a yawn. "We saw most of the island from the air and visited with the local drug growers."

"What?" Marion and Allison exclaimed in unison.

"Yeah," Jennifer said. "It was cool. We were held hostage and saw the cops chase the drug dealers away."

Allison grabbed Jennifer and hugged her. "We need to end this so-called vacation. We're going back to the mainland right now."

Denny held up a hand. "Whoa. Everything turned out fine."

Allison released Jennifer and stomped over to Denny, thrusting a finger into his chest. "You endangered our daughter."

Denny stepped back and held his hands up as if to fend off an attacking tiger. "It was an unfortunate situation that none of us could avoid."

"You and I are going to have a talk." Allison grabbed Denny's arm and dragged him into the adjoining room and slammed the door.

Marion, Jennifer and I sat there in stunned silence as we heard Allison's shrill voice screaming. I couldn't make out any words, but I clearly understood the context.

"I don't think your mom will let you go on a helicopter again," I said to Jennifer.

"No kidding."

Marion shot me daggers. "Can you blame her, Paul? What were you men thinking?"

"Aw, Marion. It was exciting. And three detectives interrogated Grandpa. He's one of their favorite persons of interest."

"Not again," Marion said.

"Here we go with this *again* bit," I said. "This is getting old."

"But as you like to say, Grandpa, not as old as you are."

"Something like that."

We resumed sitting with our thoughts to ourselves. Allison had reason to be upset, but the good news was no one had been hurt. Finally, Denny and Allison returned.

I jumped to my feet. "Nothing like that will happen again."

Allison put her hands on her hips. "I should hope not. I still have half a mind to take Jennifer and go to the airport right now."

"Please, Mom. We have fun stuff to do here. There won't be any more problems."

"I don't know."

Jennifer went over and gave her mom a hug. Then Denny joined in.

When they broke their huddle, Allison announced, "From now on we do things as a group."

Denny and I nodded our heads so hard, I thought I'd get whiplash.

"In all the commotion, I forgot to mention Madeline called," Allison said. "She wants us to come to Kaneohe this evening for a dinner and to discuss wedding plans. I called her back to accept."

"So we're drafted for the event whether we want to go or not," I said.

Marion swatted me on the arm. "Quit being a curmudgeon. You always like to eat."

"You're right, and speaking of eating, I could use a little late afternoon snack since we missed lunch."

Later, Denny gathered the whole tribe for a trip out to see Meyer, Henry and Madeline in Kaneohe. We ate at a Thai restaurant, and I did my share of slurping noodles, rice and various delicacies.

Partway through dinner Madeline dropped her chopsticks on a plate and pounded her fist on the table. "Okay, jerk and relatives. I want your attention. I'm going to tell you the plans for the upcoming nuptials."

I saluted, "Yes, General."

"That would be Admiral, jerk. Okay, here's the plan. The

festivities start on the day after Christmas."

"Ah, you want to make sure that Santa Claus has a day's rest first," I said.

"No matter what honeybunch says, I like you." Madeline poked a thick finger into my chest, knocking the wind out of me. "You have a good sense of humor. But don't interrupt me again." She punctuated this with another jab, causing me to gasp. "To continue. We're going to have a rehearsal and dinner on the twenty-sixth. I expect all of you to attend."

"Yes, Admiral," we said in unison.

"Both the rehearsal dinner and the wedding will be at the Kaneohe Yacht Club," Madeline informed us.

"Isn't that a private club?" Marion asked. "I thought only members could hold events there."

Henry smiled. "That's true, but members can sponsor events. It turns out Madeline is quite the yacht person with a worldwide reputation. She looked up one of her friends, and he's sponsoring the rehearsal dinner, the wedding and the reception."

I shook my head in amazement. "Ain't she a beaut?"

Madeline gave me a warning glare and pressed on. "On the twenty-seventh, we're having bachelor and bachelorette parties. Marion, Allison, Jennifer and I will go celebrate while Meyer, the jerk and Denny take honeybunch to prepare him for the big day. Any problems?"

All heads shook.

"Good. Finally, on the twenty-eighth we tie the knot." Madeline leaned over, hugged Henry and kissed him on the cheek, leaving a bright red smear of lipstick that matched the color Henry turned as the air was squeezed out of his lungs. "You will report promptly at seventeen hundred hours."

"Yes, Admiral," we syncopated, except for Henry who struggled to catch his breath.

"Now the assignments on the wedding day. Marion, I'd like

you to handle the flowers, Denny can set up the sound system, while the jerk and Jennifer take care of decorating the reception room. Meyer will be conducting the ceremony, and Henry and I will be getting ready for the big event. Anything I've forgotten?"

"Who's going to do your wedding photography?" I asked.

Madeline slapped her forehead. "Tarnation. I forgot. It'll be too late to line up a photographer on this short notice."

I waved my hand. "I have a suggestion. Allison can take pictures."

Madeline clapped her hands together. "Good. Allison, you're hired."

A smile crept across Allison's face.

"Your first professional gig," I said to her.

After depleting the island's supply of Thai food, Madeline ordered us to stop by the care home for a nightcap.

"Do they allow alcohol?" I asked.

She winked. "I keep a little stash in Henry's room."

We adjourned and headed out to our cars. I was the first of our party to reach Denny's rental SUV. In the light from the parking lot, I saw broken glass on the ground. *Uh-oh.* The driver's-side window was smashed. A note rested on the seat. I carefully reached through the nonexistent window and picked up the paper. It read, "Go back to the mainland now."

CHAPTER 16

On that happy note, Denny called Detective Saito to inform him of our situation. He arrived within thirty minutes along with a woman who snapped on rubber gloves and checked the car and note for fingerprints.

"You seem to have caught someone's attention, Mr. Jacobson," Saito informed me.

"Yeah, you're right. I don't think that note was meant for Jennifer."

Once the police completed inspection of the SUV, we cleaned away the glass and drove back to the care home without having to resort to any air conditioning. Jennifer sat in the back seat behind the open window and let her hair blow in the breeze.

"I'll go turn it in for a new SUV first thing in the morning," Denny said.

"Does your automobile insurance cover damage from scumbags attacking and mutilating the car?" I asked.

"I'm sure I'll end up paying for it," he replied. "The insurance deductible will probably be more than the cost of a new window."

"At least our newfound friend didn't take a hammer to the whole car, preferring to send a simple message."

"What kind of people are these anyway?" Allison asked.

"Not nice ones," I replied.

We stopped at the care home to have our nightcap with Madeline. While she prepared drinks, I struck up a conversation with Mrs. Wilson. "How are your kids and grandkids?"

"They're doing fine, Mr. Jacobson. It's good to see your granddaughter here again."

Meyer, who stood beside me, grabbed my arm and said to Mrs. Wilson. "You remember Paul's name and his grand-daughter?"

"Of course. I met them here before." Her eyes turned to Meyer, and she smiled. "You're looking very dapper in your suit, Mr. Ohana."

Meyer reddened. "Thank you, Mrs. Wilson."

"You can call me Hattie." She let out a sigh. "What a wonderful evening. I read part of a mystery book earlier. I don't know the last time I read a good book. Lately things have been so muddled, I've only been able to knit."

Meyer and I looked at each other. I remembered reading in my journal regarding Mrs. Wilson's usual single-thread speech. Finally, he said, "Hattie, you usually say the same thing over and over again about your children and grandchildren. I've never heard you carry on this kind of conversation."

She actually giggled. "As I said, my brain has really been jumbled lately. Tonight, things are clear again. You're right. I have been repeating myself too much."

I left Meyer and Hattie to continue their talk and stepped over to the presiding nurse sitting at a desk inside the entryway. "Excuse me, my name is Paul Jacobson, and I'm a friend of Meyer Ohana and Henry Palmer."

"Yes, Mr. Jacobson. I remember you from the night of the . . . unfortunate situation with Louise Kincaid."

"I apologize, but I don't know your name."

"I'm Pamela Newsome."

That name rang a bell from my journal. "Uh, Ms. Newsome. Mrs. Wilson used to say the same thing over and over again. I'm sure you noticed."

She nodded. "Poor dear has dementia."

"But tonight she's carrying on an intelligible conversation and not repeating the same tagline. Has her medication changed?"

"Why, no. In fact, her doctor has prescribed only one baby aspirin a day for her."

"And no other medication changes in the last few days?"

"None at all."

I returned to Meyer and Hattie Wilson.

Meyer looked very perplexed. "Paul, Hattie told me something quite disturbing. She said that Louise Kincaid talked her into changing her will."

My gut clenched. "How so?"

Hattie bit her lip. "I don't exactly remember, but my money's going to some group that helps orphans."

Uh-oh. I wondered if that might be drug-dealer orphans.

I stepped over to where Denny sat with a drink in his hand. "Use your cell phone thingy to call Detective Saito. I need to speak with him again."

Denny punched in some digits and handed it to me. I put it to my ear.

"Dad, you have it upside down."

"Oh, right." I turned it over as I heard the sound of Saito's voice answer.

"Detective, this is Paul Jacobson."

"Something else happen to you tonight?"

"Not to me, but you better come right away to the Hale Po-hai care home where Meyer Ohana and Henry Palmer live. Something that relates to the death of Louise Kincaid bears looking into."

When Saito arrived, I caught him at the door and motioned him to join me outside. He arched an eyebrow, "Why the secrecy?"

"I want to give you a heads-up. The woman Louise Kincaid gave marijuana brownies to is named Hattie Wilson."

"Yes, I interviewed her the night of the murder. She acted out-of-it and repetitive."

"That's the way she's been for some time. But tonight, after being off her brownies for a few days, she can converse like a normal person. I think Louise Kincaid spiked the brownies with more than marijuana. Do you have a sample of the brownie Louise planned to give to Hattie the night of the murder?"

"In our evidence room."

"You should have someone check it out. Also, Louise Kincaid convinced Hattie to change her will. I think she intended to scam the old broad out of her money."

"Interesting speculation. I'll look into it immediately."

Saito headed inside and sat down to speak with Hattie Wilson.

I pulled Meyer aside. "Detective Saito plans to check on Hattie's will and on the brownies that Louise Kincaid gave her."

He shook his head. "All this time Hattie acted like she suffered from dementia, and it was probably drug-induced. Louise Kincaid seemed nice but obviously had an agenda."

"And something went wrong, and one of her drug partners must have killed her, since it certainly wasn't Henry."

Saito and Hattie went into her room. They returned in a few moments with Saito holding a document in his hand. He headed toward the door and stopped next to me. "Mr. Jacobson, thanks for the lead." Then he disappeared into the night.

The next morning I woke up in my usual state of confusion, and the nice woman in bed with me explained my marital status and said I hadn't been abducted by aliens. I read my journal, apparently updated the night before, and everything became as clear as pig slop.

While Marion dressed, I sat in a semi-stupor trying to fathom the life of one Paul Jacobson—vacationer and crime magnet. With no new insights, I joined my family for some French toast and a large glass of freshly squeezed orange juice.

Jennifer informed us we'd be climbing to the top of Diamond Head today. Denny indicated that we would do that as soon as he replaced the SUV, once again. Even though Allison wanted us to do things together as a group, she declined the offer to stand on the top of a mountain, and Marion agreed to share pool duty with her.

"And I got an email from Austin," Jennifer said. "He's been doing some surfing too, at Venice Beach. He has to wear a wet suit, whereas here I don't need more than a swimsuit."

"And I can surf the sand," I added.

"It sure would be nice if I could call Austin on a cell phone once in a while." Jennifer gave her mom a preteen glare.

Allison crossed her arms. "We've been over that before. You have your laptop with you so you can stick with email."

We left the dining room, and Denny took off to turn in the damaged car.

When Denny returned with a new shiny white SUV, we bade adieu to the ladies, and Denny, Jennifer and I set off on our next adventure. After navigating through the mean streets of Waikiki, we drove between the Honolulu Zoo and Kapi'olani Park and took Monsarrat Avenue until we reached a right turn and passed through a tunnel into the extinct volcano crater, where I sprang for the parking and admission fee. Denny donned a backpack with water bottles and snacks, we applied sunscreen, and I put on my hat for our hike to the top of seven-hundred-sixty-foot Mount Leahi, known worldwide as Diamond Head.

We followed an arid trail along a stretch of kiawi trees and began our ascent up steps, through a dark tunnel and along a trail that brought us to a World War II bunker overlooking Waikiki and the ocean. Below, I saw the Diamond Head light-house.

"This is so cool up here," Jennifer said. "Did you know that Leahi means wreath of fire?"

"Huh? Where did my granddaughter find this random fact?"

She gave a determined nod. "I did some research on the Internet before we came on our vacation. Here're some more tidbits. The lighthouse was first built in 1899 and rebuilt in 1917. It uses a thousand-watt Fresnel lens that can be seen eighteen miles out to sea."

"Imagine that. No problem with your memory."

"Nope. Like you during the day, Grandpa, I have a photo-graphic memory. Once I read something, I remember it."

"That must help you at school."

"Yep. I don't have any trouble memorizing stuff." She pointed. "Look, there's an airplane taking off from Honolulu Airport."

I watched a 747 lumber into the air and make a turn out to sea. "I'm amazed that those things can get into the air."

"A simple matter of aerodynamics," Jennifer said.

"If you say so."

"Lookouts checked the ocean from here during World War II," Jennifer said. "They could direct gunfire if any Japanese ships showed up."

"Fortunately, that wasn't necessary." I leaned out of the bunker and looked straight down to watch surfers paddling out to catch waves, breaking over the reef. "Good thing your mom didn't come along."

"Yeah. She'd really freak out up here."

I spotted a large estate with a swimming pool and tennis court. Off to the right, the towers of Waikiki lined up like dominos ready to fall into each other. After identifying our hotel in the distance, I turned my gaze in the direction of Koko Head. What a panorama.

A group of Japanese tourists arrived, so we gave up our view to allow them to do their own ooh-ing and ah-ing. We started wending our way back down the stairs and trail. As we reached the bottom, I heard a ping in the cliff a foot from my head followed by the sound of a gunshot.

"Someone's shooting at us," Denny shouted. "Get down."

I dropped like a load of bricks and skinned my knee as another shot ricocheted off the rock, pelting me with pebbles.

Denny pulled out his cell phone and placed a call. "Detective Chun, this is Denny Jacobson. My dad, daughter and I are inside Diamond Head and someone is shooting at us. Okay. We'll stay low and await assistance."

Another shot rang out, this time kicking up dirt by my foot. I pulled my leg in behind a kiawe tree. In moments a siren sounded in the distance. Peering around the trunk of the tree, I saw a police cruiser pull into the parking lot. The cavalry had arrived.

We stayed put until a police officer trudged up the trail to where we huddled. "You the ones who called Detective Chun?" the skinny cop asked.

"Yeah," Denny replied. "Someone took potshots at us."

"Did you see which direction?"

Jennifer pointed toward a clump of kiawi trees. "I think over there."

"I'll escort you back to your car and, once backup arrives, go check it out."

We made it safely to the SUV as two other cars pulled up. Two other police officers joined the skinny guy in walking toward where the shots had originated. Detective Chun stepped out of the other car. "Ah, Mr. Jacobson, I spoke with Detective

Saito this morning and heard you had a problem last night as well. Seems like you've angered a mongoose."

"What's a mongoose have to do with this?"

Chun rubbed the wart on his left hand. "The mongoose hides in the bushes but is vicious when it attacks. You have a mongoose after you."

"Or, from what I read in my journal, someone involved in the local drug trade."

"Exactly. Did you see anyone?"

All three of us shook our heads.

One of the officers returned. "No sign of anyone, but we did find some nine-millimeter shells." He held up a paper sack as if presenting his lunch for inspection.

After taking our statements, we were dismissed.

"Lucky you come Hawaii," I said in parting.

CHAPTER 17

Later that afternoon as I sat out on our balcony admiring the
ocean—it was out there and I was nowhere close to it—Jennifer
came through the adjoining doors into our room. "Grandpa,
there's a big event going on in Waikiki. We have to go see it."

"Geezer recognition day?"

Jennifer stomped her foot. "Even better. It's the Spam Jam."

"What the hell is that?" I asked in my most pleasant manner.

"It's a chance to eat lots of Spam."

I thought back to World War II and all the Spam I had
consumed, which satisfied any further craving for many years
afterward. "I can't see making jelly out of Spam."

Jennifer tsked. "Grandpa, this is completely different. It's a
big celebration with bands playing on two stages—one outside
the Outrigger Waikiki Hotel and the other by the International
Market Place—concession booths with all kinds of goodies and
loads of people."

"Sounds as exciting as a dentists' convention."

"Oh, Grandpa, we're going. Go put your sandals on."

I lifted myself out of the chair, knowing I couldn't argue with
the twelve-year-old tigress. We assembled and took the elevator
down to street level.

"Are we driving?" Allison asked.

"No," Denny replied. "Kalakaua Avenue is blocked off, and
we couldn't park closer anyway. It's a little walk, but we're in
good shape."

"I'm warmed up from our little stroll to the top of Diamond Head this morning," I said. "As long as you promise no one will shoot at us."

"The Spam Jam will be safe and fun, Grandpa."

Upon that endorsement, we set off. Once we reached Kalakaua Avenue, the place was bedlam. People in crazy hats and wild outfits coursed through the packed street. Concession stands sold every imaginable food item made out of Spam. Choices included Spamburgers, Spamdogs, Spam salad, Spam sandwiches, Spam tacos, Spamakopita, Spam katsu, Spam lau lau, teriyaki Spam, sautéed Spam, Spam soup. The only thing I didn't see—Spam cola.

Jennifer licked her lips. "Let's eat."

She ordered some Spam jambalaya, Denny and Allison went with Spam chow mein, Marion had a Spam tostada and I picked out Spam musubi—Spam around rice and tied together with seaweed. I figured this would be my revenge on the ocean— eliminating some seaweed.

We wandered around as the sun set, the crowd grew larger, and the bands played louder. I found a brochure and read how Spam was introduced by Hormel in 1937 and that Hawaii consumed more Spam per capita than any other state. I believed that statistic by the way people around us gobbled the wonder meat.

After a second course of filling our tummies with some Spam pizza, we walked around the booths selling Spam paraphernalia. Denny came up to me as the others strolled ahead. "I don't know if you remember, but on the ti leaf sliding trip several days ago, I mentioned my interest in painting again."

"I read that in my journal."

"I followed your advice and spoke to Allison. She didn't freak out. She suggested that we might combine her interest in photography with mine in art."

"Good idea."

"Yeah, I agreed with her. We both may take some classes back in Colorado. Jennifer is old enough to take care of herself if we're gone an evening a week."

"Sounds like a good solution."

"Nothing decided yet, but we're considering it."

Allison came back to retrieve Denny to show him something she wanted to buy at one of the booths.

My head began to throb, and as darkness fell, I paused by a white tent selling T-shirts and hats with the word "Spam" in large bright letters. Suddenly, a can of Spam went whizzing inches from my head. The force of the throw ripped a hole in the tent.

I dropped to the ground.

Denny ran over. "What was that?"

I pulled myself upright. "Someone tried to nail me with a can of Spam. In addition to providing these culinary delights, that thing's turned into a lethal weapon."

We both looked around but didn't spot anyone acting suspicious. I thought of reporting this to the police, but they'd never catch anyone, and we'd have to stick around for hours to give our report.

"It's getting late," I said. "After the hiking today, I'm pooped."

Denny gathered the others, and we headed back to the hotel, with me grateful to have escaped being dispatched by a can of Spam.

Back in our room I drank a large glass of water and felt better. I must have become dehydrated from the salty Spam dishes and not drinking enough liquid refreshment. After documenting my latest adventures in my journal, I adjourned to get some sleep. When I turned off the lights, Marion gave me a kiss on the cheek. I returned the favor with a kiss on the lips. She put her arm around me. This was getting interesting. I caressed some nice parts of her body. One thing led to another. I found myself with my pajamas off, and Marion dispensed with her nightgown. Fortunately, my old body knew what to do with this nubile woman in bed with me.

CHAPTER 18

I awoke with the memory of a twenty-year-old and not a care in the world. Well, except murders, and some yahoo or yahoos trying to kill me. For once I didn't have to review my journal. I remembered it word for word from reading it yesterday. Yesterday. Someone shooting at me inside Diamond Head and aiming a can of Spam at my aged locks. I burped from the remnants of overdosing on the salty meat. Quite a day.

After we were up and dressed, someone pounded on the adjoining door. I opened it to find Jennifer standing there in her swimsuit. "Let's get going, Grandpa. This is a big day."

"I know. I'm celebrating that I'm still alive."

"No, it's Christmas Eve. Can you imagine we're going to spend Christmas Eve and Christmas day at the beach?"

"I forgot Christmas was coming. I better check with my consultant."

Jennifer returned to her room, and I said to Marion, "I haven't been paying attention to the date. I didn't do any Christmas shopping."

"That's okay. I've brought presents for Jennifer, Denny and Allison."

"Thanks for covering that." But I knew that didn't get me off the hook. I needed to buy something for Marion.

When my family headed off to the beach, I told them I'd meet them later and decided to do some shopping. This was a sacrifice because shopping and I got along as well as a new hairdo and a wind storm. Nonetheless, I needed to select something for my bride. Meandering through Waikiki to check out shops displaying all kinds of Hawaiian clothes, jewelry and souvenirs, I passed a white-bearded Santa wearing a red hat with white tassel, gold Hawaiian shirt, wild blue and green swimming trunks and sandals. Only in Hawaii.

I refocused on my mission. What would Marion want? Other than a husband who didn't have a brain like a dribble glass? Since I couldn't provide that, I sought a second choice.

I passed a storefront that said, "Pot Pourri." That was a thought. I bet my bride might enjoy some fragrant plant material stashed in a nice decorative vase of some sort or an appropriate knickknack. I entered the shop, and a bell jangled. I sniffed the air. A pungent aroma tickled my nose. I surveyed a number of plant arrangements, but they all contained the same type of pointy leaves. A glass counter held a collection of water pipes and regular pipes. This didn't make any sense to me. No one yet appeared from the back of the shop, so I moseyed over to the counter and picked up a magazine. The cover showed a plate of brownies with a tag line, "The world's ten best marijuana brownie recipes." *Uh-oh.*

A woman in an orange muumuu came through a back curtain. "May I help you?"

"Um . . . ah . . . just browsing."

"If you have your medical marijuana card, I can provide whatever you need. We have a new supply of the best plants on the island."

"I don't have one of those."

She graced me with a gapped-tooth smile. "If you have glaucoma or arthritis, we have a doctor in the back who can provide a prescription for you."

"No thanks." I darted out of there before you could say cannabis incubus.

Obviously, Hattie Wilson could have obtained her brownies with a prescription in that shop. I wondered if the drug growers in the Waianae Mountains supplied medical marijuana outlets. Regaining my focus, I decided I'd next survey the bauble option for Marion and selected a jewelry store.

Inside, I looked through glass cases containing diamond, emerald, ruby and sapphire rings and necklaces. What would Marion like? Being a typical male, I'd failed to notice what she wore. Dang. I should have been paying more attention.

I approached a smiling young woman wearing a pikake lei and a blue and white muumuu. "I'm looking for some jewelry for my wife."

"We have some nice tennis bracelets."

"She doesn't play tennis."

The clerk brushed back her sparkling black hair and graced me with another smile. "No, no. It isn't for playing tennis. Here, let me show you some."

She pulled out three diamond bracelets and set them on the counter in front of me. "These are very popular with our older customers."

The clerk obviously assumed I wasn't married to some young trophy wife. Still, Marion was younger than I was, and I considered her quite a trophy.

I regarded the bracelets carefully. Which one would Marion like? They looked the same to me. I closed my eyes and reached out, touching one. "I'll take this one."

"A good choice."

She put it in a velvet box and wrapped it up in Christmas paper for me. I forked over my credit card, and the woman happily processed it to deplete my life savings. Actually, it wasn't that bad. I had achieved the right balance of finding something of value while not ending up insolvent.

The saleswoman also gave me a card, so I wrote a note to

Marion wishing her a Merry Christmas and thanking her for putting up with an old poop like me.

With my Christmas shopping completed, I returned to the room and turned on the television. I found the History Channel and watched the end of a show that described the five most dangerous animals in the ocean from the standpoint of killing people. The list included the Orca, giant squid, great white shark, ocean crocodile and box jellyfish. Now I knew what I needed to avoid. It reinforced my opinion that the ocean offered no hospitality for members of the human race. And here my granddaughter was at this very moment tempting the fates with these vicious animals swimming around with her. I clicked off the TV and decided to go check on the beach scene.

After a brief jaunt I located Marion and Allison sitting on beach towels. "Where are Jennifer and Denny?"

Marion patted the sand beside her. "Have a seat and relax. Jennifer went surfing, and Denny is taking a swim."

After the sun caused my forehead to break out in a sweat, Marion jumped up and grabbed my hand. "Come on. You ventured into the ocean the other day. You can try it again."

"I don't know. I watched a program describing the evil creatures in the ocean." I recited the top five killers mentioned on television.

"Oh, posh. Ocean crocodiles and jellyfish live mainly around Australia and Asia. Orcas, giant squid and great white sharks don't frequent the shallows of Waikiki Beach. You worry too much. We're only going to splash around near shore."

"Maybe those dangerous sea creatures become tourists like we do and come here for a vacation. They might be lurking anywhere."

"Quit thinking up excuses. Don't be a wimp."

With my manhood once again challenged, I agreed to take a dip. Marion led me into the water until waves lapped at my calves.

"See, this isn't so bad," Marion informed me.

"Easy for you to say."

She dragged me out a little deeper until the water reached my knees.

"See? You're safe. Nothing has happened."

I took a deep breath and then another. I felt dizzy. Would I hyperventilate and pass out?

"Think how calm and beautiful the ocean is. Let it relax you. It's like meditating. Think happy thoughts."

"You and Peter Pan."

Marion tugged on my arm again.

"I can't relax with things swimming and crawling around under there." Suddenly, I gasped in pain as if a dozen bees had stung my leg. "Ow! A box jellyfish got me! I'm going to die!" I raced for shore, expecting to find a huge clear glob attached to my leg. Instead I saw a small purple thread connected to a dime-sized bluish bubble.

Marion threw sand on my leg and wiped it off. "It's only a Portuguese man-of-war."

"It stings like crazy." I hopped around.

"You'll live."

CHAPTER 19

After Jennifer and Denny returned from exploring Davy Jones's depths, we headed back to the hotel to shower and change. I had a welt on my leg, but as Marion predicted, I survived to harass my family for another day.

Jennifer knocked on the door between our rooms and invited us into the one she shared with her parents, where she proceeded to set up a poinsettia plant for a Christmas tree. She added some shiny candy bar wrappers for tinsel and stood back to admire it. "Not bad," she informed us.

"Best Hawaiian Christmas tree I've ever seen," I said, "but I don't know how Santa Claus will get here. No chimney."

Jennifer rolled her eyes. "I don't believe in Santa anymore."

"I don't know. I saw him a little while ago walking around the Hilton Hawaiian Village in his best beach gear."

We put our various presents under the tree, providing enough gifts for an exciting Christmas morning.

Jennifer rubbed her hands together. "Now we're set."

On Christmas morning, a loud banging on the door to the adjacent room caught my attention. I opened it to find Jennifer standing there hopping back and forth on her feet.

"Come on, Grandpa. It's time to open presents."

Marion and I joined the rest of the Jacobson clan around the packages under the poinsettia plant. Denny ordered room service so we slurped coffee and juice and munched on sweet rolls and croissants. Jennifer bounced around as if she were only twelve years old. Wait a minute, she *was* twelve.

I said to Jennifer, "I don't know if you're allowed to open presents. You revealed something to me yesterday that I read in my journal first thing this morning. You told me you don't believe in Santa Claus."

She waggled an eyebrow at me. "But I believe in presents."

Spoken like a true twelve-year-old.

I made out like a bandito. Allison and Denny gave me a new Hawaiian shirt that practically pulsated with color. Jennifer presented me with a baseball hat with the inscription, "Geezers rule." And the pièce de résistance, I received a new waterproof watch from Marion. It was beautiful—bright silver with big numbers and a button to light it in the dark.

"And best of all, if you wear it in the water, you won't ruin it," my bride informed me as she picked up the wrapping paper accumulated on the carpet.

"It would also be perfect if I ever take up scuba diving, which I won't."

"You might forget to take your watch off before going in the shower."

I tapped the side of my head. "As you might recall, I have an excellent memory during the day. I won't forget that."

"That's right." Marion gave me a peck on the cheek. "I read part of your journal yesterday. You describe everything that's happened very accurately."

"Yep. And I'm fortunate that once I review my journal, everything I read stays with me until I fall asleep. That's the way my quirky brain works. Two modes—photographic memory during the day and overnight—wipeout. Say, I hope you didn't read the part about what present I got for you since you haven't opened it yet."

"No, I'm waiting to be surprised. So I might as well open it now." Marion unwrapped the present and gave a squeal of delight. "This is beautiful, Paul." She put the bracelet on her wrist and gave me a kiss on the cheek.

Whew. I done good.

Since I didn't know what Marion had bought Jennifer, I was as surprised as my granddaughter when she tore open a box to reveal some snazzy video game. Jennifer gave Marion and me hugs. Another success.

Denny opened the next present, from Allison, and his eyes widened as he pulled out an oil painting set containing tubes of paint, three small canvases, brushes and the various mixing agents. "This is great. My old paints stashed in the closet at home have dried up."

"That's cool, Dad. You'll have to paint a picture of the view from our balcony."

Allison opened a package from Denny that contained a Nikon digital single-lens reflex camera. She threw her arms around his neck. "How did you know?"

"I saw you eyeing this very model at the camera shop we passed on our way to the Spam Jam the other day."

After all the packages had been opened, Jennifer bit her lip. "Is this all? I hoped there might be one other present."

"I don't know," Denny said. "Let me look around." He peeked under the bed. "Hey. What's this?" He pulled a small package out and handed it to Jennifer.

She tore it open. "A cell phone!" She hugged her mom and dad.

I shook my head in amazement. How could a little dipstick electronic doodad evoke so much emotion?

"I'm going to call Austin. Can I use your room, Grandpa?"

"Have at it."

She raced through the adjoining door and didn't return for ten minutes. She held up her phone as if displaying a prize for winning a marathon. "His parents gave him a new surfboard for Christmas. And, Grandpa, he thanked you and Marion for the Wii games you gave him."

I turned to Marion. "Imagine that."

Jennifer handed the cell phone to Marion. "Austin and his parents want to talk to you."

Marion took the device and jabbered away, waving her unencumbered arm as she recounted our activities to her daughter, son-in-law and grandson.

"There's a speakerphone setting," Jennifer said. "Let me activate it for you." She pushed a button, and I heard the sound of commotion coming out of the gadget.

We sang, "We Wish You a Merry Christmas," and Marion's family reciprocated with "Jingle Bells."

After both sides bellowed "Merry Christmas," Marion closed the phone. "I should call my brother in Kansas."

"You can use my phone again," Jennifer said. "We need to get it broken in." She winked at her dad.

Marion placed another call, and we went through the same speakerphone routine of singing and shouting. The wonders of modern electronic communications. I had a hard time imagining phones working without cords and phone lines. But then again, I was a dinosaur.

After we gorged on the remaining sweet rolls, we changed into our swimming togs and headed to the beach for Jennifer to surf. I was resplendent in my new hat.

After plunking down on the sand, I entertained myself by watching my family enjoy the ocean. Marion, Denny and Allison went swimming. Jennifer paddled out, ducked in and out among the breakers and caught a ride partway into shore. My ocean view suddenly became blocked by a woman standing in front of me with her hands planted firmly on her hips. She looked like she had the muscle to give Madeline Hightower a tussle in a mud-wrestling ring. She unfurled a long arm and pointed at me. "That hat disgusts me."

"What?"

"I'm offended. 'Geezer' is a despicable word. How dare you wear that to the beach!"

I eyed her carefully, wondering what planet she inhabited. "You've got to be kidding. I'm a geezer, and I'm not offended. What's the matter with you?"

"What's the matter with me? What's the matter with you is what's the matter with me."

I determined this debate wasn't going anywhere. I gave her my most indulgent smile. "Have a nice day."

She harrumphed and stomped away to go harass some other innocent tourist.

I shook my head in amazement. The things that upset people. Maybe I should start a twelve-step program for Geezers Anonymous. If you're older than dirt, join and we'll teach you how to maintain your sense of humor and stay entertained by wearing hats that offend others.

I thought of an article describing a twelve-step program I had read before my memory went to the South Pole. I could see it. Come join Paul Jacobson in these steps:

1. Admit that you are powerless over being a geezer.
2. Believe that something greater than you can rescue you from geezerhood.
3. Decide to turn yourself over to that power.
4. Look into all aspects of your geezerhood.
5. Admit to everyone the wrongness of your geezerhood.
6. Be ready to have a power beyond yourself remove your character defects.
7. Beseech the power to fix your shortcomings.

8. Write a list of everyone you've offended and rectify the situation.
9. Then go take care of this business without injuring anyone.
10. Keep looking into your geezerhood and admit the errors of your ways.
11. Pray to carry out what the power beyond you asks.
12. Carry this message to other geezers.

I slapped my cheek and pulled the hat further down over my eyes. Obviously the sun was getting to me.

With nothing better to do, I periodically checked for sand crabs. I suffered no bites other than when Marion returned and leaned over to nibble on my ear.

Later, I took a stroll down the beach with my bride. We held hands like newlyweds, but then again, we'd only been married five months, and almost every morning seemed like my first day of marriage anyway.

"Are you enjoying our vacation?" Marion asked as we skirted a beached catamaran.

"I enjoy being with you, and it's great having Denny, Allison and Jennifer with us. I'm disconcerted by the murders and strange incidents with the local drug dealers."

She leaned close to me. "I'm sure Detectives Chun and Saito will get everything sorted out."

"I hope so. I'd like to live a few more years without someone trying to push me into an imu or taking shots at me. Hopefully, the bad guys have taken a Christmas break today."

We paused to watch a gaggle of kids building a sand castle. Jennifer would have done that in the past, but now she had foregone sand structures for the allure of surfing.

Upon returning to our towels, Marion insisted that I stick my toe in the water. After trying to convince her otherwise, I gave in to the inevitable. I put my hat down next to my sandals and allowed myself to be led to my doom.

As the water reached my knees, a note in my journal came to mind. "Okay, this is deep enough. I don't want to risk an encounter with a box jellyfish or Portuguese man-of-war."

"That isn't going to happen again." Marion splashed water in my face.

Not to be outdone, I splashed back. Soon we were going at it like immature adults. At that moment Jennifer paddled up to us on her surfboard. "Now children, behave."

I reached over and tipped her off the surfboard. She joined the antics until I was sopping wet. Good thing I had left my new hat on the sand.

After I dunked Jennifer and she teamed up with Marion to knock me into the water, I spluttered to the surface. "I give up. You win."

"Girls rule," Jennifer shouted.

I held my fist in the air. "No, geezers rule."

As we headed up the beach to dry off, Marion said, "See, Paul, that wasn't so bad."

"No, other than almost drowning when you two wild women attacked me, nothing bit or stung me."

I reached down for my towel and couldn't find my hat. "Uh-oh. Someone swiped my Christmas present."

"It has to be around here somewhere," Jennifer said. "Maybe the wind blew it away. I'll help you look."

"There's been no wind," I said. "It's been perfectly calm today. Some thief has absconded with my hat."

We scoured the beach and headed up to a walkway that separated the sand from grass. Jennifer peered in a garbage can. "Found it, Grandpa." She handed me my hat, desecrated with a smudge of mustard.

"I bet I know who did this," I said.

"Who, Grandpa?"

"A crazy lady verbally attacked me earlier. She didn't like me

155

wearing a geezer hat." I scanned the beach. "In fact, there she is."

With Jennifer following, I marched over to Crazy Lady, who sat in a beach chair under a large green umbrella reading a *Glamour* magazine. I kicked some sand on her feet to gain her attention. "Did you throw my hat in a trash can?"

"Yeah, so what?"

"You might not like it, but it was given to me by my grand-daughter. I don't appreciate your inconsiderate action. How'd you like it if I threw your magazine in the trash?"

"Go pound sand, you old coot."

I stared at her. "You can call someone an old coot but not a geezer?"

"Come on, Grandpa." Jennifer tugged me away. As we returned to our towels, she whispered in my ear. "You're not going to convince her, but you have your hat back."

Jennifer turned in her rental surfboard and said she wanted to stay at the beach a little longer, but the rest of us headed back to the hotel.

After a shower to wash off the salt and sand, I went through the adjoining door to find Jennifer writing something at the desk.

"Whatcha doin'?" I asked.

She gave me a Cheshire cat smile. "A little project." She picked up her sheets of paper and headed to the door. "I'll be back in half an hour."

"Don't take longer than that," Allison said. "It's almost time to go to dinner."

Later as we walked to a nearby Red Lobster Restaurant for our Christmas feeding frenzy, Jennifer whispered in my ear. "I waited at the beach and followed that lady who took your hat. She's staying in our hotel on the eleventh floor. I got some tape from the front desk, made ten signs that said, 'Geezers rule' and stuck them on her door."

Ah, if the world's problems could only be solved so simply.

CHAPTER 20

I actually slept late the next morning and read my journal at the suggestion of an attractive woman in bed with me. Good thing I read fast because I had a lot to cover. After completing the diary, I sat there in amazement at my crazy world. Then I sucked it up and joined my family for some fine island fare.

After breakfast Jennifer informed me that we would be going to Hanauma Bay to swim with the fishes.

"From what I read in my diary this morning, I already saw a guy named Sammy Malo swimming with the fishes in the yacht harbor."

Jennifer gave me an exaggerated eye roll. "Oh, Grandpa, we're going to look at the fishes. Dad rented snorkels and face masks."

"Let's go to the aquarium to watch fishes instead," I suggested. "There'd be glass protecting us, and I wouldn't get my tootsies wet."

"You're going to have to be brave and go in the water." Jennifer set her mouth in her determined twelve-year-old manner.

After collecting enough paraphernalia for an army, we took the elevator to the basement parking area. Denny pushed a button on the key and lights flashed on a white SUV. As I approached the driver's side, I flinched at what I saw. *Uh-oh.* Someone had gouged the words, "No more whites."

Denny gawked. "It looks like racial hate vandalism. I'm going to call hotel security." Denny diddled with his cell phone and in five minutes a uniformed guard appeared.

"This has never happened before," the beefy security man said. "I'll report it to the police."

So we stood around waiting for another half hour until a police officer arrived. He took our statements and snapped several photographs. "Pretty hard to catch someone who did this and took off," he informed us.

"I'm not driving around with that on my car," Denny said. "We'll go trade this in at the car rental agency before going to Hanauma Bay."

We made the trek to replace our vehicle and, as before, Denny insisted on a white SUV. Allison tried to talk Denny into taking another color, but Denny possessed the same stubborn streak as his father.

"You're in luck," the agent informed us. "The car you returned with the smashed window has been repaired."

Allison tugged at the sleeve of his T-shirt. "Let's get a brand new blue or black SUV. Those colors will do."

Denny sloughed her off. "The one we had before will be fine. We'll take it."

After transferring our gear and bodies, we began our journey to Hanauma Bay.

Jennifer used the back seat for a fanny trampoline. "This is the coolest place to see millions of fish. Aren't you excited, Grandpa?"

"I'd be more excited if the fish came up on the sand to see me. Do you remember the prehistoric fish that climbed out of the water on their fins? I'd like to see some of those."

From my vulnerable backseat position, I ducked before either Marion or Jennifer pummeled me.

We entered the packed parking lot. Denny drove around until he spotted one remaining open place.

"They saved the best one for us," Denny said. "It's under a banyan tree so we'll have lots of shade to keep the car cool."

I volunteered to reach into my Social Security stash to fund the expedition and forked over $7.50 per person and a dollar for parking. Jennifer got in for free. We watched a film and then walked down the steep paved road to the beach. We plunked down our stuff and slathered on sunscreen.

"Too bad your new camera doesn't work underwater," I said to Allison. "You could photograph fish today."

She held up a yellow plastic gadget. "I bought an underwater camera, so I will photograph sea life today."

"Ah, the talent of the younger generations."

Rocky cliffs on both sides of us bounded a beautiful, curved sandy beach. The ocean pulsated in a brilliant blue, punctuated by bobbing heads of the fish-watchers. "What a view," I said. "Makes me want to sit right here and not go in the water."

"Come on, Grandpa. You have to try snorkeling."

I blew my nose into a tissue Allison had given me to wipe off excess sunscreen. "I'm pretty good at snorking."

"That doesn't count." Jennifer kicked sand on my feet. "If I tell you a geezer joke, will you come in the water with me?"

"Only if it's a good one."

She set her lips. "Okay, here's one that Austin sent me. Why is life for a geezer like a roll of toilet paper?"

"I give."

Jennifer grinned. "It goes faster at the end."

"You have that right. Days whiz by."

"Now, you need to uphold your part of the bargain, Grandpa. Here's your mask and snorkel."

I eyed the contraptions as if Jennifer had handed me a live snake. With some finagling, I adjusted the face mask and tried putting the snorkel in my mouth. "Du . . . ma .. ik . . . tu . . . ite," I said.

Jennifer gave an exasperated sigh. "Take it out of your mouth to speak."

Oh. "The mask is too tight."

My granddaughter adjusted it for me. I was being taken care of like a prince, but I'd prefer to have dancing girls cooling me with fans and feeding me grapes.

Everyone waded into the water. I remained with my toes touching the foam from the expired gentle surge. I looked out to sea and saw larger waves, tamed by passing over a section of reef.

Jennifer came back and took my hand. "Come on."

I ventured in up to my knees. The water felt warm, but I shivered nonetheless. I remembered reading in my journal about being attacked by a Portuguese man-of-war. "Do you see any vicious blue bubbles in the water?" I asked.

"It's safe today, Grandpa. Nothing's going to get you."

"You better be right."

Jennifer tugged on my arm and dragged me deeper until the water covered my belly button. "Okay, Grandpa, tighten your mask, look in the water and try breathing through the snorkel."

I adjusted the mask, stuck the snorkel in my mouth, bent over and put my head in the water. Water came into my mouth, and I shot upright, coughing.

"You need to bite down on the mouthpiece so water doesn't come in. Do it like this." Jennifer gave me a demonstration, and I imitated her.

"I think I'm too incompetent for this," I said.

"You can do it, Grandpa. Try again."

So as not to disappoint my granddaughter, I gave it another shot. I clamped down on the mouthpiece, and this time I managed to breathe through the tube. An orange fish darted past. This wasn't so bad. I clearly saw my feet. I needed to cut my toenails.

A half dozen silver stick-like fish swam by showing absolutely no interest in my toes. I brought my head up and removed the mouth piece and gulped in air that didn't taste like plastic. "Okay, I've been snorkeling. I'm ready to bask on the beach."

"No way, Grandpa. You have to try swimming with your mask and snorkel on."

"I don't swim."

"Try it. Stretch out and look through the mask."

I reattached the equipment, took a deep breath and flopped out in the water. My body dropped as fast as a fishing line full of lead weight, and I settled onto the sandy bottom. Water poured into my snorkel tube, and I came up gasping and spitting.

"I've never seen anything like that," Jennifer said. "You sank like a rock."

"I told you."

"Let's try this. You can walk around the edge of the reef where it's not too deep. That way you can see the sea life without having to swim."

So I followed Jennifer's instructions and watched as Jennifer floated alongside me. Periodically, she'd point to a fish, and I'd watch it feeding on the plants attached to the reef. Jennifer kept trying to get me to go out deeper, but I only went up to my chest. An angel fish meandered in front of me and fluttered away. Finally, I stood and removed my mask and snorkel. "I'm slowing you down. You swim ahead, and I'll go sit on the beach."

"You did good, Grandpa."

"I'm retiring for the second time. I'm retiring from snorkeling."

I headed back to shore, dried myself and sat on the damp towel. I nodded to a man sitting two feet away on the crowded beach.

"You must be a tourist," he said.

I regarded him. He was a local man with a dark tan, probably in his late sixties or early seventies. He wore dark glasses and a Primo Beer baseball cap.

"How can you tell?"

"No tan."

"You got me. I lived in the islands at one time but now am visiting from the mainland with my family."

"This used to be a quiet bay," he said. "Now look at how crowded it is. I remember coming here in the 1950s when you didn't have to worry that people would trample you."

"That's the problem," I said. "Something becomes popular, and everyone shows up . . . myself included. But you can understand the attraction. The ocean here is such a beautiful blue."

"That's for sure." He straightened his beach mat. "In the early sixties a commercial was shot in Hanauma Bay for Newport cigarettes. They found places with the correct shade of blue, and this was an ideal spot."

I looked at the sun sparkling on the ocean—a blue, green and blue-green panorama sprinkled with the brown of reef. The man's mention of cigarettes made me think of the funny cigarettes being distributed by some of the marijuana growers and dealers. I hoped they were taking the day off from trying to harass me.

"Did you grow up around here?" I asked.

"Yep. Born at Queens Hospital and raised in Nuuanu Valley."

Remembering recent events documented in my diary, I said, "I've been to both places. Did you live here when Hawaii became a state?"

"I was in high school at the time. We had quite a celebration." His eyes lit up, and it wasn't from the sun. "With the announcement of statehood, school was cancelled for the day."

No unexpected days off from school for me as a kid growing up in California, without statehood celebrations or snow days like in other parts of the country. We trudged to school every day, rain or shine. Of course, I only had to walk six blocks, and the weather was good most of the time, but what the heck, I could feel sorry for myself anyway.

Marion soon returned followed by Denny and Allison. Finally, Jennifer emerged from the ocean looking like a soggy sea monster. She charged up to where we sat. "You won't believe what I saw—trigger fish, parrot fish, butterfly fish and two green sea turtles."

"You won't believe what I saw," I said. "The beach here and the ocean staying out there where it belongs."

We bought lunch, and the others returned for another view of the sea life. I contented myself with watching from the shore. After even Jennifer had been in the water long enough to turn into a wrinkled prune, we gathered our gear and headed up the hill to the parking lot. Upon reaching our car, I heard the sound of a thousand myna birds having a party in the banyan tree above our car and celebrating by leaving gifts all over the roof. No longer white, every inch of the top of the SUV had turned a putrid gray.

"The only consolation—this time it wasn't a human messing up your vehicle," I said to Denny.

He snorted in disgust. "I need to replace it again."

"Why not settle for going through a car wash instead."

"I guess so."

"Can we do a little sightseeing before we go back to the hotel?" Jennifer asked.

Denny looked at his watch. "We have time."

From Hanauma Bay we took the windy road that went along the jagged rocky coastline. We stopped at the Blow Hole and watched spray shoot into the air.

"Reminds me of sneezing the last time I had a cold," I said, earning a wifely glare from Marion.

We proceeded past Sandy Beach and came to the overlook high above Makapuu Beach.

"We should go bodysurfing there," Jennifer said.

"No way, young lady," Allison replied. "It's too dangerous."

"Oh, Mom. I'm a good swimmer."

"Look how rough it is. Being a good swimmer doesn't help if you get crushed in large waves, and there's undertow."

"I'm an expert on undertoe," I said. "While at Hanauma Bay I looked through my mask and saw my under toes."

It was a good thing my family didn't throw me off the cliff, although they were tempted.

On our way back to the hotel, Denny followed my earlier advice and took the car through a car wash. After that he was in a better mood.

But I couldn't help worrying what the Hawaiian drug cartel was up to.

CHAPTER 21

In the late afternoon we gathered to go to Kaneohe for Henry and Madeline's rehearsal dinner. As we drove, excitement reigned in the back seat, with Jennifer expounding on her snorkeling experience.

We arrived at the Kaneohe Yacht Club, me bedecked in a tie at the insistence of my beautiful bride, whom I could not refuse. Madeline greeted us at the door, wearing a gold sequined dress that reminded me of a giant version of some of the fish I had snorkeled with earlier. She gave me a handshake that crushed two finger bones. I even saw Jennifer grimace after Madeline grabbed her hand. We entered a room where Meyer and Henry stood, confined in dark suits and ties.

"This looks more like a funeral than a rehearsal," I said.

"This is the only suit I kept," Meyer replied.

"Hello, jerk," Henry said. "About time you arrived."

"The top of the evening to you too, Henry. I see your engagement hasn't improved your sweet disposition."

"Watch what you say about my honeybunch." Madeline leaned menacingly toward me.

I imagined being swallowed whole by a gold shark. "Yes, ma'am."

She showed me her right fist. "Don't 'ma'am' me. You call me Madeline if you know what's good for you, jerk."

I massaged my sore knuckles. "Yes, Madeline."

"That's more like it." Madeline gave Henry a hug that made

him squeak. I pictured a large cat ready to eat a captured mouse.

Madeline rubbed her hands together. "Let's get this rehearsal on the road. I'm starving." She looked toward Henry. I wondered again if she intended to devour him on the spot.

Meyer took charge and told Madeline and Jennifer to wait outside the room. He positioned Henry and me in the front.

"Not bad work for a guy who can't see a chair from a caboose," I said.

Meyer shrugged. "I can see shapes. Henry's the smaller of you two."

I rubbed Henry on his bald head. "And to think this squirt is getting hitched. I can see Madeline carrying you under her arm all over the island."

Henry only grinned. "Ain't she a pistol?"

We went through the motions. Madeline and Jennifer came into the room. To my relief, Madeline didn't try to carry Jennifer under her arm. They stopped in front of Meyer, who said his magic words. I gave Henry an imaginary ring. He pretended to put it on Madeline's hand.

Meyer said, "You may kiss the bride."

Madeline picked Henry up and planted a smacker right on his lips, loud enough to wake a teenager on a Saturday morning.

I whispered in Meyer's ear. "I don't know if Henry will survive the ceremony, much less the honeymoon."

We adjourned for dinner, and Madeline and Henry competed to see who could eat the most shrimp cocktails. Madeline won by a tail.

During dinner three people came up and asked for Madeline's autograph. She obliged like the Queen of Sheba granting requests from the peasants. When a fourth man appeared with a pen and photograph of a boat in his hand and practically bowed as he handed them to Madeline, I could stand it no longer.

"Why this interest in Madeline?"

The man, bald as Henry, looked at me with wide eyes. "Don't you know? She's the oldest woman to ever circumnavigate the globe alone in an Islander 36 sloop."

I wouldn't know an Islander 36 from the Daytona 500, but I guessed this was a big deal for the nautical set.

Jennifer seemed impressed though. "Wasn't that scary, being out in the ocean by yourself for all that time?"

"Hah!" Madeline waved her arm, almost knocking over a water glass. "I've been sailing since I was your age. Did my first Transpac race at eighteen and never looked back." She reached over and gave Henry's cheek a pinch that left a red mark. "Honeybunch and I will sail to Lahaina the morning after our ceremony. I've lined up a rental, and everything is ready for a romantic cruise and then a week of marital bliss on Maui."

"Henry, have you ever been sailing?" I asked.

Madeline gave his cheek another pinch, leaving an even redder mark this time. "He doesn't need to do anything. He can sit back and enjoy the ride. I'll do the sailing, and we'll stay at the Pioneer Inn right by the Lahaina Harbor."

"Sounds like you have everything planned," Allison added.

Madeline tweaked Henry's chin, causing his head to snap back as if from whiplash. "Yup. All Henry has to do is show up."

Henry smiled through his bruises. "Ain't she a gem?"

As Denny drove us back to the Hibiscus Hotel, I remained deep in thought. Try as I might not to think about it, I kept puzzling over what had happened to Louise Kincaid. Illegal drugs seemed to be at the core of the whole situation. Louise Kincaid had spiked Hattie Wilson's brownies with marijuana and with something else that kept her practically a vegetable.

Then Louise had convinced Hattie to change her will, obviously to put her money in the hands of the wrong type of people. No one had knocked off Hattie to get her money right away, but someone had taken Henry's Swiss Army knife to kill Louise. And Louise was linked to Sammy Malo, who ended up dead in the Honolulu Ala Wai Yacht Harbor. And Sammy had ties to the band of illegal growers in the hills above Waianae where our helicopter had landed. How did the strands of this spider web tie together? All very confusing.

"Penny for your thoughts, Grandpa."

I turned toward Jennifer. "It will take a whole leprechaun's pot of gold for my fuddled thinking. I've been reviewing what I read in my journal this morning and trying to figure out who did what to whom and why regarding the murders."

Jennifer leaned close to whisper in my ear. "It's pretty simple, actually, Grandpa. Louise worked with Sammy Malo. I bet they came up with a scheme to scam money from older people like Hattie Wilson. They probably got at cross purposes with other members of the drug mob and were bumped off."

"Hmmm. Could be."

"Yep. Maybe one of those guys in the mountains killed both of them. We know that one of them was with Sammy the night he died. The guy with the big nose named Manuel Hiaka."

"There's probably a lot of money involved in the local drug trade. When the stakes get high, people die."

"Good phrase, Grandpa."

I was too worked up to accept my granddaughter's compliment. "But why is someone trying to get at us?"

"What conspiracy are you two up to?" Allison asked from the front seat.

"Grandpa and I are trying to help the detectives solve the murders."

"You shouldn't even be thinking about that," Allison said. "This is supposed to be a relaxing vacation."

"Yeah, but Grandpa has this way of getting in the middle of stuff. He'll get it figured out, and I'm trying to help him."

"Look out," Allison shrieked.

CHAPTER 22

A pickup truck veered in front of us.

Denny slammed on the brakes and turned the wheel to the right as the SUV scraped the railing that kept us from falling fifty feet into the valley below the Pali highway.

My heart beat double time as the seat belt jerked me back into the seat. The taillights from the truck disappeared in the distance.

"He tried to run us off the road." Denny's voice shook.

"And you're going to have to get another new SUV," I added helpfully.

Once our breathing returned to normal, Denny stepped out to look at the damage. He climbed back inside to inform us the car had suffered no structural damage, but a gash ran along the whole right side.

As we resumed our trip, I leaned toward Jennifer and whispered, "As I was saying before being rudely interrupted, I can't figure out why someone keeps harassing us."

Jennifer whispered back. "We know too much that someone doesn't want to get out."

"But what the hell is it?"

Jennifer looked out the window for a moment before putting her mouth close to my ear. "We'll have to figure that out before they try to hurt us again."

The next morning after I read my journal and dressed, Jennifer came bopping into our room. "It's the day before Henry and

Madeline's wedding. I'm going surfing, then we're going to the *Arizona* Memorial, and finally, this evening, we have the bachelor and bachelorette parties."

"Sounds like I have my day planned. I went to the *Arizona* Memorial back in my ancient past before my memory sprung a leak."

"We need to go there for my school assignment. I'm supposed to write a report on something of historical significance that I saw over winter break. I've been putting it off, but now I have to do my research."

"The *Arizona* is definitely significant. Where's your dad?"

"He went to the airport to replace the damaged SUV. You ready to have breakfast and then come to the beach with me?"

"Why not?"

So after ridding the island of more papaya, bananas and coconut syrup on macadamia nut pancakes, I joined my granddaughter out on the sands while she paddled through the waves and I avoided Jacques Cousteau's domain.

The good news—I survived the expedition with no one trying to shoot me, drown me or treat my body with disrespect other than a slight sunburn.

That afternoon we hopped in the replacement SUV and drove to Pearl Harbor. After Denny found a parking spot, we entered the visitors' center and obtained tickets for the next available shuttle out to the memorial. With a little time to kill, we watched a movie before boarding a small white Navy boat for the trip to the *Arizona* Memorial. While the little boat bobbed back and forth, I held on for dear life, doing the white-knuckle bit. Fortunately, I'd never suffered from seasickness.

As we approached the memorial, I told Jennifer, "When this was completed, critics called it a crushed milk cartoon because of the sagging middle to the white building."

"It looks like a bridge," Jennifer said.

"Exactly. It bridges the hull of the sunken battleship."

We disembarked and entered the structure. One marble wall displayed the names of the men killed on the *Arizona* on December 7, 1941. It brought back memories of the many friends of mine who died in World War II—Ralph, my best buddy in elementary school, shot in the Battle of the Bulge; Willy, who wanted to kill every German in Europe and ended up the victim of machine gun fire on Omaha Beach; and Ted, downed by a grenade on Iwo Jima. So many people with potential whose lives were cut short through the violence of war. I had been lucky. Being a paper-pusher with the Navy in England, I helped with the logistics for Operation Overlord, the Battle of Normandy. I wanted to be in the action to do my part, but settled for a background role. In hindsight, I probably would have ended up like one of my departed friends and wouldn't have spawned Denny, who in turn begot Jennifer.

I stepped to one of the twenty-one windows, looked out at Pearl Harbor and spotted a battleship moored with its bow pointing toward us. Jennifer stepped over and placed her hand on my arm. "What's that ship?"

"The *Missouri*. On its decks, Japan surrendered to end World War II. The *Arizona* commemorates the first deaths of Americans during the conflict, and the *Missouri* represents the conclusion of the war."

"I'll have to put that in my report."

Memories continued to flood through the part of my brain that still worked. All the people whose lives had been disrupted or lost, all the turmoil in the world, all the changes in our country after the war.

Jennifer recognized I needed time to myself, so she patted me on the arm and went to explore the rest of the memorial.

Smaller boats traversed the harbor. Even after over seventy

years, oil seeped from the sunken hull below us. I fought back tears at the thought of the terror and destruction on the day of infamy. That Sunday morning I heard the news over our old RCA radio. I wasn't quite old enough to enlist, but wanted to do nothing more than go fight the bastards who had killed Americans. I had to bide my time, but eventually chose the Navy, influenced by the posters proclaiming, "Join the Navy and see the world." I guess I was a sucker for advertisements.

How ironic. I, who hated the ocean, ended up in the Navy. I felt comfortable on large ships, but small ones scared the piss out of me.

I shuffled over to the hole in the center of the floor where I leaned over to view the murky water below. It was as clear as my short-term memory. A woman in a long, flowing blue muumuu dropped plumerias into the water. Allison snapped a picture with her new camera. There would be lots of photographs of this vacation for me to look at after I forgot everything. Hey, I didn't need a memory. Allison could store everything I saw in her little magic camera. I didn't understand how those things worked without film. Oh, well, I would go with the flow.

Jennifer and Marion appeared at my side.

"I should have brought a lei like the ones I made with Hina," Jennifer said. "I could have put it in the water."

"You can't drop leis in the water any longer," Marion said. "I read that there are new restrictions. The strings endanger sea life."

We returned on the shuttle boat, and I survived without it sinking. As we walked to the parking lot, Jennifer remained pensive. Finally, she turned to me. "Makes you think, doesn't it, Grandpa?"

"That it does."

Denny came to an abrupt stop. "I don't see our white SUV."

"Try the alarm on your key," Jennifer said.

Denny pushed it, but nothing happened.

"We should have heard beeping," Jennifer said.

"Are you sure we're at the right place?" Allison asked.

Denny nodded vigorously. "I parked right here."

"Dad's right," Jennifer said. "We parked right in front of this light post, and now there's no car here."

I raised my hand. "I agree. I remember the blue Subaru and the gray Honda on either side. The old daytime memory remains intact." Anger surged through my body. Much like Pearl Harbor had been hit by a sneak attack, my family had been struck by someone bent on harassing us.

Denny pulled out his cell phone and called the car rental office. He said "yeah" and "uh-huh" several times and snapped the phone shut. He faced the rest of us. "They'll report it to the police and said to come back to the airport office to get another car." He tapped the phone thoughtfully. "The car rental agent indicated there have been a number of thefts recently."

"We enjoyed a ride with a nice cab driver named Moki coming back from the hospital," Marion said. "I have his card in my purse." She retrieved it, and Denny made the call.

In half an hour a black cab pulled up with the name Moki's Cabs on the orange sign on top of the vehicle.

After we crammed in, Moki welcomed us with a big grin. "Aloha, everybody. Good to see you."

Denny only scowled, not appreciating having to go retrieve yet another rental car.

"You're probably depleting the whole island supply of white SUVs," I said, which didn't improve Denny's disposition.

Jennifer was scrunched up against me in the back seat. I nudged her. "In addition to the *Arizona* Memorial, you can add the incident of the stolen car to your school report."

"That wasn't of historical significance, Grandpa."

"I don't know. If you look at your dad fuming in the front

seat, you may see an explosion as big as one of those bombs that hit the *Arizona*."

Moki dropped us off at the car rental lot in no time at all, and Denny negotiated with the clerk in the office.

"We only have one white SUV left," he said. "And that hasn't been cleaned yet. We have plenty of black or blue ones."

"Get another color," Allison insisted.

"No way," Denny pounded his fist on the counter. "Dark colors get too hot. We'll take the white one even if it isn't clean.

The clerk shrugged. "Okay."

As Marion, Jennifer and I climbed in the backseat of the replacement vehicle, I cleared away a candy wrapper and a half finished bag of pretzels. On the road back to Waikiki, I said, "I thought at first the drug gang damaged our rental cars, but now I believe otherwise. Those guys have taken pot shots at me, but vandalizing and stealing our cars makes no sense. This has to be someone else's work."

Jennifer thumped up and down on the seat. "I bet you're right, Grandpa. We have to track down who would be doing this."

Back at the hotel Jennifer scampered off to find her friend Hina.

That evening we headed back to Kaneohe and assembled at the Hale Pohai care home. I dutifully took the clipboard from Pamela Newsome to sign out Meyer and Henry. "Where are we taking these yahoos?" I asked.

"To the Black Pearl Restaurant," Denny answered.

I finished filling out the form.

Madeline told us what restaurant the gals would be going to and invited Marion to join her in the Corvette. She shot off like a bat out of Gehenna. Denny followed and dropped off Allison and Jennifer. I figured the bride's pre-wedding shindig wouldn't be that risqué with Jennifer being included.

We men folk took off for the groom's stag event at the Black Pearl, where we could inebriate and humiliate Henry. The place resembled a dive on the outside—peeling paint, a door handle that looked like a pit bull had chewed on it and something that appeared suspiciously like a bullet hole in the outside wall. Inside was surprisingly cozy. A gas fire burned in a lava rock fireplace, oak tables with matching chairs stood in the middle of the room with plush-covered booths around the side. We settled at a table, and my eyes adjusted to the dim light as a scantily clad hostess came up to take our order. "What will it be for you boys?"

I pointed to Henry. "We need the special treatment for this doofus. He's getting married tomorrow."

The hostess raised an eyebrow. "That so." She reached over and gave Henry a kiss on the top of his bald pate.

Henry's face turned as red as the lipstick marks on his head.

"It's a good thing Madeline isn't here." I said. "She'd probably punch out the young lady."

Henry's eyes turned glassy. "Yeah. Ain't she a winner?"

We ordered beer on tap and two huge pupu platters of fried cheese, buffalo wings, calamari, onion rings and veggies. We were soon slurping and munching to the beat of the band.

"Henry," I said. "Are you prepared to be a married man again?"

"If you can do it, so can I, jerk."

"Ah, I love the endearing way you talk."

A group of men arrived and sat at a booth across the room. From their raucous conversation, it became obvious this wasn't the first bar they had visited.

"Poor Meyer will be without your charming company, Henry. Meyer, you'll have to hook up with Hattie Wilson now that she's coherent. She's not a bad looker."

Meyer almost choked on his buffalo wing.

"Hit a vulnerable spot, I see."

"Paul's right, Meyer," Denny said. "Of the three widowers who used to sit together at the retirement home, you'll soon be the only unmarried one. Might as well make your move."

"We'll see if her mental faculties stay sharp," Meyer replied. "Tonight the subject is Henry. Tell us more about your honeymoon plans."

Henry shrugged. "I'm going along for the ride. Madeline has it all set."

I speared a piece of fried cheese. "You may never have to make another decision in your life. That woman will take care of everything. She'll probably carry you under her arm whenever you need to go pee."

"Yeah, ain't she a beaut?"

We ordered another round of drinks, which would be my limit, and a plate of teriyaki steak and chicken on skewers.

When the food arrived, I reached for a stick but Henry grabbed it first.

"Kind of greedy, aren't you, Henry?"

"I like that piece."

"Since it's your night, have at it." I took a different skewer.

"Uh-oh," Denny said. "That loud group of men over there. The guy with the eye patch. He's a member of the drug gang in the Waianae Mountains."

Surreptitiously, I looked over and, since my eyes had adjusted to the ambient light, saw the creep with the patch. I wouldn't have recognized him if he had held a knife in his teeth and sported a parrot on his shoulder, but from my journal I recalled the name, Snake Laka.

"Probably not someone we want to invite over to wish Henry a happy marriage."

"No, but I'm going to call Detective Saito." Denny took out

his cell phone and punched keys.

I listened as he informed Saito that one of the drug growers had come to the Black Pearl. He snapped his phone shut. "Saito is dispatching a police car immediately and will be here himself as soon as he can."

I used the opportunity to get up to go use the little boy's room. After taking care of business, I noticed Snake Laka and another man with a black ponytail in heated debate inside the restaurant's entryway. Snake pushed a bony finger into Ponytail's chest and shoved him out the door. Being a nosy coot, I followed and stuck my head outside. The two men stood in the corner of the parking lot, waving arms at each other. Snake pulled out a knife and put it against Ponytail's throat. I looked around. No one else in sight. I couldn't allow another murder to take place. I stepped outside and shouted, "Hey, what's the commotion?"

Snake looked in my direction. That gave Ponytail a moment to whack Snake's hand, sending the knife skidding across the parking lot.

I heard a siren.

Snake punched Ponytail, and I heard something clatter to the pavement. Ponytail reeled but recovered from being hit.

A police car pulled into the parking lot.

Snake and Ponytail shot off in different directions.

I ambled over to where the combatants had stood. I crinkled my nose at the sour aroma emanating from a nearby dumpster. Looking down, I noticed, next to a grimy oil spot, a small key. I picked it up and held it as it sparkled in the reflected light.

Off to the side I saw Snake Laka watching me before he disappeared into the undergrowth.

I dropped the key into my pocket.

Chapter 23

A police officer jumped out of a car and raced over to where I stood in the restaurant parking lot. Footfalls from the two combatants receded into the undergrowth.

"A fight took place between a man named Snake Laka and a guy with a ponytail," I said. "My son spoke with Detective Saito a little while ago."

The officer nodded. "Dispatch notified me."

At that moment an unmarked car bounced into the lot and skidded to a stop. A guy in a suit scrambled over to where we stood.

"Ah, Mr. Jacobson. Your son called me. You attract problems like a squished mango attracts flies."

"Detective Saito, I presume. Merely one more unexplained coincidence."

Saito gave an exaggerated eye roll.

I held up my hands. "I know. You don't believe in coincidences. I don't either after all that has happened. Something is going on with this drug dealer crowd. You should know that Snake Laka tried to kill a man with a ponytail. They both ran away."

"I need to speak with you and your son, but I have a few things to take care of out here first."

"I'll be inside. Come join us, and I'll buy you a drink."

He glared at me. "I don't drink when on duty, but I'll see you in the restaurant as soon as I can."

I rejoined the prenuptial group at our table.

"What's happening?" Denny asked.

"Nothing much. Snake Laka tried to knife a guy in the parking lot."

Denny spewed out a mouthful of beer. "Not another crime scene?"

I sighed. "Apparently so. Saito's out there. He'll come join us in a little while."

"The police going to arrest you, jerk?"

"No, Henry. The same as you didn't have anything to do with Louise Kincaid's death, I'm not responsible for these crimes."

"You do have a way of being around trouble," Meyer said. "And you always resisted hiring an attorney."

"Damn right. I have a retired judge in my corner if required. Right now I'm trying to figure out what's what with these drug dealers and how half of them are ending up dead or almost dead around me."

"If you're going to yammer so much and not eat your meat-on-the-stick, jerk, I'll finish it."

"Have at it Henry. I've lost my appetite."

Henry happily munched away while I remained deep in thought, trying to figure out my predicament. My mind refused to give up the image of Snake holding the knife to Ponytail's throat. My own throat constricted. "What happened to the rest of Snake's group?"

"They split around the time you went to the restroom," Denny said.

When Saito arrived, he pulled over a chair in front of Denny. "Tell me specifically what prompted your call."

"I recognized Snake Laka from the group of marijuana growers who held us hostage in the Waianae Mountains," Denny said. "He had a black patch over his eye."

Saito chewed his gum vigorously. "Anyone else associated with Snake or the guy with the ponytail still around?" Saito asked.

I looked over to the vacated table. "Nope. Denny said they took off."

"Did any of Snake Laka's other associates look familiar to you?"

Denny shook his head. "No."

"I didn't recognize any of them, but with my memory I wouldn't," I added.

"I don't know, Mr. Jacobson. You often surprise me with what you do remember."

I looked up at the ceiling as the fan circled to push a small amount of air down toward us. I felt as if I were caught on a blade of that fan, going around and around in circles. "Sometimes the old brain cells work better than others. Oh, by the way. I found this in the parking lot where the confrontation took place." I reached in my pocket and dropped the key on the table.

Saito eyed it as if he were the early bird ready to pounce on the first worm and picked it up with a napkin. "Probably won't have any useful prints other than yours, Mr. Jacobson."

"You can check it out, Detective. You need a sample of my prints to verify?"

His mouth opened a slit, revealing even white teeth. "That won't be necessary. Your prints are already on file."

"Oh. Also, Snake Laka saw me holding the key."

Saito frowned. "That's not good, Mr. Jacobson. This may be important to him."

Although my heart beat faster, I gave my best geezer shrug. "It's out of my hands now, so to speak. What will you do with the key?"

"I'll see if we can identify what it goes to."

"How're you going to do that?" I asked.

Saito chuckled. "Trade secret. If you think of anything else useful, give me a call." He stood and strode out the door.

"Intense fellow," I said.

"He has a lot on his mind," Denny replied.

After all the excitement, I used a napkin to wipe a little spittle from the corner of my mouth. "That would be a hell of a life, having to be around criminals all the time."

"Speak for yourself, jerk."

I reached over and patted Henry on his bald head. "You have this way of putting everything in perspective."

After Henry finished all the food and licked his fingers clean, Denny signaled the waitress. "We're done."

"No you're not." She whistled and two other scantily clad nubile women came over. One carried a cupcake with a candle in it, and the other sat in Henry's lap. They launched into a loud rendition of "Happy marriage to you," to the tune of "Happy Birthday." When the song ended, they kissed the top of Henry's head and his cheeks. He looked like he had come down with a new variety of measles.

"Don't wipe off the lipstick," I said. "Madeline will enjoy the sight."

After Henry gobbled the cupcake, he raced off to the restroom to get rid of the smooching evidence while Denny paid the bill.

After Henry waddled back clean and spiffy, I asked him, "Are you sure you had enough to eat?"

"For now. I may want a bowl of ice cream back at Hale Pohai." He belched loudly.

"Does Madeline know what she's getting into with your appetite and after-dinner manners?"

"Sure. She likes to cook, and I like to eat. We're a perfect couple." He pounded on his chest and burped again.

We drove back to the ladies' restaurant to retrieve Allison and Jennifer. They were waiting for us. "What took you so long?" Madeline bellowed.

"A little incident," I replied. "We needed to talk to the constabulary."

Madeline glared at me. "I hope you took good care of my honeybunch."

"Oh, the best."

We got in the two cars, this time with Jennifer riding with Madeline, and returned to Meyer and Henry's place of residence.

As we gathered in the living room while Denny signed the necessary paperwork to readmit the inmates, Jennifer said, "Madeline does magic. She wowed everyone at the restaurant. Show my grandpa the disappearing orange trick."

Madeline scooped up Henry to give him a hug strong enough to squeeze out a burp before dropping him back to the floor. "I'll need a piece of fruit."

"Should be something in the kitchen," Meyer said.

"I'll take a look." Jennifer shot off like a mini-rocket and returned in moments with an apple, fortunately having discovered no dead bodies. "Couldn't find an orange, but this should work."

"Okay," Madeline said. "Everyone gather around."

We shuffled, strolled or hopped (Jennifer) over to where Madeline stood, awaiting whatever this woman would do.

Madeline rolled up her sleeves and held the apple in her large right hand. "As you can see, I have an ordinary apple here. She brought her hand down onto Jennifer's head.

Jennifer winced but held her ground.

Madeline held her hand out. The apple had disappeared.

Jennifer patted herself all over. "And the apple isn't on me anywhere."

"That's right." Madeline reached into Henry's pants.

His eyes expanded to the size of the apple. "Ooh."

Madeline pulled her hand out, displaying the apple.

Henry grinned. "She's always trying to get into my pants. Ain't she a treasure?"

"Quite a trick, Madeline," I said. "Too bad you can't make Henry disappear."

She stomped over and put her face an inch from mine. "What did you say?"

I put my hands up for protection from violence. "Just kidding. Is there anything you can't do?"

"I don't do dishes. Henry can do those."

I remembered that I hadn't thanked Meyer for giving us a helicopter ride, even if it hadn't ended in the best of circumstances.

"Hey, Meyer, you old coot. I appreciate your lining up a free helicopter ride for us."

He looked at me blankly. "What helicopter ride?"

"Don't tell me your memory has gone in the crapper like mine?"

He regarded me indignantly. "I remember things fine, Paul. I didn't arrange any helicopter ride."

I scratched my head. "It was given to me by a friend. You're my only friend on the island. It couldn't have been Henry, could it? Henry, did you provide a free helicopter ride to me and my family?"

Henry snorted. "I'd never do anything like that, jerk."

"Who the hell left the letter for me at the hotel?"

Everyone stared at me blankly. One more strange occurrence.

After Madeline refused Jennifer's request to do an encore, we adjourned for the night. As we drove along the Pali Highway heading back to Honolulu, Jennifer squirmed around in the backseat. "Tomorrow we're going to Waimea Falls, and in the late afternoon we're going to help set up for the wedding."

"I'm sure it will rival a royal wedding in excitement," I said. "With those two, anything could happen. Maybe Madeline will make Henry disappear during the ceremony."

"Nope. She likes him." Jennifer waved her hands. "And, Grandpa, you and I have the assignment to blow up balloons to decorate the reception room at the yacht club."

"I've been told I'm full of hot air, so I guess I can contribute."

I looked out the window as we passed through the forest on the Honolulu side of the tunnel. A light rain made leaves glisten in the light from oncoming cars. I retraced my journal summary of the strange events of the last week and a half. So many co-incidences, so many dead bodies and so much exposure to danger for Jennifer. I couldn't believe these happenstances occurring to us for no good reason.

Although people had told me I was a dead-body magnet, none of this made any sense. That first body in the Honolulu Ala Wai Yacht Harbor. How had I happened to be there? Then my eyes must have grown as large as Henry's when Madeline goosed him pulling out the apple.

I slapped my forehead. Yes, it was too slick. How had I missed the connection? I would have to check on one item upon returning to the hotel.

CHAPTER 24

Back at our Hibiscus Hotel hideaway, I stopped at the front desk. A woman in a bright blue muumuu with a hibiscus in her hair greeted me with a smile.

"I'm looking for a clerk who has bushy eyebrows."

She laughed. "You must mean Hal Hayashi. He works the morning shift."

"Will he be here tomorrow?"

"Let me check the schedule." She pulled out a sheet of paper and scanned it. "Yes. He'll be on duty from six until noon."

"Good. I'll catch up with him then."

Rather than immediately going up to my room, I moseyed out onto the hotel patio that overlooked the yacht harbor. With the place to myself, I leaned on the railing and watched the lights on the mast of a bobbing sailboat. My troubles started there when I spotted Sammy Malo's hand in the murky water. I remained in murky water myself, trying to put the puzzle pieces together. After following up with Hal Hayashi in the morning, I hoped to be one step closer.

But I needed to get some sleep. I yawned, stretched my arms and turned back toward the hotel.

A man stood there pointing a gun at me.

"Who the hell are you?" I asked in my most inquisitive fashion.

"Your worst nightmare. Kenny Keonu."

"Oh, yeah. The guy who works with Snake Laka."

"No. Snake works for me. And you have a little item we want back."

I looked around hoping someone would appear. No one did. "And what would that be?"

"A lockbox key dropped in the parking lot of the Black Pearl. Snake saw you pick it up."

"Oh, that item." I tried to give a casual shrug. "I don't have it."

Kenny took a step closer to me and pushed the gun into my stomach. "I think you do. Either you give me the key or I'll leave your body like Sammy Malo's."

"So you whacked Sammy."

He shook his head. "No, I don't know who did that, but I can let someone find your body in the same condition as Sammy's."

"But you must be the guy who's been messing up my son's SUV."

He gave a disgusted snort. "What do you mean? Why would I bother with your son's car? I only want the key you have."

Something didn't make sense. "I bet you took shots at me inside Diamond Head."

"I don't know what you're talking about. Only one thing matters. Where's the key?"

"I told you I don't have it."

"We'll see. You're going to come on a little ride with me."

I pushed the fear down my throat. Wouldn't these guys ever give up? I had to figure out a way to stall this nutcase.

My thoughts were interrupted by a large woman stepping between us and sticking a massive finger in my chest. "Why did you put those Geezers Rule signs on my door?"

The crazy lady from the beach. I didn't know if I should laugh or cry. Her appearance might distract my assailant. I thought back to my journal. "My granddaughter put up those signs, and I apologize for her behavior."

Kenny snarled, "Move it, lady."

She spun to face him. "Out of my way." In a lightning-fast move, she grabbed his gun with her left hand and decked him with her right hand.

Kenny did not bounce back up.

"Thank you, ma'am. You've taken a dangerous drug dealer out of commission."

She turned around to face me. "You doing a drug deal right here at the hotel?"

"Not me. He wanted to kill me. I gave the police a lockbox key he wanted. Would you happen to have a cell phone to call the police?"

She whipped one out of her purse, poked at it with her large fingers and handed it to me. In a moment the 9-1-1 operator answered and I explained that a suspect being sought by Detective Chun had been captured at the Hibiscus Hotel.

Crazy Lady arched a large eyebrow. "You really serious that this is a drug dealer?"

"Yeah. And I appreciate that you showed up and saved me."

Soon a police officer raced onto the scene. He bent over Kenny. "We've been looking for this guy." He snapped handcuffs on the unconscious scumbag.

Fifteen minutes later, Detective Chun showed up. I wouldn't have recognized him until he started rubbing a wart on his hand.

"I see you captured a member of the drug gang, Mr. Jacobson."

I waved my hands in a crossing motion. "I had nothing to do with it. This nice young lady deserves all the credit. She saved my sorry butt."

In the ambient light I saw Crazy Lady actually blush.

Detective Chun turned to my huge angel and flinched as if

overwhelmed by her size. "Thank you, ma'am."

She put her hands on her hips. "I hate it when people call me ma'am. My name is Fredricka Falcone."

"Thank you, Fredricka," I said.

After Kenny revived, another officer led him away. He made one attempt to kick me but fortunately missed by a foot, so to speak. Detective Chun took our statements and then took off. He probably needed to spend the rest of the night completing paperwork.

I turned to Fredricka. "Thanks again. I'm sorry for the misunderstanding with the signs on your door."

She flicked her gigantic wrist in a dismissive gesture that would have killed on contact. "I guess I overreacted. I've been having some problems with my hormone treatment." She gave an immense sigh. "The word 'geezer' fries me."

"Yeah, I got that impression. What's the big deal? I think it's a humorous way of describing an old fart like me."

Her eyes met mine. "You're right, but I have an emotional problem with the word. You see I'm a transgender person. I used to be known as Fighting Freddy, the professional wrestler."

My jaw dropped. "I remember you. I saw one of your fights on television back when my memory worked. No wonder you're so big."

She kicked at the ground as if trying to dislodge a section of cement. "I realized something wasn't right with me being a man. I enjoyed the sweaty, male bodies too much. I decided to go out with one last victory before retiring to have a sex change operation. In my final match I met an opponent named Geezer Gus. He wasn't that old but had a bald head and a prematurely gray beard. He whooped me, and I've never liked the word 'geezer' since."

"I can understand. An attorney once took advantage of me, and after that time I've hated the word 'lawyer.' "

We shook hands, and she was kind enough not to break any bones. Afterward, I headed back to tell Marion of being saved by someone even larger and stronger than Madeline. And speaking of Madeline, if she ever tired of Henry, I'd have to introduce him to Fredricka.

CHAPTER 25

When I returned to my hotel room, my bride greeted me with anger in her eyes, "Where have you been? I was ready to pound on Denny's door and ask him to go look for you."

"I'm sorry to have been delayed." I proceeded to give the account of my encounter with Kenny Keonu and Fredricka Falcone.

"I can't leave you alone for even a minute without you getting in trouble."

"I know. I need protection from strong women."

I documented the latest adventures in my diary and left a large note to remind my feeble brain to track down Hal Hayashi at the front desk in the morning.

Marion and I turned out the lights, and we fell asleep.

I awoke to find a woman snuggled up against me in bed. I carefully extracted myself from her embrace and padded into the bathroom I found. When I returned, I spotted a note on the nightstand on my side of the bed. I began reading the journal underneath.

After finishing the diary, I set it back on the nightstand. Holy crapola. What a life I led. The places I'd been, the things I'd witnessed, the dead bodies I'd found. This was too much excitement for someone in my age category.

Marion opened her eyes. "Why don't you come back to bed?" she asked.

With an invitation like that, how could I refuse?

Marion sighed. "Another wedding today. We had a wonderful ceremony. Too bad you don't remember it."

I held her closely. "I'm working on trying to remember the bride."

"I may have to give your memory a little boost. You keeping any apples in your pajamas?" She reached inside my PJ bottoms and something other than an apple came alive. "My goodness. What do we have here?"

Duly inspired, I reciprocated by exploring interesting parts of her body, and soon we were making the mattress springs hum.

Marion fell back asleep after our assignation, but I decided to get up to admire the beautiful sunny morning. I shaved, pulled on Bermuda shorts and a T-shirt with a curling wave on it (as close as I wanted to get to the ocean today) and caught the elevator to the lobby. I needed to complete a self-assigned mission.

Sure enough, as my journal indicated, I found a man with bushy eyebrows behind the counter. I approached him. "Are you Hal Hayashi?"

"Yes. How may I help you?"

"My name is Paul Jacobson. A week and a half ago I picked up an envelope here that someone left for me. You were on duty at the time."

His mouth turned up in a smile. "I remember, Mr. Jacobson. You also had me call nine-one-one."

"That's right. Did you happen to get a look at whoever left the envelope for me?" '

Hal bit his lip for a moment, and then his eyes lit up. "Yes. Now I recall."

Good. He didn't have any memory problems like yours truly. "And a description?"

"It was an old man, dressed very poorly. There are a lot of homeless people who spend the night in Ala Moana Park. He looked like one of them. Now that you remind me, I was surprised that he would be delivering something to the front desk."

Bingo. This made one more puzzle piece fall into place. "Thanks for your assistance."

Next stop, the office of Tourist Air Tours, which, according to my journal, was on the next block. I headed along the yacht harbor, consciously not going close enough to look in the water. I didn't want to risk that again. I passed a restaurant, a real estate office and lo and behold, the next office was what I wanted.

A bell jangled as I entered. A small table held travel magazines, and a woman with her black hair pinned back in a bun appeared through a curtain behind the counter. "May I assist you?" Everyone was being so helpful to me this morning.

"I'm looking for Dex Tanaka."

"I'm sorry. He's at the airport preparing for a tour."

"You know when he'll be back in the office?"

She looked at her watch. "He'll be here by three to complete his daily paperwork. You can catch him then."

"I heard that he force-landed near Waianae recently. Did the helicopter get recovered?"

She nodded. "Yes. Apparently, it was only a minor mechanical problem, and Dex flew it back the same day."

Interesting.

"Is there anything I can do to help you in Dex's absence?"

My brain, working well at the moment, came up with an idea. As long as I was here, I might do a little snooping. "Thank you, but I need to see him in person. May I use your restroom?"

"Sure. Go through the curtains. It's at the back on the left side."

I followed the directions, noticing no one in the back office. Figuring I only had a short time, I scanned around. Travel brochures cluttered one desk. I picked one up and found an ad for Tourist Air Tours. Another desk contained piles of invoices. On a third desk I found a large log book. I opened it. Bingo. It contained the schedule of their recent tours.

I leafed back to the day of our trip and located an entry for the Jacobson party, three people. All kosher. Then I gawked. At first I didn't believe what I saw.

The account showed nineteen hundred dollars paid in cash the day of our flight. Our tour was supposedly a gift from a friend of mine, but neither Meyer nor Henry claimed responsibility. And a cash payment the day we flew? No one I knew had that much cash lying around to fork over for an anonymous present. This didn't make sense. Unless . . .

My devious mind put two and two together and got four hundred. I realized I needed to skedaddle before the woman became suspicious. I quickly stepped in the restroom, flushed the toilet, returned to the front, waved and said, "Thanks," as I headed out the door.

More of the crime-saw puzzle pieces fit together, but I couldn't tie in the death of Louise Kincaid at Hale Pohai. I would have to noodle on that during my day of being a tourist.

I rejoined my clan for breakfast, and then the ladies and I packed up for our trip to Waimea Falls while Denny went down to retrieve our car and bring it to the front entrance. We stuffed beach bags with towels, sunscreen, water bottles and snacks.

In five minutes Denny came stomping back into the room. "I went to the garage to get the SUV and found four flat tires. It looked like someone slashed them. I called the car rental and they have a spare SUV but can't send anyone right now to bring us the replacement. They said we needed to come to their lot, so we'll have to take a cab."

"Can you call that cabbie we used yesterday?" Allison asked.

"Yeah. I should have his number in my call list." Denny punched some buttons on his cell phone and reached the taxi driver.

In fifteen minutes we headed down to the lobby and met Moki and his black cab. "Howzit, everybody. I remember all of you. Hop in."

Moki was becoming like a member of the family.

We climbed in and headed to the car rental lot at the airport where a sparkling new white SUV awaited us. "Last one in the fleet," the attendant informed us.

"Yes," Allison said. "We've tried all the other ones."

After transferring our gear into the new SUV, we were on our way.

"What's the big attraction at Waimea Falls?" I asked.

"I Googled it," Jennifer said.

"What's that have to do with a big number?" I asked.

"Huh?"

"A googol is a large number—ten raised to the hundredth power."

"Oh, Grandpa. Google is a search engine. I checked out Waimea Falls on the Internet."

"Is that like a fishing net?"

"You're impossible."

"No, I'm your feeble-minded Grandpa."

Jennifer reached over and gave me a hug, as much as her seat belt would allow. "Not feeble-minded. Only stubborn and unwilling to use computers."

"You have that right. So tell me the scoop on our destination."

Jennifer treated the seat as if it were a trampoline. "We're going to see all kinds of birds, plants, Hawaiian shows and swim under a waterfall."

"Everything sounds good except for the last item. I enjoy waterfalls from afar."

"Oh, Grandpa. I'm going to swim in the pool and splash under the waterfall. That's the best part. And we'll see people jumping off the cliff by the waterfall."

"And as long as I don't have to climb up the waterfall," Allison added from the front seat.

"You and I can be the landlubbers on flat ground, Allison," I replied. "We'll leave the waterfall to Jennifer."

Denny drove us across the center of the island through what had once been sugar cane fields, now converted to residential real estate. On the other side of Wahiawa we stopped at the Dole Plantation to snack on pineapple.

After we finished our refreshments, Jennifer pointed to a sign advertising the world's largest maze, which resided on the plantation grounds. "We have to try it. Come on everybody."

"I'm game. Marion and I will team up with Jennifer and let you middle-agers go together." I pointed to Denny and Allison. "Last team out buys lunch."

"You're on," Denny replied, rubbing his hands together, his competitive juices obviously flowing.

"I don't know," Allison said.

But Denny grabbed her hand and led her outside.

"I guess I'll chaperone you two," Marion said to Jennifer and me as we headed to the maze entrance.

I looked around at the pineapples growing in neat rows with their spiked leaves poking up. The volcanic red soil stuck to my shoes but apparently provided the correct nutrients for pineapples. I thought of all the work to grow and harvest crops of these juicy fruit. I had never been much of a farmer, having tried a vegetable garden once, which only produced weeds.

Denny placed his toe at the start of the maze. "Ready, set, go." He grabbed Allison's hand and they disappeared.

Our team followed and inside the maze, we began meandering through passageways bounded by tall hedges. I imagined being trapped in here for days and having to have food and water airlifted to us by helicopter. "This is a-mazing," I said.

Marion punched me in the shoulder.

"Ouch." I rubbed the point of contact.

"Don't give me that. I barely touched you."

"It's so cool, Grandpa. Pay attention to where the sun is. I learned in Girl Scouts to find my way by orienting to the position of the sun."

"Good thing we have an expert along," I said.

We traipsed around, and in no time at all Jennifer led us to the center where the vegetation formed a large pineapple shape.

"While we wait for Mom and Dad, we can tell some geezer jokes, Grandpa. I have a good one that Austin found on the Internet and emailed to me. Ready?"

"Sure."

"Instead of catching the West Nile Virus, what did the geezer get?"

"You got me."

"C-nile."

Marion groaned, and I chuckled. Before we had an opportunity to explore more geezer humor, Denny and Allison appeared, looking bedraggled.

"I told you to take that turn," Allison said, shaking her fist at Denny. "But you never listen."

"Now, now, children, don't fight." I spread my arms like the Pope conducting a service on Easter morning.

Denny glared at me. "Let's hit the road."

So we walked back to the SUV.

Upon clicking my seat belt in place, I whispered in Jennifer's ear, "I detect your dad didn't use the sun to navigate like you did."

"That's because he wasn't a Girl Scout." Jennifer giggled.

We continued our journey and made a stop at Waimea Bay to get out and look at the surf. Denny and Allison had reconciled and held hands. Out in the ocean huge breakers crashed. In my chest my heart thumped at the sight of those horrendous waves.

"Wow," Jennifer said. "Look at that. They're much too big for me to surf."

"I remember this place from before my memory went on the fritz," I said. "In the summer it can be as smooth as a lake but during the winter, look out. Waves can reach as high as forty feet." And I wouldn't have gone in that water even when it was calm.

Allison made us stand on the edge of the cliff and took several pictures with the crashing waves in the background. I felt oh so proud to be once again immortalized inside one of those crazy cameras that didn't use film.

We arrived at the Waimea Falls parking area with no further damage to SUVs or people. I sprang for the fees (Jennifer, Marion and I getting in for the lower rate as a kid and seniors). It paid to be a young pup or an old fart.

We moseyed along a well-groomed path, sniffing the tropical aromas and looking at flora and fauna. The fauna chirped and the flora fluttered in the breeze. We came to a rock wall with a sign for a Heiau.

"You know what a Heiau is, Jennifer?" I asked.

She gave a quick nod. "Of course. It's a Hawaiian sacred spot."

"No," I replied. "It's a place where if you walk barefoot on the sharp lava, you shout out, 'Hey, ow!' "

Jennifer raised her fist to slug me, but I did the geezer shuffle to avoid being pummeled. From what I read in my journal, a number of females had tried to bruise me recently.

We passed a peacock with its dark blue body, light blue head and fan of feathers with what looked like blue iridescent eyes. I found one feather lying on the ground and presented it to Jennifer. "Here. Maybe this will make up for my bad pun."

She took the peace offering. "I don't know about you sometimes, Grandpa."

"You and me both."

With the rest of our troop having walked ahead, Jennifer said to me, "I have another geezer joke for you, Grandpa."

"I guess you can tell me since your mom's out of hearing range."

"Why'd the geezer go to all the funerals in town?"

I shrugged. "I have no clue."

"He was social networking." Jennifer bent over laughing and slapped her thigh.

I looked at Jennifer as if she were a zebra at a horse show. "I don't get it. What's social networking?"

"Oh, come on. You must have heard of social networking, Grandpa."

"Nope. It's not something that my brain retained before it went haywire."

Jennifer stopped to pick up a leaf to go with her feather. "Social networking is the best way to communicate with friends on the Internet."

"Uh-oh. There's the damn Internet thingy again."

"You're impossible."

"That's what Marion says as well."

We caught up with the rest of our party and reached a pool with lily pads in front of the objective of our destination—a spectacular forty-five-foot waterfall. We arrived as a show began that included cliff divers. Allison snapped pictures nonstop. As each diver dropped gracefully into the pool, my stomach lurched. They disappeared and then popped to the surface. If it had been me, I would have gone to the bottom and never re-appeared.

Afterward, the announcer indicated that the pool was open again for swimming. Jennifer took off her shorts and tank top to reveal her swimsuit and jumped in. "Brr. It's much colder than the ocean." She stroked out and swam under the waterfall.

I found a place to sit and watch.

Jennifer swam around the pool demonstrating all the swim strokes she knew. The only one I ever learned was the sinker. Finally, she stroked over and clung to the rock siding where I sat.

"You look like a water sprite."

She wiped the drops off her face and leaned her head back in the sunlight. "Too bad you don't want to swim with me."

"I'm fine sitting on this rock."

Jennifer's head continued to tilt upward toward the cliff. "Lots of plants grow along the rim up there. What's that? Look out!" She grabbed my arm and pulled me.

I crashed into the pool.

I heard a loud splash next to me and came up sputtering. My arms flailed as I tried to gain purchase in the cold water. I sank again. I kicked, and my head came above water momentarily. As I went under for the third time, Jennifer grabbed my arm to help me to shore.

"Why'd you pull me into the pool?" I demanded once safely back on dry land.

"A large rock fell off the cliff. It would have hit you on the head."

I noticed where I had been sitting. Dirt and rock fragments littered the surface. I gulped. Then I looked upward. I saw a figure disappear over the crest above.

CHAPTER 26

As we hiked back to the car, I kept my soggy tennis shoes on so I wouldn't have to say, "Hey, ow." Along the dirt path, I felt as if I were walking on soaked sponges as each step I took squeaked and sloshed.

Denny put his arm around my shoulder. "I didn't see anyone, and the park ranger said no one was supposed to be climbing above where you sat, Dad."

"I don't care what he spouted. I saw someone up there. And that someone tried to make my cranium even mushier than it already is."

"Grandpa's right. It wasn't an accident. Someone threw a rock off the cliff and almost hit him on the head."

"But fortunately my quick-thinking granddaughter saved my hide."

Jennifer reddened and gave me an aw-shucks smile.

"I think you're overreacting," Denny said.

"I don't agree. Think back to what's happened." On my fingers I began ticking off the events documented in my journal. "Being pushed and almost falling into the imu. The broken window and threatening note left in the SUV. Something put in my papaya that made Marion sick. The car being run off Pali Highway. Being shot at on Diamond Head. A can of Spam thrown at my head. And now someone trying to bash me with a rock. This all ties to the murders and the drug dealers. With Kenny Keonu accosting me and being arrested last night, I thought all my problems would be over, but someone else still wants me out of the way."

"The park ranger said he'd report the incident to the police, but he didn't sound very convincing," Denny said.

"No," I replied. "There isn't much that Detectives Saito or Chun can do right now. I'm trying to piece it together myself."

"Things have become too dangerous," Allison said. "We should cut our trip short and go back to the mainland."

Denny pounded his hand on the steering wheel, causing the car to swerve. "No way. We can't give in to intimidation."

"Besides," Jennifer said, "we have Henry and Madeline's wedding we need to go to. Grandpa will figure it out."

Back at the Hibiscus Hotel, I took a quick shower, changed and stuck my head into the adjoining room.

Jennifer waved to me. "Grandpa, come look at this email message from Austin. I asked him to do some research for us."

I strolled over to her computer. "On what subject?"

"The illegal drug business in Hawaii."

"Ah, like all the thugs we've run into."

"Yeah." She tapped the screen. "They often get involved in money laundering as well as growing marijuana and selling drugs. You learned about money laundering last summer in Venice Beach."

I scratched my head. "Don't remember squat on that subject."

Jennifer giggled. "That's what he wrote, so he wanted to remind you. Take a look at his message."

I bent over and read how in most drug gangs, they have one or more legitimate businesses that they pour cash into to hide the source of their illegal gains, making cash transactions in denominations less than ten thousand dollars to avoid any government reporting requirements. The legitimate business could show a profit and the earnings could be distributed to the business owners, who were, you'd never guess, the drug lords. Made sense. Then an idea occurred to me, and I realized I needed to check one other thing before we headed to Kaneohe for the wedding festivities.

After leaving Jennifer to send a message back to Austin, I strolled over to Tourist Air Tours. Eager tourists packed the sidewalk as I navigated my way. At the office, the door jangled when I entered. The same woman I had spoken to in the morning appeared from the back. No customers were there, so I didn't have to wait.

"I'm back to speak with Dex Tanaka."

"Just a moment." She disappeared behind the curtain.

I didn't have to "pay no attention to that man behind the curtain" because in moments he appeared. Dex's eyes widened as they focused on me.

"Dex, so good to see you again."

"Uh . . . yes . . . Mr. Jacobson."

I paused for a moment trying to figure out how I wanted to handle this. I decided on the direct confrontation. "That's right. I recall our little trip last week. First of all, it was no coincidence that your helicopter landed in the Waianae Mountains." I shook my right index finger at him. "You staged that event. My question is why?"

Sweat appeared on his forehead, and he looked from side to side as if expecting the walls to collapse around him. "I . . . uh . . . don't know what you're talking about."

"Yes you do. Someone directed me to you in the first place. The whole bit with a homeless man leaving a packet for me at the hotel was a setup. And by the way, one of your cohorts killed him so he wouldn't be able to testify. When we went on the helicopter ride, you conveniently landed where the drug growers hung out, making it seem like the helicopter had been shot down. But that was staged. The helicopter wasn't really damaged. You pretended it had been hit. You even acted like you didn't know any of the drug gang, but the intention was to get rid of me. I may not have that long to live, but I resent that you put my son and granddaughter at risk as well."

"I . . . I have a tour waiting for me." Dex came out from behind the counter, pushed me aside, dashed out the front door and disappeared.

The echo from the jangling bell hadn't subsided as the door slammed shut. I heard a car start and, pushing through the glass door, I saw Dex roar away in a blue Toyota. "The police are going to nail you, Dex," I shouted, but he had disappeared out of hearing range.

So much for an intelligent discussion with one of the slime-balls. I suspected Dex would be going into hiding.

When I returned to the hotel, I spotted a sign saying there would be a lecture on Hawaiian statehood. From my journal I recalled the discussion with the man at Hanauma Bay. I looked at my watch. The program should have just started. I could spare a few minutes and was curious, so I ambled into the appropriate meeting room and sat down in the back behind a dozen or so tourists. A young man in a green Hawaiian shirt proceeded to educate us on the history of statehood. I learned that there had been a heated debate in Congress with much racial prejudice around admitting to statehood a territory with a minority of Caucasians. Only after Alaska became the forty-ninth state did the proponents muster enough votes to admit Hawaii as state number fifty. The presenter showed slides of the Hawaiian statehood celebrations. One picture caught my attention of a paperboy with a gap-toothed smile holding up a newspaper announcing, "Statehood."

The opening in the boy's teeth reminded me that I had a few gaps to fill in this world of drug dealers and murder. I knew what I needed to do.

When I returned to our adjoining rooms, I asked Denny to call Detective Chun. He wasn't available. Next, I asked him to try Detective Saito. Also, not answering. I'd have to wait to recount Dex's involvement in this weird chain of events.

I turned in my casual wear for the nuptial costume of a jacket and tie. What I had to go through for Henry. I hoped he appreciated the sacrifice of having my throat constricted. Nope. He wouldn't.

Jennifer had invited Hina and Keoki to join us, so we had a full load as we piled into the SUV for Denny to chauffeur us to the Kaneohe Yacht Club.

"You're not performing tonight at a luau?" I asked Keoki.

"Nope. It's my night off."

"You could perform a fire dance at the wedding," Jennifer said.

"I think there'll be enough fireworks as it is," I replied. "Madeline will do something to entertain the crowd. With two more men Henry's size, she could perform a juggling act."

"Oh, Grandpa." Jennifer turned toward Keoki. "Tell us a Menehune story."

"Okay. As you know the Menehunes play tricks on people. They particularly like to fool visiting people from the mainland. So one day this haole guy, who thought he was hot stuff, went up in the mountains to pick guavas. He came across a group of Menehunes eating ripe guavas from a tree. The haole picked up some rotten guavas and began pelting the Menehunes. They, of course, didn't like that, so they cast a spell on him and turned him into a lava tree. So if you ever see a lava tree you know the Menehunes have punished someone. The moral—don't mess with Menehunes."

Thinking over the story, something clicked. The lecture I attended earlier mentioning racial prejudice against Hawaiian statehood and Keoki's story somehow caused a connection in my weirdly wired brain. "Hey, the writing on the side of our car the other day that read, 'No more whites.' That wasn't a racial reference."

"Why not?" Denny asked from the front.

"Because in Hawaii it would have said, 'No more haoles.' Local people always call whites haoles."

"That's right," Keoki said. "Everybody here uses the word 'haole.' "

I pounded my hand against the back of the front seat. "And another thing. The vandalism done to our car can't be from the drug dealers because they wouldn't mess with something that petty, preferring instead to dispatch me into a fire pit, with poison papaya, bullets, a can of Spam or a rock. And since the car vandalism can't be racially based, there has to be some other reason for it."

CHAPTER 27

I sat in silence, trying to figure out why someone constantly tried to damage our rental cars. There had to be a simple answer.

"Someone doesn't like our cars?" Jennifer asked.

I snapped my fingers. "Bingo. Maybe the reference to white was because we've been in nothing but white cars, not a racial reference. If so, we still need to find out who's doing it and why."

None of us came up with a good reason by the time we reached the Kaneohe Yacht Club. Once out of the car, we deployed to our assignments like the troops landing on the beaches of Normandy. Marion took care of the flower arrangements, Allison began taking photographs, Denny checked out the sound system, Keoki helped with chairs, and Jennifer, Hina and I blew up balloons. When my cheeks reached the aching point, I quit huffing and puffing, stuffed a handful of extra balloons in my pocket and started hanging the blown-up ones on the walls. One popped, so I pulled a replacement out of my pocket and inflated it. With our task completed, Hina went to help Keoki. Jennifer and I gave each other a high-five before we stood back to admire our work.

"Not bad, Grandpa."

"What we go through for Henry."

"And Madeline too. I like her."

"Yeah," I replied. "Ain't she a beaut?"

Jennifer gave me a conspiratorial wink. "Now Keoki, Hina

and I need to go decorate Madeline's car. I found a trash bin full of discarded tennis ball cans next to the tennis courts here at the yacht club, and we brought along a bunch of other stuff. I borrowed Dad's shaving cream. Keoki got a fishing net and duct tape. We're going to turn her Corvette into an artistic creation." She skipped off, ready to contribute to the world of graffiti.

With nothing better to do, I followed to watch the kids decorate Madeline's car. They assembled their paraphernalia and began attaching tennis ball cans to the fishing net with the duct tape. I remembered my first marriage. We departed in a 1938 Buick with a sign saying "Just married" attached to the rear bumper. And my second marriage? Unfortunately, I didn't remember any of the specifics. Marion would have to be my memory for that. But so much for the past. By necessity I focused on the present and the future, awaiting whatever it had in store for me.

"Jennifer, I have a geezer joke for you," I said as I watched them work.

"Go for it, Grandpa."

"Do you know what a geezer triathlon is?"

"Nope."

I cleared my throat. "You ride a stationary bike for a minute, take a walk to the Jacuzzi and soak in the hot tub."

Hina looked up from attaching tennis ball cans to the net with duct tape. "Do you always tell dumb jokes?"

"Absolutely. It's what I was born to do."

"Grandpa, here's one that Austin emailed to me. You know what the geezer did when he lost an hour in the morning?"

"I give up."

"He spent all day looking for it."

"I've had days like that. That reminds me—" A loud pounding noise interrupted me. I snapped my head to the side and peered in the direction of the banging to see a ragged jean-clad young man with long blond hair, who reminded me of a California surfer dude, slamming a hammer into the hood of our white SUV.

"Hey!" I shouted and dashed toward him. "What the hell are you doing?"

He took one more swing and started to run. He pushed past me before I could do anything but step aside to avoid being knocked over. "Stop him!" I called out.

He headed right to where Jennifer and her friends were working. As he reached them, Jennifer and Hina stretched out the fishing net. The vandal ran right into the net, stumbled, became fully entangled and dropped to the pavement as the hammer flew out of his hand. As he struggled, Jennifer pulled off strips of duct tape and wound them around the fishing net, firmly securing the man in the tangles. The kids had caught a giant fish.

Keoki put a knee on the man's chest. "I'll hold him, Mr. Jacobson."

"Jennifer, go inside and have your dad call the police," I said. "This guy isn't going anywhere." I picked up the hammer.

Jennifer dashed off, and I kept an eye on the car basher, brandishing the hammer as if to whack him over the head if he tried to get up. Between Keoki and me, he got the message and quit thrashing. He lay there quietly with eyes wide and mouth opening and closing like a beached fish.

"Why have you been damaging and stealing our cars?" I asked.

The blond guy made a fist and tried to raise it but was unsuccessful at getting very far in his confinement. "It's part of our protest. Go back to the mainland. We don't want you messing up the island by driving gas-guzzling cars and polluting the air."

I chuckled. "I get it. All the tourists should shove off. Ain't going to happen."

He tried to struggle to a sitting position but Keoki held him down.

"We want to put the car rental companies out of business. They're exploiting their workers and contributing to you tourists coming to destroy the island."

"Why are you targeting white SUVs?" I asked.

The guy tried to move again, but Keoki kept him pinned to the ground. Blondie gasped. "White is the color of purity. We want the purity of the island back."

While we waited for the police to arrive, Jennifer and Hina returned to their decorating project, going with only the shaving cream since the fishing net was occupied.

Fifteen minutes later a police car pulled up to retrieve the activist. As he was led away, he raised a fist in the air and shouted, "Stop wars!"

Denny, who had come out of the yacht club moments before, regarded the commotion with perplexity. "We've been dealing with an anti-war demonstrator?"

"That is one confused protestor," I said.

As he was pushed into the backseat of the patrol car, a sheet of paper fluttered to the ground. I ambled over to pick it up and read, "Stop White Auto Rental Suvs. Bring back the purity of our island. No more tourists."

I now knew what had been happening to our rental cars. We'd been the victims of a crazy fruitcake protest. I shook my head in amazement at this latest weirdness. The blond surfer dude probably arrived here as a tourist before going native.

Now we only needed to rid ourselves of the threat from the drug gang.

Denny stepped over to the SUV and ran his hand over the bashed hood, a look of sadness in his eyes. "I'll have to pick up another new car tomorrow."

I patted him on the back. "As your wife has been pointing out, get a color other than white if you want to avoid further problems."

★ ★ ★ ★ ★

Soon everyone congregated for the big event. Henry and I sat on chairs outside the room where the ceremony would be conducted. He wore a dark suit with a red tie.

"You clean up pretty good, Henry."

He gave me a onceover. "You don't, jerk. You're missing a button on your right jacket sleeve."

I inspected my arm and sure enough, the doofus was right. Somehow I'd lost a button, leaving a brown thread hanging forlornly on its lonesome. I patted my jacket pocket to make sure I had the jewelry box containing the ring. I was prepared to do my part.

Meyer appeared wearing a black robe and the three of us entered the room. The guests consisted of Denny, Allison, Keoki, Hina and Hattie Wilson. Meyer and Hattie had taken a taxi from the Hale Pohai care home to join the festivities. Meyer, Henry and I waited while Pachelbel's Canon in D played.

It suddenly struck me, and I whispered in Henry's ear, "How come none of your relatives came to the wedding?"

"My kids and grandkids are on a Mediterranean cruise right now."

"Why didn't you schedule the ceremony after they came back?"

"Madeline and I didn't want to wait. They can visit us later."

The music changed to Wagner's Bridal Chorus and sure enough, here came the bride as Madeline and Jennifer appeared at the back door and walked slowly toward us. Jennifer was decked out in a yellow flowered dress and held a matching bouquet of daisies. Madeline wore a blue dress that reminded me of the morning sky. Allison pointed her camera as Madeline and Jennifer moved toward the front, and I heard a succession of shutter clicks.

Henry gulped. "Ain't she a beaut?"

I nodded. "That she is."

Things proceeded as during the rehearsal until we reached the part where Meyer asked for the ring.

I patted my pockets frantically and whispered, "What ring?"

Henry's eyes grew the size of the daisies Jennifer held.

"Just kidding." I reached into my pocket, pulled out the box and removed the ring, which I handed to Henry. I know I shouldn't have, but I couldn't resist tweaking Henry after all the crap he gave me.

A big sloppy kiss sealed the deal. As Mendelssohn's Wedding March blared out, Madeline picked up Henry and stuffed him under her arm. "Come on, honeybunch. Let's go grab some chow before we consummate this thing."

"I'm for both of those," Henry gasped.

Madeline stepped down the aisle in time to the music with Henry firmly secured under her arm. Jennifer followed, grasping the flower bouquet.

I turned to Meyer. "Did you see that?"

"Not all that well, but it was the most unusual recessional I've ever witnessed."

We gathered in the adjoining room for food. I admired the balloons Jennifer, Hina and I had stuck to the walls and dove in to the goodies. I stuffed my face with an assortment of veggies; cow, pig and chicken parts; and a cookie or two—all right, maybe four cookies. Grabbing a glass of punch and a spoon, I moseyed up to a lectern in the front of the room and tapped the spoon on the glass until everyone stopped talking and looked in my direction.

"I have a few words to say." I pulled out a sheet of paper from my jacket pocket. "For the occasion, I composed a poem for the newlyweds." I cleared my throat, looked around the room once and focused on my notes.

"Although Henry is bald, weird and short.

"He has found the ideal consort.

"Madeline is tall, brave and strong.

"And in Henry's eyes can do no wrong.

"They make the ideal couple.

"And will keep each other out of trouble."

I paused, looking around the room again. "Now everyone raise your glasses in a toast to the bride and groom." I lifted my glass. "To Henry and Madeline. May you have a long and happy life together. And may Madeline learn to put up with Henry's idiosyncrasies. Cheers."

Everyone held their glasses up.

"Thanks, jerk," Henry called out. "Next time wipe the mustard off your mouth."

I ran my hand over my puss and noticed a streak of yellow. I shrugged. Hey, what could you expect from a geezer my age?

Madeline picked up Henry, tucked him under her left arm and raised her right hand to execute a perfect military salute. "Let's go consummate this marriage."

"Hold on," Allison called out, waving her hand frantically. "You can't leave yet. We need to take some more pictures."

Madeline set Henry down on the floor. "I guess we can wait a few more minutes, honey pot." She rubbed him on the top of his bald head.

"Ain't she a beaut?" Henry beamed.

Marion came up to me and hugged my arm. "I didn't know you wrote poetry."

"I don't, but I thought the occasion deserved something different."

"You didn't write a poem for our wedding ceremony."

"I don't remember, but I probably was too distracted by sheer terror."

Marion put her hands on her hips. "What's that supposed to mean?"

"Uh . . . er . . . in sheer terror because I didn't deserve someone as good as you."

Marion laughed. "Good recovery."

"Phew." I wiped my brow. "I can't stand having my bride mad at me."

Marion went over to speak with Jennifer, who was grazing at the food table, and I used the opportunity to step over to speak with Hattie Wilson, who stood holding Meyer's hand.

"Thanks for joining the festivities, Hattie," I said.

"Meyer needed a date." She snuggled close to him.

Meyer didn't seem to resist the attention.

"Would you get me a glass of iced tea?" Hattie asked Meyer.

"Sure." He released her hand and hopped over to the refreshment table. Well, actually he kind of shuffled over.

"You seem in good spirits this evening, Hattie."

"Yes, indeed. I seem to be less fuzzy every day. My memory has returned."

This gave me an idea. "Speaking of memory, do you remember the evening when Louise Kincaid died?"

Hattie bit her lip. "Yes. A most unfortunate occurrence."

"Did you happen to notice anyone going into the kitchen before I found Louise dead?"

She put her hand over her mouth for a moment and nodded her head. "I hadn't realized it before, but our nurse Pamela Newsome did."

CHAPTER 28

I excused myself from Hattie Wilson and hustled over to where Denny stood speaking with Allison and Jennifer. I waited for him to turn in my direction.

"You need to call Detective Saito on your cell thingy," I said.

"How come?"

"I have some news to pass along to him."

Denny opened the device, punched some buttons and handed it to me. It cut over to voicemail, and I said, "Detective, this is Paul Jacobson. I'm at the Kaneohe Yacht Club and have some important information for you. Please call back on my son's cell phone."

"What's up?" Denny asked.

I handed him the phone. "I think I've put together more pieces of the puzzle."

At that moment Madeline came up to Allison. "Take the final pictures of my honeybunch and me before we go consummate."

Allison lined them up and motioned Jennifer over to join the picture. Madeline gave a huge smile and squeezed Henry. He tried to smile, but it came out more of a grimace.

"Let's try it again," Allison said.

This time Madeline released her grip, and Henry managed a real smile.

I needed some fresh air and time to think things through, so I headed outside and walked down to the water's edge. I caught a glimpse of a sliver of moon and a few stars in spite of the light from the parking lot. I thought back to my journal notation of the night I found Louise Kincaid's body in the kitchen at Hale Pohai. I punched my right fist into my left hand. "That's it," I said out loud. "Pamela Newsome was in cahoots with the drug dealers."

"Very good, Mr. Jacobson."

I jerked my head up to see a man pointing a handgun at me.

He stepped closer, and I saw he had a large nose. I ran through more of what had been in my journal. "You're Manuel Hiaka."

He grinned. "I told Kenny you knew too much. You should have been killed sooner."

I didn't like the sound of that. I needed to keep him talking. "You're one of Sammy Malo's henchman."

He leered at me, and light from the parking lot reflected off large incisors. "Not any longer. I've taken over for Sammy after his timely death. Move."

He propelled me into the parking lot. I stumbled, and he pushed the gun in my back once as a not-too-subtle reminder to move my fanny.

We reached a black Lincoln Town Car. He flicked a button on his key chain, the lights flashed, and he opened the back door. With a shove, he sent me flying, and I landed with a thud on the seat. Good thing I had some padding on my backside.

Before I even had a chance to reach for the door handle to attempt to escape, he climbed in the driver's seat. I tested the handle and found that the childproof lock had been engaged. Crap. It felt like being locked in the back of a cop car, which I would have preferred.

A woman sat in the passenger seat, and although I didn't recognize her, I knew who it must be. "Ah, nurse Pamela New-some. Murder accomplice."

She glared at me momentarily and turned toward Manuel. "I

told you this old coot was interfering."

"Not to worry," Manuel said. "He won't be bothering us much longer."

Uh-oh. "Pamela, I thought you were responsible for watching the inmates. How did you break away from Hale Pohai?"

She brushed back her hair with her hand. "I'm off duty."

The puzzle pieces swirled in my head. I reviewed some of the pertinent information from my recent journal perusal. Then, like a lock clicking into place, everything fit. In spite of my situation, I laughed.

"What's so funny, old man?" Manuel asked.

"All of this. What a setup. It started when you and Sammy Malo sat at the table next to ours at the top of the Hibiscus Hotel. These coincidences go back to that one evening. You overheard my family mention a helicopter ride and Hale Pohai."

Manuel started the engine, and we tore out of the parking lot like a winged mammal out of Hades. "You definitely know too much."

"But the police will put it together as well. They'll nail you better than spikes in a two-by-four."

"I don't think so. You'll never have a chance to tell them."

"Oh, they already know," I bluffed. "It's a matter of time before they arrest both of you. Your hours are numbered."

"You told me the cops wouldn't catch on." Pamela gave Manuel a swat on the arm. "What are we going to do?"

"Don't listen to the old geezer."

Another note from my journal flashed into my mind. "And I saw you driving this very same car when you picked up the old transient near the Hibiscus Hotel. You thought I could identify you, and that's why you've been trying to kill me. You're also the one I saw running away from Hale Pohai after murdering Louise Kincaid. You and Pamela wanted to take over the operation from Sammy Malo and Louise."

Manuel turned his face partially toward me. "That was your mistake, old man. You were the only witness, and witnesses have to be eliminated." He gave me an evil, one-sided grin. "No witness to testify against me."

Crap. From what I read in my diary, I never got a good look at the driver or the running figure but inadvertently convinced him I had. "The police will figure it out. I wouldn't be surprised if they have a warrant for your arrests and are looking for both of you at this moment."

"Manuel," Pamela whined.

Manuel clenched the steering wheel. "Pamela, cool it. He's bluffing. No one else has figured this out."

"Nah, everyone knows. You had a homeless guy deliver an invitation to me for a free helicopter ride. When I went to claim it, that same guy was waiting at the yacht harbor to point out Sammy's body in the water. The transient then conveniently disappeared. The police at first suspected me of killing Sammy because I argued with him the night before, which you conveniently witnessed. How soon after that altercation did you whack Sammy and drop his body in the yacht harbor?"

Since he didn't answer, I continued to babble. "Now you're going to an awful lot of trouble for little old me."

"It's no trouble at all." Manuel snickered. "I'm enjoying this."

I looked behind me out the window hoping to see a police cruiser with its lights flashing following us. Nothing. "I don't share your enthusiasm."

"Sit back and savor the ride. It's your last. But buckle up. Wouldn't want you to be injured along the way."

Damn. I'd hoped we'd be pulled over because I wasn't wearing a seat belt. I hitched it up. "The police found a murder victim, an old homeless man. I bet that was the same guy you used to deliver the letter to me and point out where to look for Sammy in the yacht harbor. You killed that transient to eliminate, as you like to say, another witness."

Manuel didn't respond.

Being on a roll, I continued. "And the thing with Dex Tanaka of Tourist Air Tours. That was beautiful. We go for a ride with him and he fakes a landing so that we end up in your territory. Everyone acts like the helicopter was forced down, but you and Dex planned it."

Manuel slammed on the brakes, turned and pointed the gun at me. "I can shoot you right now if you don't shut up."

I held up my hands. "Okay, okay."

He started driving again and so did I. "You even tried to push me in the imu."

Manuel gave a snort. "Old men have balance problems."

"And you shot at me inside Diamond Head. I bet you poisoned my papaya at breakfast that one morning as well."

Manuel chuckled this time. "I thought that would get rid of you. You must have the constitution of a wild boar to have survived."

"I didn't appreciate that little stunt. It made my wife sick."

"Too bad you didn't eat it instead. Then we wouldn't have to bother with this trip."

Feeling my oats, I continued. "And, Pamela, since you knew where I was going with Meyer and Henry, you alerted your partners in crime. That's how you knew I'd be at the Kaneohe Yacht Club tonight and how a gang of thugs ended up at the Black Pearl the night of Henry's bachelor party where Snake Laka confronted that guy with the ponytail." I scratched my head. "I don't know why he did that."

"See, you're not as smart as you think you are, old man. Snake was trying to get rid of an undercover cop."

Another piece of the puzzle fit into place. "I bet the undercover cop dropped a lockbox key. Probably something he didn't want Snake to get his hands on. I'd speculate it goes to a lockbox where some serious drug money is stashed. That's why your buddy Kenny Keonu was so anxious to get it back."

Without taking his eyes off the road, Manuel threw his right arm back and hit me on the jaw.

I fell back in the seat, stunned.

"Quit your yammering. That's only a sample of what will happen to you later."

As my senses, whatever was left of them, returned, I considered my predicament. Cars came toward us in the other lane, briefly illuminating the crazed maniac driving me who knows where. We were traveling too fast for me to contemplate jumping out, and I was locked in anyway.

"I don't understand the business you're trying to do in a care home like Hale Pohai," I said once my head cleared.

Manuel chuckled. "It's part of my diversification plan. I'm working with people I've set up in a dozen care homes so far. People like Pamela work for me as well as hold jobs at the care homes. We have a whole new set of clientele. Great source of new revenue."

"That's all we need. Scum like you preying on older people who should be protected."

"It's the new economy." Manuel tapped out a happy beat with his hand on the steering wheel.

I didn't know how to get my aging body out of this predicament. I'd have to wait and see what Manuel planned to do.

A few minutes later, we swerved into a dirt parking area and skidded to a stop at a boat landing by Kaneohe Bay. I scanned in all directions. No one else in sight.

Manuel got out and yanked open the back door. "Out of the car."

"But I'm admiring the scenery."

He grabbed me by the collar and dragged me out.

"Easy does it," I said. "Don't crumple my jacket."

After receiving a poke in the ribs, I stumbled toward the bay. "Keep moving."

I took several more steps and looked over my shoulder, expecting to be shoved again. No one else in sight.

Manuel returned to the car and removed something from the trunk.

The faint light from the parking area reflected off metal.

Uh-oh. Manuel held a shotgun and a duffel bag.

"You going to blast me into pieces?"

He jogged up to where I stood. "No. I have something much better in mind for you."

"You planning to shoot a duck for my last meal?"

"Nope." He patted the barrel. "But it will help you with your final swim."

"I don't swim."

He cackled. "That's the point."

CHAPTER 29

I staggered along with Manuel periodically nudging me with the shotgun. I felt like a prisoner being led to a firing squad. I hadn't figured out what he intended to do to me. Part of me wanted to find out, but the majority of me wanted to be back at the wedding reception.

We arrived at a dock. He fiddled with a rope, jumped down into a motorboat and quickly tied a nearby aluminum rowboat behind it. He hopped back onto the swaying dock where I stood.

What was he going to do? I looked around. I squinted at the black town car where Pamela remained in the passenger's seat. Periodically, a car went by on the road, but no one bothered to turn into the parking lot. I looked out into the bay. No one there at this time of night. Overhead I again saw stars and the sliver of moon. They wouldn't do me any good.

Reaching in the duffel bag, Manuel took out a piece of cloth with dangling cords. "Slip your arms though the straps."

"What the hell is this?"

"It's a climbing harness. Perfect for scaling peaks. One of my hobbies. I want you to put it on backwards."

"I wouldn't know backwards from upside down."

"Push your arms through here." He thrust it toward me.

I pushed it away, but he grabbed my arm and twisted. I winced as a sharp pain shot through my elbow.

"Now, do as I say."

I followed his orders, my arm throbbing. This didn't make

any sense. Why a climbing harness by the ocean?

He began snapping interlocking pieces together. Each click made me flinch as if sealing my doom.

"There, old man. You're all set."

I felt like I'd been imprisoned in a strait jacket.

"Sit on the dock," he ordered me.

I complied, and he reached down into the rowboat and slipped a piece of rope under and around the metal bench-like seat. As he perched precariously leaning into the boat, I considered pushing him into the water, but I'd only have made him mad, and I couldn't have escaped anyway.

He stood holding the rope and proceeded to connect it to my back. After a moment he tethered me to the rowboat. I tried to reach behind my back, but was unable to stretch my arm enough to make contact with the spot where the rope connected.

"I don't understand why you have this contraption on me."

He laughed. "It's a protective device. I wouldn't want you to fall out of the boat and hurt yourself."

Yeah, right.

Next he unhooked the power boat from the dock.

"Into the rowboat," Manuel said.

"It doesn't look very stable to me."

"Don't give me any more lip or I'll show you what unstable is." He raised his arm, ready to deal me another blow.

I put up my hands. "Okay. Message received loud and clear. Give me a moment to maneuver into it."

I didn't like this one little bit. I lowered my creaking bones down onto the dock, dangled my legs over the boat and gingerly dropped into it. I hit hard enough that I thought I'd puncture a hole in the hull, but the aluminum shell held fast. The boat rocked back and forth with the impact. I grabbed the gunwales to steady the motion. My stomach lurched, but it wasn't from feeling seasick. I may have hated water, but I didn't plan to toss my cookies.

Once I steadied myself, I watched as Manuel jumped into the motorboat and fired up the engine. With a roar his boat took off, and in seconds the line between our boats went taut and my craft shot after his. I held on tight to the seat. We had a tag team boat trip in store for us until Manuel implemented whatever evil intent he had in mind.

"Aren't you forgetting Pamela?" I shouted. "You shouldn't leave her alone. You can't tell what might happen to her sitting there by herself."

"She's fine," Manuel called out. "I won't be gone that long anyway."

Uh-oh. How would I get out of this fix?

We sped onward, and the shoreline receded. The sliver of moon hung above the mountains, silhouetted against a faint blue residue of dusk. Lights from a few houses twinkled in the distance. The air remained warm as I stuck a finger in the water. Not that cold, but the temperature wasn't conducive to my idea of a pleasant swim, not that any swim was pleasant for me.

Manuel actually hummed a tune that sounded a little like the Beatles "Yellow Submarine." He was enjoying this. The same didn't hold for yours truly. Being in the middle of a large bay in the dark of night with a homicidal maniac wasn't my idea of evening entertainment. *Think.* What could I do? What would happen to me?

The most likely scenario, I imagined, entailed Manuel drowning me. Why else did he go to all this boat trouble? And with me swimming like a lead weight, that wouldn't take much doing. My eyes darted back and forth as I surveyed my craft. Anything here to help me? No paddles, no life vests, no Royal Canadian Mounted Police. I shuffled my feet around but encountered nothing other than the metal hull. I felt under the metal seat.

Ouch! I had cut my hand.

Then a thought occurred to me. I carefully felt under the seat again and found the metal protrusion, sharp as a knife blade. A part of the metal seat support had been ripped up, leaving a jagged edge. I grabbed the tether between both hands and began rubbing a section of the rope over the sharp metal lip.

I sawed like trying to fell a redwood in one minute. My arms ached as I continued to move the rope back and forth.

I lifted my head to make sure Manuel couldn't see what I was doing. He looked straight ahead, navigating his boat to some destination. I returned to my task and continued to saw the rope on the ragged metal.

The pitch of the motor changed, and we began to slow. *Uh-oh.* I needed to get the rope cut completely.

I sawed like mad.

Manuel looked back toward me for a moment.

I stopped my work and tried to look harmless.

His gaze returned forward.

I sawed again with all my might until my arms felt like they would fall off.

Finally, I heard a snap.

I had cut through the rope!

Catching my breath after the exertion, I adjusted the tether to hide from Manuel that it was no longer connected. I had freed myself from the rowboat, whatever good that would do.

I continued to gaze around the bay. Not another craft or person in sight. Only me and the shotgun-toting Manuel.

He cut the engine and we drifted slowly. I scanned the horizon again. We appeared to be smack in the middle of the bay. It had to be a mile to shore in any direction.

Manuel tugged on the line to my boat until it bumped against his. In the faint light I saw him fiddle with the rope until he untied it. My boat drifted free from his, two feet away. He stood up, raised his shotgun and pointed it toward me.

"Any last words, old man?"

"You'll never get away with this."

"You'll never know."

Then he fired.

CHAPTER 30

The shotgun blast reverberated in my ears. My hands flew to my chest. Had I been hit? I heard a gurgling sound. *Uh-oh.* Was that my blood draining away? I didn't feel any pain. Had I gone into shock from the loss of blood? I patted my chest again. Nothing felt damaged. I pulled my hand away from my chest and looked at it in the faint light. No blood. The gurgling sound became louder. Peering down, I saw water filling the rowboat.

A motor roared to life, and Manuel's boat raced away. A sense of relief surged through my old body at the sight of him departing. Then I realized my predicament.

The bastard had blasted a hole in the bottom of my boat. I gaped as water seeped in over my shoes. My surprise at being alive quickly changed to a gripping fear in my belly. The boat would sink out from under me, and I'd go down with the ship, given that I swam like a rock.

I needed to stem the flow of water into the boat. I put both shoes over the hole to try to cover it. That helped a little. I needed to find a way to stay afloat. *Think.*

I thought back to a survival course in the Navy during World War II. Use anything at hand in an emergency. Make something that floats. Make a bubble from a shirt. My shirt breathed air like a jet engine. It wouldn't hold a bubble. And I couldn't get my jacket or shirt off with the climbing harness confining me anyway. What could float?

Then I remembered. *Yes!* The balloons I'd stuffed in my

pocket earlier. I could inflate the balloons, although I'd have a hell of a time trying to hold onto a balloon while flailing toward shore. I huffed and puffed and blew one until it reached three inches in diameter, but it started deflating. Damn. It had a pin hole. I tossed it overboard and reached for another balloon. When this reached the right size, I tied it off.

Water kissed my calves. Good thing it was Hawaii and not California in December. I shivered in spite of the warm water and air.

Water lapped at my knees.

Double uh-oh. How much longer would the boat stay afloat?

Water soaked my pants above my knees.

I looked wildly around, not spotting anyone or anything to save me. The water covered the gunwales. Then the boat slipped away beneath me. Would I be sucked under like those people on the *Titanic*?

I clutched the balloon as I sank up to my neck.

Would it hold me?

I pushed down a rising wave of panic.

Be calm.

I put the balloon under my chin and clutched it as if holding a life preserver, which it would have to be.

There. My head floated secure above water.

I took a deep breath.

Bobbing from side to side, I stabilized myself.

I registered the shock of water gripping my chest. It pressed in on me. I had images of not being able to breathe.

I panted like a dog after a long run.

Stay calm.

I gained control of my breathing. My chest hadn't collapsed. I hadn't sunk yet. But I remained out in the middle of this huge bay.

Yikes. All kinds of creatures swam underneath me. Would

something come up and bite me? Would a shark drag me down into the depths and shred my decrepit body into bits?

Think positive. I had to reach shore.

Above the balloon, I spotted the sliver of moon to the west. I oriented my body in that direction and saw the lights of a car traversing the road near the shoreline. To the left shone the lights of several houses. Might as well head that direction.

I started paddling with one arm for all I was worth. Unfortunately, I wasn't worth very much. I didn't make much headway. *Keep paddling.* I held the balloon with one hand and splashed forward with the other arm thrashing like a seagull with a dislocated wing.

Now I started kicking.

Keep paddling.

I needed to keep my legs and one arm going, and that would heat my body. My legs were in pretty good shape from walking, but I hadn't done much to exercise my arms lately.

I had to give it my best.

I stroked and kicked until my arm and legs felt like strings of putty.

I gasped for breath and rested for a moment. As my feet settled below me, I again wondered what creatures lived in the ocean. I imagined a Kaneohe version of the Loch Ness monster grabbing my feet or a great white shark circling for the kill.

Keep focused.

I switched arms, careful not to lose hold of my flotation device, and started kicking and stroking again.

I had to think positive.

I remembered seeing Esther Williams and Red Skelton in the movie *Bathing Beauty* in the mid-1940s. I imagined being in a water ballet. I raised my free hand gracefully. Only difference— Esther Williams knew how to swim.

I looked up to make sure I was headed in the right direction.

The moon had disappeared, but I still saw the lights from the houses. I didn't want to swim around in circles and waste my energy needlessly.

The exertion seemed to help. Either that or I was getting used to the water.

I settled into a regular rhythm. Kick, kick, stroke. Kick, kick, stroke.

I imagined a pendulum moving back and forth as my arm flew forward and returned back through the water.

Mark Spitz would have been proud of me.

Damn. I actually swam like a wounded duck.

I spotted another car traversing the road along the bay.

Was I closer?

I had to think so.

Keep paddling.

I needed to keep the old body in motion.

Kick, kick, stroke. Kick, kick, stroke.

My arm ached. My legs felt like lead weights.

I paused to change arms again. *Don't lose your grip, you old coot.*

I couldn't give up. I had to keep going.

How did I end up in this situation?

The one saving grace—Manuel hadn't broken my neck with his hands or used the shotgun on me. I had to be thankful for that. I had to survive this swim and reach shore. Easy for someone younger, who knew how to swim.

Play through the pain.

It didn't matter how much my muscles hurt, the alternative was worse.

I gasped for breath. Would my old ticker give out? Would my arms and legs quit? Would I sink into a coma?

Then another predicament presented itself.

I needed to relieve myself.

Crap. I hated to pollute the bay, but I had no choice.

With that taken care of, I redirected my attention to the task of reaching shore.

Keep moving.

My achy limbs couldn't take this anymore. I came to a stop, and my feet sank beneath me.

After a few deep breaths, I focused on a spot on the bay and resumed paddling toward it.

I had to stay alive to finger Manuel.

I thrashed forward.

I heard a loud pop, and my chin hit water.

Damn. I lost my balloon.

I started sinking. I kicked frantically to bob back to the surface. I needed another balloon. I reached in my pocket, which caused me to sink again. My fingers touched a balloon. I tried to grab it but couldn't gain purchase. My head went under water. I kicked again and came up to gasp air. My fingers grasped the balloon. I pulled it out of my pocket, put it to my lips and blew. My head went under again, but I floated back to the surface with the help of a partially filled balloon. I blew again. This time it helped me stay afloat.

I gulped in air and rested. Once I caught my breath, I blew to make the balloon larger. After another rest break, I tied it off. I was safe again for the moment. I clutched the balloon for dear life.

I had to reach shore.

So tired. I only wanted to sleep. I almost nodded off but caught myself.

Keep moving, you old poop.

You can't die now. You have to reach land, contact Saito and Chun to nail Manuel.

With that motivation, I continued my sporadic kicking and one-handed stroke.

I had to keep going.

More lame stroking and more kicking.

I let my feet down.

Nothing.

Back to my kicking and pathetic one-handed stroke.

I looked toward shore. Crapola. I had a long way to go.

My legs felt like dead weight. I paused to let my feet sink again.

Contact!

What was going on? I remained in the middle of the bay, yet my feet rested on solid, not squishy, ground. I slithered my feet forward. I was able to stand. I peered ahead. I saw a small mound of sand. I had reached a sand bar.

CHAPTER 31

I pulled my aching body up onto the small spit of sand in the middle of Kaneohe Bay. I shivered as a breeze rippled through my clothes. I clutched my jacket close to my body for some protection. One thing for sure: I intended to get rid of the damn tie. I ripped if off, considered throwing it in the water and thought better of the idea. I might need it for something, as I had little with me. I stuffed it in my coat pocket.

Now that I was safe from immediate drowning, what should I do next? I squinted toward shore, too far to try swimming. I shivered again. Besides, I didn't want to tempt my fate in the water again. My balloons might not last, a shark might get me or I might have a heart attack. No, thank you. I decided I'd put my fate in the hands of the sandbar.

Exploring my new domain, I discovered it was three feet wide by ten feet long and reached a stunning altitude of two feet above the water line. Good thing Kaneohe Bay remained calm. If surf came in here, I'd be washed off in no time.

Another thought occurred to me. I didn't know if the tide was low or high. *Let's see.* The sun and moon had set, so they should be pulling the oceans that way. I gulped. That meant that this was probably low tide. Come midnight, the tide should come in. I wondered how much tidal difference there was here between high and low tide. Not like the Bay of Fundy. I'd expect several feet. I swallowed hard. Several feet would take away my sandbar.

I positioned myself on the top of Mount Jacobson, the highest part of the sandbar, and scanned the horizon. A periodic car traversed the road by the bay, a few house lights shone, but no rescue craft approached. It was just old me on my lonesome out here in the middle of nowhere. No dancing girls, no live bands, no nothing.

Trying to find something to occupy my mind, I began thinking up geezer jokes. When I next saw Jennifer, I'd have something to entertain her with. This continued for several hours as I registered a sequence of jokes in my mind. My mental systems continued to function—if what went on in my addled brain resembled functioning. I was so tired. My arms ached, my legs hurt, and I felt the onset of a headache. My age had caught up with me. I put my head down. I needed to rest.

My eyes snapped open as water washed into my mouth. I spat and coughed. I remembered where I was—on a sandbar in the middle of Kaneohe Bay. A thought occurred to me. I wouldn't remember this at all, if not for the little romp with Marion the previous morning.

My newfound home was awash. I stood to get my face out of the water. Seaweed covered my shoes. Hell's bells. How much more tide would be coming in? I checked my watch. It hadn't stopped from the effects of the ocean water. Marion's Christmas present to me really was waterproof.

The dial showed five minutes past midnight. I wasn't sure when the tide would start going out again. Would I have to stand up the whole rest of the night? Would the tide come up higher than to my shoes? Would I be back in the ocean, struggling to survive?

If so, I'd need my balloons. I reached in my pocket and found only one left. I'd have to protect it for an emergency. If I used up several balloons to reach this sandbar, I didn't have much confidence one balloon would get me the rest of the way to shore. I took in several panting breaths. I really needed to stay on the sandbar until someone rescued me.

Then I realized another problem. I needed to relieve myself again. Darn old bladder. I waded in so as not to foul the shallows. With that taken care of, I returned to the submerged peak of Mount Jacobson. The water reached my ankles. I wasn't able to lie down to sleep, which I wouldn't want to do anyway. If I fell asleep again, I'd forget everything, and I had a lot of news to share with my detective buddies, assuming I survived and got off this sandbar. With nothing better to do, I reviewed the recent life and times of Paul Jacobson.

The first night in Honolulu, we had dinner at the top of the Hibiscus Hotel. The party at the next table included Sammy Malo and Manuel Hiaka. Manuel had overheard our conversation. Later I had an altercation with Sammy Malo out on the sidewalk. This had apparently inspired Manuel to knock off his boss and take over the group of drug dealers Sammy controlled. Manuel had orchestrated an elaborate plot, which included having a homeless man leave an invitation for a free helicopter ride provided by Tourist Air Tours. The homeless man was told to wait by the yacht harbor for me to show up. There he directed my attention to the dead body in the water. That put suspicion on me because of the confrontation I'd had with Sammy the night before. Later I saw the homeless man get in a black town car, and I shouted at the driver. Although I didn't recognize Manuel at the time, he thought I had seen him.

When we took the helicopter ride, Dex Tanaka had faked a problem and landed where Manuel could take care of me permanently. Fortunately, the police raid saved Denny, Jennifer and me. And the events at the Hale Pohai care home. Louise Kincaid worked with Sammy Malo, gave drugs to Hattie Wilson and convinced Hattie to change her will. Louise probably intended to kill Hattie to reap the reward of her subterfuge. Instead, Manuel had done away with Louise, in this case casting suspicion on Henry. And I had seen Manuel running away. By shouting at him, I gave the impression I had seen him, another reason he needed to eliminate me as a witness. And Manuel had this plan of infiltrating care homes all over the island to boost his illegal drug business.

What a mess my sorry behind had plunked into. Manuel made numerous attempts on my life to get rid of me as he had done with the homeless man—a shove into an imu, a poisoned papaya, gunshots at Diamond Head, throwing a can of Spam at me, trying to drop a rock on my head at Waimea Falls and finally this little stunt here in Kaneohe Bay.

And those other incidents of damage to Denny's white SUV, which I thought at first the drug mob caused, turned out instead to be the work of a psycho protestor. But so far I had survived. And Pamela Newsome had provided Manuel with a running account of where I'd be from the information gleaned during my visits to Hale Pohai. I had witnessed an altercation in the parking lot of the Black Pearl where Snake Laka had almost killed the ponytail guy, an undercover cop. I had found a lockbox key, now in Detective Saito's hot little hand. The drug gang wanted that back, and Kenny Keonu had accosted me to reclaim the key. So much to share with Detectives Saito and Chun. So how the hell would I get off this spit of wet sand?

Periodically, I pushed the button to light up my watch. The time passed oh, so slowly. At two-thirty-five with my legs and back aching, I noticed the water receding. Enough sand had been uncovered to allow me to sit down. I hunched my knees against my chest. I felt sleepy again. I pinched my cheek. I needed to stay awake. No nodding off.

I watched the sky and after a time saw a shooting star. I remembered as a kid the wonder of seeing one for the first time. Crazy old coot. I remembered vividly events like this from childhood. Too bad the last six years or so of my life had disappeared into the fog.

A middle-of-the-night fear seized my chest. What if I didn't make it until daylight? What if I had a heart attack and my body was washed out to sea? Then a wave a sadness passed through me. What was I doing out here? What had I accomplished in my life? What did I regret?

I took a deep breath and tried to calm my jangled nerves. Regrets. I regretted not hitting a home run in Little League when I came to bat with two outs, a runner on first and my team behind by one run. I regretted having only one kid, but Denny was the only one who popped out. I regretted not being able to stop the spread of cancer in my first wife, Rhonda. I supposed I could have helped people more during my life; I could have been a better neighbor. On the other hand, I never took advantage of people. I ran an honest business, provided needed products and treated my customers with respect. I had no regrets regarding anything that had happened to me in the last few years because I couldn't remember those years. That might have been the only benefit of my defective memory.

Regrets. Maybe I should have written a great novel or painted a Mona Lisa, but that wasn't me. I was a plain old guy, doing my thing, not causing a ruckus and trying to make my contribution in my own small way. And I had been blessed with not one, but now two, wonderful wives. It was a miracle that either of them put up with me. All of these thoughts swirled in my decrepit brain. I supposed I had some regrets, but on the whole I had lived a good life. I clenched my fist. And I'd be damned if I'd allow it to end on this spit of sand.

After continuing to review my life for several hours, out to sea I noticed a faint glow along the horizon from my old friend, Sol, ready to light the day. Within half an hour the sun rose, as did my hopes. Surely someone would be out in the bay in a boat soon. The sun continued its upward journey. No one appeared. Where were the early-morning fishermen?

My throat and lips felt dry and rough as sandpaper. So much useless water around me. My stomach growled. I hadn't eaten anything since the wedding reception. Off in the distance I saw a fishing boat. I waved my hands, but the boat kept on its merry way without changing direction toward me.

The sun continued to climb in the sky, and sweat formed on my forehead. I'd get sunburned out here. I wrapped the tie around my forehead and continued to squat on Mount Jacobson. Periodically, I stood to stretch my legs and survey all directions.

I spotted a little motor boat off in the distance, but, in spite of my frantic signaling, it puttered along the shore and disappeared around a bend in the coast. Damn unobservant people. Where was the Coast Guard when I needed guarding?

A small plane flew overhead. I hoped it would spot me and circle to call attention to my plight. I waved my hands in the air, but it continued on its way.

Off in the distance I saw a sailboat. It luffed, and I watched the sunlight strike the sparkling white mainsail. It was too far off to see me. I hoped it would continue in my direction. I kept a close watch as it sailed toward me. It turned, aiming toward the open sea. "No," I shouted. "Come back this way!"

I waved my tie in the air. No good. An idea occurred to me. I aimed the dial of my shiny new watch so the sunlight reflected off it toward the sailboat. I kept jiggling my wrist back and forth hoping that someone on the sailboat would see the reflection. I paused and waved my tie again, before resuming to flash my watch at them.

The sailboat made no correction to its course but continued on. I waved and flashed, waved and flashed. I had almost given up, when I noticed the sailboat turning toward me. I kept up my signaling. They had seen me!

I reattached the tie around my forehead as I waited.

The sailboat came within twenty yards and dropped its sails and an anchor. "Help," I croaked.

A dinghy was launched. I felt a little dingie myself.

The skiff rowed toward me. I blinked in the bright sunlight. Was I imagining things? No, I definitely recognized the occupant. It was Madeline.

She scraped the little boat onto my sandbar and jumped out. "Where the hell did you go to last night, jerk, and how did you end up here?"

"Nice to see you too, Madeline."

"Climb aboard."

I wasted no time clambering in. Madeline pushed off and jumped in before rowing me back to the sailboat.

She shouted up, "Henry, looked what the sea puked up. The missing best man."

Henry looked over the side of the sailboat. "Hey, jerk. I thought you bailed on me during the reception."

"No, Henry. I would have stuck around, but a drug dealer kidnapped me and tried to turn me into fish bait."

"You look like a pirate," Henry said.

I realized my tie had slipped down over one eye. I removed it and stuck it in my jacket pocket.

"Too bad you missed the excitement," Madeline said as she pushed me up the ladder. "Jennifer decorated my car with shaving cream."

"Yeah, I remember her doing that."

As I landed on the deck, Madeline stood over me like an Amazon warrior. "I thought you couldn't remember things from the day before."

I scooted back for fear that she might stomp me with one of

her oak-like legs. "Once in a while I remember overnight."

Madeline reached an arm out and dragged me to my feet as if lifting a tinker toy. "You have one fine granddaughter."

"Yeah, she's a beaut," I replied.

Madeline tossed me a water bottle, and I greedily gulped the cool liquid. She dispensed with any further conversation and focused on sailing the boat. She raised the anchor, set the sails, and in moments we took off like the wind, actually in the wind. Henry and I didn't need to do anything other than gawk as Madeline dashed back and forth, adjusting sails and spinning the wheel.

Once she had everything shipshape, I asked, "Do you have some way of contacting my son and Detective Saito of the Kaneohe police?"

"Sure do. I have my radio."

"Is your car at the yacht club?"

"With all of Jennifer's artwork still on it."

"Good. If you can drive me to the Hale Pohai care home, tell my son and Detective Saito to meet us there as soon as possible."

"Snookums, keep us on this course."

"Yes, Admiral." Henry jumped up and grabbed the wheel.

I arched an eyebrow. Henry had learned to be polite.

Madeline disappeared below deck and soon reappeared to announce, "All set up." She wrinkled her nose at me. "What's that contraption on your back?"

"A climbing harness. Would you be kind enough to remove it?"

Madeline reached over and unsnapped the connections behind my back and dropped the harness onto the deck.

I felt much more comfortable.

Madeline waved a large hand. "Have a seat and enjoy the

ride." She wrested the steering from Henry. He eagerly returned to his life of leisure beside me.

Spray kicked up in my face, and I held on tight. Given my hate–hate relationship with the ocean, I didn't feel comfortable being out here, but it beat flapping around holding a balloon or sitting on a water-swamped sandbar.

In no time at all, Madeline sailed back to the Kaneohe Yacht Club, moored up and ushered us ashore.

I resisted the urge to kiss the ground.

We climbed into her Corvette with Henry on my lap in the passenger's seat.

"Don't get too cozy, you two," Madeline said. She stomped on the gas and shot out of the parking lot, practically pushing Henry through my innards.

I rubbed Henry on the top of his bald head and said, "I think this is the beginning of a beautiful friendship."

We pulled into the parking area at Hale Pohai, sending a cloud of dust into the air. Henry tumbled out, and I gave a sigh of relief over surviving with nothing worse than a dented lap. At that moment I saw Pamela Newsome race out the door and head for her car. "Stop her!" I shouted.

In two gigantic steps Madeline stood alongside Pamela's old silver Honda, her hands on her hips, blocking the door.

"Out of my way," Pamela shouted.

Madeline crossed her arms over her large bosom. "I don't think so."

Pamela reached in her purse and pulled out a switchblade, which she clicked open.

Henry and I both gasped at the same time.

Madeline chuckled. "Oh, looky. A toy knife." With a lightning-fast movement of her arm, she knocked the switchblade away, twisted Pamela's wrist and dropped her to the ground. "Henry, pick up the knife."

"Yes, sweet cakes." Henry scampered over and retrieved the weapon.

Madeline raised her head toward me. "Jerk, go inside and get some duct tape."

"Yes, sweet cakes." I galumphed into the care home and found Meyer and Hattie sitting on the couch holding hands in front of a rerun of a *Seinfeld* show on TV. "Know where to find some duct tape?"

"Paul," Meyer shouted. "Everyone's been looking for you."

"Madeline and Henry found me. I need to get some duct tape to wrap up a little business."

"There should be some in the first kitchen drawer on the left," Hattie said.

I regarded her. She had changed from stuck-in-one-groove lady to memory woman. I dashed into the kitchen and, sure enough, found a gray roll where directed. I ran past the happy couple and went outside to find Madeline standing with her foot on Pamela's chest.

Madeline grabbed the duct tape out of my hand and before you could say "gift wrap," she bound Pamela like a packaged ham. Madeline tucked Pamela under her arm and carried her inside.

Henry and I followed. I elbowed Henry. "You mind your Ps and Qs, or you'll end up like that—a trussed Thanksgiving turkey."

"Ain't she a beaut?"

When I entered the living room, Meyer stood next to Madeline, who had her foot on a struggling, swaddled Pamela Newsome.

"I can't see that well, but this doesn't look like a normal way to treat our nurse," Meyer said.

"That's because your nurse was part of the twosome that

kidnapped me last night. She's in like Flynn with the drug dealers."

Madeline eyed her package on the floor and dusted her hands. "Any other scum needing attention?"

Hattie looked up from watching the television show. "Yes, there might be one other person to deal with. When Pamela saw your car pulling into the parking area, she spoke on her cell phone and told someone named Manuel to come finish the business. Then she ran outside."

Uh-oh. "Any sign of Denny or Detective Saito?" I asked.

Meyer shook his head. "You're the first visitors this morning."

The door burst open, and Manuel planted his feet in the entryway, a gun pointing directly at me.

CHAPTER 32

I gulped at the sight of Manuel, his large nose throbbing and his trigger finger twitching. Here I thought I'd escaped him, and he showed up again like a bad penny.

"Well, well. How the hell did you end up here alive, Mr. Jacobson?" He pointed his gun right at my chest.

In spite of my dry mouth, I tried to compose myself and act as nonchalant as possible. "Stuff happens."

"Look what these lunatics did to me," Pamela bellowed from the floor. "Do something. Get me untied."

"Would this help?" Henry flicked open the switchblade.

Manuel's eyes darted from Pamela to Henry. In that brief moment, Madeline stepped in front of Manuel. With lightning-fast movements she wrenched the gun out of his hand, kneed him in the groin and punched him in the jaw.

He dropped like a sack of fertilizer.

Madeline looked down with a snarl on her large lips and put her foot on Manuel's throat. "Make my day, scumbag."

Upon this happy scene, Detective Saito arrived.

"You can arrest these two for the murder of Louise Kincaid and for the kidnapping of one Paul Jacobson," I announced. "You should be able to clean up a whole lot of crimes today, Detective Saito. Manuel Hiaka also whacked Sammy Malo and a homeless man."

"I sense that you have a lot to tell me, Mr. Jacobson." Saito's jaw worked overtime as he chomped on his gum.

"Darn tootin'. How much time do you have?"

"All the time it takes as soon as I take care of these two suspects."

Saito took out his phone to summon backup. Then he leaned over to examine Manuel and patted the slimebag's cheek.

Manuel regained consciousness. "Get this Amazon's foot off me." He gagged.

"I'll take it from here," Saito said.

Madeline removed her foot.

Manuel made a grab for Madeline's leg.

She sidestepped as Manuel's hand missed her leg by inches. Without a wasted motion, she kicked him in the side of the head.

Manuel returned to his unconscious state, lying sprawled on the floor with his mouth wide open as if trying to catch flies.

"Some people never learn," Madeline said.

After two police cars arrived to escort Pamela and Manuel to awaiting cozy jail cells, Marion, Denny, Allison and Jennifer came running into the care home.

"Grandpa, you're okay!" My granddaughter gave me a huge hug. My wife, son and daughter-in-law joined in for a family embrace, and I felt like the luckiest guy in the world.

After I emerged from the group love-in, Saito tapped me on the shoulder. "I hate to interrupt, but I need to get a statement from you."

I sat down to recount my latest adventures. I explained how Manuel Hiaka caused my recent problems and his link with the helicopter business.

"We'll have to look into Tourist Air Tours." Saito scribbled notes on his pad. "I'll get in touch with Detective Chun right away."

"You'll find something else interesting with that outfit. When we took our tour, they logged in cash received of nineteen hundred dollars. I don't think that was a legitimate payment. Since Dex was linked to the drug dealers, I have a hunch that Tourist Air Tours served as a front to launder drug money. Get a warrant for their financial records. I bet you'll find a lot of cash payments for helicopter trips that were probably nothing more than surveillance flights for the drug dealers."

Saito continued to madly write notes.

"And Manuel killed a homeless man. From what I read in my journal, Detective Chun showed me a picture of an old bearded man killed with a knife. That was the same man who left the helicopter invitation for me and later directed me to Sammy's body in the yacht harbor." I smacked my forehead. "I may have saved the envelope used to deliver the helicopter invitation. I'll have to check for it back in our hotel room."

"You're a wealth of information, Mr. Jacobson."

"I'm just getting started. And the death of Louise Kincaid. Manuel and Pamela Newsome teamed up for that one. And Manuel had a scheme going in care homes. He infiltrated his people into a number of care facilities to scam unsuspecting senior citizens." I pointed to Hattie Wilson. "Louise Kincaid drugged this woman and tried to take advantage of her financially. Louise worked with Sammy Malo, and Manuel wanted to take over the operation. He took out Louise, so Pamela could keep the drug business going here. Louise provided medication to a number of care homes, and Manuel knew when she'd be at Hale Pohai, so he came here to whack her. Detective, you'll want to check at other care homes to find what Manuel put in place."

Saito smiled. "You never cease to amaze me with what you discover."

I opened my hands. "That's what we geezers do. And remember I told you before how Snake Laka attacked the guy with a ponytail and I found the lockbox key—the one I gave you. Anything new on that?"

Saito nodded. "We were able to track down the location. With a search warrant we discovered a lockbox with gold bullion."

"Earned from illegal drug dealings."

"Exactly, Mr. Jacobson. We greatly appreciated your assistance."

"Always willing to oblige. The final event occurred after the wedding last night. Manuel and Pamela abducted me. Manuel took me out into Kaneohe Bay to drown me and sink my body into the depths, but I managed to escape." I went through the details and my timely rescue by Madeline and Henry. "Then we came here and Madeline apprehended the thugs."

Detective Saito shook his head. "Man, I'd like to have her on our police force."

"I think she has other plans." I pointed to Henry and Madeline smooching on the couch as they sat next to Meyer and Hattie, who held hands. "The air is full of romance."

Once the confusion was sorted out, we headed outside to get in our vehicles. As Madeline approached her red Corvette, a cockroach scurried across the driveway.

"Eek!" she shouted and jumped into Henry's arms.

Henry staggered, holding the large woman as if hoisting bags of sand.

The miniscule brain, which had allowed the cockroach species to survive since the time of the dinosaurs but apparently went lacking in this one particular specimen, sent signals causing it to scamper back toward Henry.

Madeline clutched her new husband tighter and shouted, "Do something!"

In the manner of all knights since the days of King Arthur, Henry responded. He somehow lifted a foot while holding the immense burden and brought his foot down, unceremoniously dispatching the offending bug.

Madeline gave her man a kiss on the top of his head. "My hero. Ain't he a beaut?"

CHAPTER 33

We waved as Madeline and Henry drove off to head back to the yacht club and resume their sailing trip to Lahaina. I looked around the garden at the side of the care home, admiring the hibiscus bushes and the flowering plumeria trees. The bad guys and gals were in custody. All was good in the universe.

That was until Detective Saito came running out of the house. "Before you leave, I have some news for you. I spoke with Detective Silva in Waianae. They rounded up a number of the drug gang. Unfortunately, Snake Laka escaped. Snake thinks you have the lockbox key, Mr. Jacobson, so I want you to be careful."

"Great. Now I have an angry snake after me. What's his real name, Detective?"

"Snake's not a nickname. That *is* his real name. His father named his other kids Spider and Mongoose."

"Sounds like one big happy family."

Denny grabbed Detective Saito's sleeve. "I'm concerned. Can you provide police protection for my father?"

"I'll call Detective Chun in Honolulu and see if he can arrange for someone to watch your hotel room until we apprehend Snake Laka."

On that encouraging note, we climbed into the unmolested blue Denny-mobile and headed back to Waikiki.

"I see you went with a color other than white," I commented.

Denny let out a sigh of disappointment. "With you and Allison harassing me, I caved in."

Allison punched Denny in the shoulder. "You didn't have any choice." She turned her head toward me. "Paul, when we went to get a new SUV this morning, the car rental agency had completely run out of white."

"Good thing," I said.

Our commute back to Honolulu passed uneventfully, and to my surprise, a police officer met us in the lobby of the Hibiscus Hotel. He was a tall, lanky young man who introduced himself as Officer Baang. I thought that an appropriate name and figured he would be a good replacement for Madeline as bodyguard and protector of my family and me.

He escorted us to our rooms, checked inside first and positioned himself on a chair in the hall outside. I wondered what the other guests would think of that. We could pretend to be in the witness protection program awaiting new identities, maybe the O'Jacobsons, escaped ex-Boston racketeers, or the Jacobellis from the Chicago mob.

The first thing I did once we were back in our room was to search for the helicopter invitation envelope. I opened the desk drawer. Bingo. There it sat. I would give it to Detective Chun the next time I saw him.

Jennifer was anxious to go surfing. I begged off, saying I needed to take a nap. Marion reminded me to update my diary before I did the Jacobson memory reset, so I sat down at the desk to perform my duty while she, Denny and Allison escorted Jennifer to the beach. It took me a good long while to recount the prior day's events, and finally, I put down my pen, yawned and settled under the covers for a little shuteye.

Before I even began counting sheep, I heard a "bang" outside my room. I jumped out of bed and galloped over to the door peephole and peeked out. A man with a patch over his eye stood there.

Uh-oh. I reassessed the noise I had heard. It wasn't a gunshot; instead, it was more the sound of someone being bashed over the head. I raced to the phone and hit the operator button. When a pleasant woman's voice answered, I gasped, "Have hotel security come to my room immediately and call the police. A wanted man named Snake Laka is trying to get in my room. He has a patch over his eye and looks like an angry pirate."

The door shook as a fist pounded on it.

I cleared my throat and tried my best high-pitched female voice impersonation. "Who's there?"

"Room service."

"Just a moment. I'm not presentable."

I shuffled around, trying to stall as long as possible.

More pounding on the door. "Open up."

"Be patient, honey."

I clomped around again.

Snake began to kick the door. It shuddered but held. The kicking continued and splinters began falling into the room. I looked around frantically for somewhere to hide. Then I remembered the adjoining room. I went through the inner door and locked it behind me. I heard a crashing sound. The outer door to my room must have given way. Heavy footsteps echoed inside my room. I opened the front door of Denny's room and peered out into the hallway. Officer Baang lay sprawled on the floor. Loud banging shook the inner door. I stepped back inside the room and realized my mistake. I had locked Denny's side of the inner door but had left my room's side open. Snake knew where I was. The inner door started to splinter. Damn. Pirate Boy must have been wearing hobnailed boots.

Time to retreat. I dashed into the hallway and raced as fast as my old legs could carry me toward the stairwell. I almost reached it when a shot rang out. Plaster struck my face from the wall next to me. I heard another shot and simultaneously ran into a man the size of a bulldozer emerging from the stairwell. He wore the blazer of hotel security. I crumpled to the floor.

Everything was happening too fast for a geezer my age. I turned on my side and saw Officer Baang sitting with his gun in his hand and Snake Laka lying in a pool of blood on the hallway floor. The officer had regained consciousness and lived up to his name.

CHAPTER 34

I sat in my room, trying to lower my blood pressure to an appropriate level for a geezer my age. Needless to say, I remained too keyed up to take a nap. Just as well. I needed to have my memory intact to report all that had happened.

When Detective Chun arrived to take my statement, I gave him the envelope used for the helicopter invitation. "An old man delivered this to the front desk of the Hibiscus Hotel. If you check for fingerprints, you'll probably find a match with those of the homeless man who was stabbed."

Detective Chun gave me a sly grin. "You remember things pretty well for someone who claims memory loss."

"With my good recollection during the day and my journal, I get by."

Detective Chun led me to an office at the lobby level. As he rubbed the wart on his hand, I told of Snake overpowering Officer Baang, my stalling tactics and my attempt to escape.

"You're lucky Snake didn't hit you with the shot he fired."

"Darn right. Fortunately, your officer was a better shot."

After I ran out of useful information, Detective Chun departed, saying he had a doctor's appointment, and I went to the front desk to make arrangements for my family and me to be moved to new rooms.

"I'm sorry, we have no adjoining rooms of the same size," the clerk informed me.

I scowled as images ran through my mind of us being

crammed into a janitor's closet. "What have you got?"

"Well, I can put you in one of our deluxe adjoining suites." He clicked on his keyboard for a few seconds. "There will be no extra charge."

"We can handle that."

I completed the arrangements by the time my seafaring family returned. Jennifer skipped along, laughing, with Marion and Allison following in animated conversation while Denny traipsed behind with an armful of towels.

"Paul, I thought you'd be sleeping." Marion came up and gave me a kiss on the cheek.

"Nah. I decided to spend some time with Snake Laka instead."

"What?" Denny shouted.

"Not to worry. It's all taken care of. But we will be moving into new rooms."

"Why's that?" Allison asked.

"Oh, merely a few minor issues. With doors kicked in and blood in the hallway, I thought we might like some new scenery."

Marion tsked. "I don't know what I'm going to do with you, Paul. You can't be left on your own for two hours without getting in trouble."

"I know. The story of my life." I handed Denny one of the new room keys. "You can relax in the new suite. It'll probably be a while before we're allowed back in our old rooms to move our possessions."

"Maybe I'll go back to the beach," Jennifer said.

"No, it's getting too late and will be dark soon." Denny looked at his watch. "I hope they let us pack our clothes soon. It's almost time for dinner."

"Are you ready to go to our new room, Paul?" Marion asked.

"Not yet. I'm too keyed up. I think I'll take a little stroll. You want to join me?"

Marion shook her head. "No, I think I'll relax in the room."

I gave her a room key and meandered out on the patio that overlooked the yacht harbor. I watched people walking along the quay. Quite a sequence of events. It was over.

CHAPTER 35

The next day I awoke in my usual muddle, but a beautiful woman coaxed me into reading my journal to make everything clear. I shook my head in amazement. For a retired auto parts store owner, I sure ended up in a lot of trouble. Then again, I wasn't one to sit around picking my nose and letting the world pass by.

After a leisurely breakfast with my clan, we headed back up to our rooms. The ladies did some organizing, while Denny and I sat out on my balcony.

"These are sure luxurious rooms," I said.

"Even better than the ones we stayed in for the last two weeks. It was a hassle repacking and moving our things last night, but we can enjoy these rooms for another day before we head back to the mainland tomorrow."

"You mean our vacation's almost over?"

"Yeah, but it's been exciting." Denny sucked on his lip for a moment. "I've been thinking more about what you and I discussed earlier on the trip."

"You'll have to refresh me on that subject."

"My job and wanting to paint again."

My clunky brain pulled back what I'd read in my journal. "Okay. Got it."

"Allison and I have continued to discuss it, and I've reached a decision."

I turned toward him. "I trust you're not going to run off to

Tahiti to paint naked women."

"No. Allison and I plan to take photography and painting classes, respectively. I'll paint on weekends as I can work it in. As you suggested, I can do more later after Jennifer goes off to college and moves out on her own. And best of all, I now know what I want to do when I retire."

"Makes sense."

Inside the room, the phone rang. Marion answered and in a moment came out on the balcony. "It's for you, Paul."

I ambled inside and found Detective Chun on the line requesting my appearance at the Honolulu Police Department.

"You going to lock me up for something?" I asked.

"No, Mr. Jacobson. We want to thank you for your assistance."

"Well, in that case I'll show up."

"Please bring your whole family."

So rather than going to the beach to increase the stock price of some sunscreen company, we assembled, and Denny drove us to the police station on Beretania Street. There we were ushered into a meeting room and found Detectives Chun, Saito and Silva waiting. I recognized them by the name badges they wore. A woman, a young man and a girl Jennifer's age also stood there.

Jennifer squealed. "Hina, I didn't expect to see you here."

"My mom, Keoki and I came to your grandpa's ceremony because he's a hero." Hina gave Jennifer a hug.

We were offered coffee and special police malasadas, the kind with extra sugar. The adults partook of coffee, and Jennifer, Hina, Keoki, Denny and I agreed to gobble malasadas while the ladies demurred in order to maintain their svelte figures.

Once we settled in to slurp and chomp, Detective Chun stood. A bandage covered his hand.

"You punch out a villain?" I asked.

"No, Mr. Jacobson. I took your advice and had my wart removed yesterday so I wouldn't be rubbing it all the time. I want to mention to you that we did match fingerprints on the envelope you gave us with the homeless homicide victim."

"Imagine that." I regarded Detective Saito. "No gum chewing today, Detective."

"No. I've gone cold turkey. No smoking. No gum."

"You gentlemen are a tribute to your departments," I replied.

They looked at each other, and I imagined them giving each other mental fist bumps.

Chun said, "The reason we asked you to stop by, Mr. Jacobson, is that we want to summarize what you've helped with these last two weeks. With your assistance we have solved the murders of Sammy Malo, Louise Kincaid and a homeless man. You also saved the life of Benny Makoku."

"Who's Benny Makoku?"

"That's my daddy," Hina shouted.

"He was an undercover narcotics officer Snake Laka tried to kill in the parking lot of the Black Pearl," Detective Saito said.

I remembered a reference in my journal. "Oh, yeah. The guy with the ponytail, who Manuel Hiaka said was an undercover cop."

"That's right." Chun looked at a notepad. "When Officer Makoku's cover was blown, Snake tried to kill him. Your intervention saved his life."

I shrugged. "I happened to stick my nose into something going on in the parking lot. Nothing more than that."

"But that provided the diversion necessary for Officer Makoku to escape," Chun said. "Under arrest are Manuel Hiaka, Kenny Keonu, Pamela Newsome and Dex Tanaka. Snake Laka would also be in jail except he was killed by Officer Baang when Snake tried to shoot you."

"And I'm mighty appreciative that Officer Baang saved me."

Chun nodded. "He did his job, but we want to show our appreciation to you, Mr. Jacobson, for your contribution in helping to solve a long list of crimes. As a result of information you provided, we have an investigation going on at a number of care homes on the island regarding Manuel Hiaka's scheme to scam residents. Finally, we have closed down Tourist Air Tours and seized their records. As you suggested, Mr. Jacobson, the business served as a front for the local drug cartel and provided a convenient means for money laundering."

"You can thank my granddaughter and my wife's grandson for that idea," I said. "My step-grandson did some research and sent a message to my granddaughter on the subject of money laundering. That's where the suggestion came from."

Detective Chun continued his spiel. "In that case, your whole family has certainly helped our investigation. Tourist Air Tours logged helicopter trips on their books where no tourists actually flew. They registered cash payments from drug money, as if the tourist trips had taken place. They also used the helicopter flown by Dex Tanaka to survey the marijuana growing areas and to alert the growers of any police activity in the area. The drug gang had surveillance, and at the same time used those flights as a means to funnel drug cash into a supposed legitimate business. Quite an operation."

"Glad to help."

Detective Saito stood up. "And in regards to the investigation in Kaneohe, Mr. Jacobson. You called attention to a brownie given to Mrs. Hattie Wilson by one of the victims, Louise Kincaid. As you suggested, we did a chemical analysis and found that the brownie recovered the night of the murder was laced with marijuana as well as a drug called scopolamine, which causes memory loss. Louise Kincaid drugged Hattie Wilson and manipulated her to change her will. Again, thanks to your efforts, things have been rectified for Mrs. Wilson."

"That's good to know," I said. "I think Meyer Ohana is enjoying Hattie Wilson having her marbles back."

"Please join us at the front of the room," Detective Saito said.

I stood and ambled up to join Chun, Saito and Silva.

Chun handed me a certificate, and Saito opened a box revealing a medal with a striped ribbon. He attached it to my lapel.

"For your contribution and bravery, we're awarding you the civilian medal of honor," Chun announced.

Everyone clapped their hands.

I felt my cheeks grow warm. All this for little old me.

"Would you like to say a few words, Mr. Jacobson?" Detective Chun asked.

I cleared my throat. "I'm lucky to be alive. As with my memory, where I need assistance from my wife and granddaughter and the journal I keep, I couldn't have accomplished anything alone. From what I read in my diary, Madeline Hightower, Fredricka Falcone and Officer Baang contributed as much or more than I did. Thank you."

I sat down to a round of applause.

Afterward while we chatted, Jennifer came up to Detective Saito and asked, "Do you still collect butterflies?"

"Yes, I do."

"Grandpa, you probably don't remember, but Detective Saito gave you mounted butterflies as a present when you lived at the Kina Nani retirement home."

"If you say so."

Marion came up and gave me a kiss. "You can add this certificate and medal to your collection of police souvenirs back in Venice Beach. You have others on your dresser."

"Imagine that."

"You should also know that we have a similar civilian medal of honor to award to Madeline Hightower when she returns

from her honeymoon on Maui and to Fredricka Falcone," Saito
said. "We held this ceremony for you today because we know
you're returning to the mainland tomorrow."

I turned to Marion. "Too bad we have to leave so soon."

"That's right. Back to California for us and back to Colorado
for Denny, Allison and Jennifer. Jennifer has school and Denny
his work."

I patted Jennifer on the arm. "You'll have to suffer through
school again."

"I like school, but this has been a cool vacation. Surfing,
sightseeing, being scared and catching criminals. Maybe I'll
become a journalist when I grow up and be on the crime beat."

Marion hugged her. "You change career ideas as often as
your grandfather gets involved in crimes."

"Yup. I have lots of options. I need to call Austin and tell him
you received an award, Grandpa." Jennifer pulled out her cell
phone and skipped away.

Back at the hotel Denny found an envelope waiting for him at
the front desk. He opened it, read a letter, snorted and handed
the sheet of paper to me. I scanned the correspondence from
Ace Car Rental Company: "Dear Mr. Jacobson. Due to the fact
that you ran through our complete Honolulu fleet of white
SUVs, damaged four of them, including one twice, and had
another stolen, we request that you do no more business with
our company."

I handed the letter back to Denny. "Seems only fair. I don't
know what's happened to you, son. I trained you to take better
care of cars than that."

Denny glared at me and stomped off.

I winked at Jennifer. "I think your dad has lost his sense of
humor."

Allison and Marion followed Denny upstairs, but Jennifer

motioned me to a couch on the side of the lobby. "Grandpa, any new geezer jokes for me?"

"Sure. Try this. How old do you have to be to be a geezer?"

"Older than dirt?" Jennifer answered.

"Yeah, that too, but here's the real answer. You're a geezer when you're too old to take advice but still young enough to give it."

She nodded her head. "That's why you never take my mom's advice to quit telling geezer jokes."

"You got it, kiddo." I spotted a large woman striding across the lobby toward us. That could be only one person—Fredricka Falcone. "Uh-oh. No more telling geezer jokes with Fredricka on the prowl."

Fredricka grabbed my hand. "I understand you're leaving tomorrow, Paul."

"That's right. Back to the mainland."

She bit her large lip. "I'm going to be taking off in a few days as well. I've decided to give Hollywood a shot." She preened for us. "Don't you think I'm a shoe-in to become a white Queen Latifah?"

Before I answered, she waved to someone across the lobby. "Oh, Lenny, wait for me." She shot off in a cloud of pikake perfume.

"Quite a woman," I said.

"You make the most interesting friends, Grandpa. Now that she's gone, you need to tell me some more geezer jokes."

"Okay. While stuck on the sandbar, I entertained myself by thinking up geezer jokes. Fortunately, I later documented them before doing the overnight Jacobson memory reset. So here goes. How can you tell you're a geezer?"

"Go ahead."

"You know you're a geezer when you spend more time reading the obituaries than the front page."

Jennifer giggled.

"You know you're a geezer when you spend more time trimming hair from your nose and your ears than the top of your head."

"Good one."

"You know you're a geezer when you wake up in the morning and something hurts but you have no clue what caused it." Seeing from Jennifer's smile that I was on a roll, I continued. "You know you're a geezer when you keep telling the same story over and over again, but people your age don't notice any difference."

"Ooh, ooh, I have one," Jennifer said. "You know you're a geezer when the highlight of your day is taking a nap."

"Yep. And you know you're a geezer when the small print really is."

Jennifer bounced up and down, getting into the spirit of this. "You know you're a geezer when it's easier to pop your joints than a pop top."

"You know you're a geezer when your yard . . ." I paused and stretched out my arms. ". . . keeps growing larger and larger. And the grand finale. You know you're a geezer if the mortician offers you a senior discount."

Jennifer gave me her best twelve-year-old smirk. "Those are cool, Grandpa. I have one more based on you."

I raised an eyebrow. "Okay."

"You know you're a geezer if you do something good and aren't concerned about getting recognition for it." She put her arms around me and gave me a big hug.

My heart went flip-flop.

When Jennifer pulled away, she asked, "Why don't geezer jokes offend you?"

"Good question. It's like this. Aging is part of the human predicament with all its ups and downs. We shouldn't get hung up on the stereotypes, but we also need to chuckle now and then. Nothing wrong with laughing at ourselves and not taking ourselves too seriously. As long as it's not done maliciously, I enjoy a joke about people my age as much as the next person. Being a geezer, I have my quirks of old age, but I love life, love my family and love laughing. Have I ever told you my philosophy of life?"

Jennifer shook her head. "Nope. Tell me."

I took a deep breath. "Each moment is unique as is each individual. Yet moments unite through time and individuals through love. What more is happiness than living and loving each moment?"

We stood there in silence for a moment. Jennifer bit her lip. "I'll remember that, Grandpa. We've sure had an awesome trip. Too bad we have to go home so soon."

I chucked her under the chin. "Lots of excitement. I'm looking forward to a nice vacation at home with no drug gangs."

Jennifer looked up and pointed across the lobby. "There's Hina. I'll catch up with you later, Grandpa. We're going to make some leis to wear to the airport tomorrow."

As she charged away, I watched my offspring in amazement. If we old coots had that much energy, we'd have to turn in our geezer club membership cards.

I decided to take a walk to stretch my old legs. When I came out of the hotel, I looked to the right and saw the yacht harbor. No way I'd go near there again. I turned and walked the other direction.

ABOUT THE AUTHOR

Mike Befeler is author of four previous novels in the Paul Jacobson Geezer-lit Mystery Series: *Retirement Homes Are Murder,*
Living with Your Kids Is Murder (a finalist for the Lefty Award
for best humorous mystery of 2009), *Senior Moments Are Murder*
and *Cruising in Your Eighties Is Murder.* Mike is co-chair of the
Boulder County Aging Advisory Council and is president of
the Rocky Mountain Chapter of Mystery Writers of America.
He grew up in Honolulu, Hawaii, and now lives in Boulder,
Colorado, with his wife, Wendy.

If you are interested in having the author speak to your book
club, contact Mike Befeler at mikebef@aol.com. His website is
http://www.mikebefeler.com.